INTRODUCTION

ANTHONY BERKELEY COX (1893–1971) was a versatile author who wrote under several names. Under his real name, he wrote humorous novels, political commentary and even a comic opera. As A. Monmouth Platts, he wrote a light-hearted thriller involving a vanishing debutante. As Francis Iles, he wrote the groundbreaking psychological crime novels *Malice Aforethought* (1931) and *Before the Fact* (1932). And, as Anthony Berkeley, he wrote 14 classic detective stories, many of which feature Roger Sheringham, an amateur investigator who works sometimes with—and sometimes against—Chief Inspector Moresby of Scotland Yard.

In some senses, Anthony Berkeley *was* Roger Sheringham; at the very least the two have much in common. Roger, like his creator, was the son of a doctor and 'born in a small English provincial town'. Both went to public school and then to Oxford, where Berkeley achieved a Third in Classics and Roger a Second in Classics and History. Both served in the First World War: Berkeley was invalided out of the army with his health permanently impaired, while Roger was 'wounded twice, not very seriously'. Roger became a bestseller with his first novel, as did Berkeley, and both men spoke disparagingly of their own fiction while being intolerant of others' criticism. Against this background, Berkeley's comment that Sheringham was 'founded on an offensive person I once knew' is likely to have been an example of the writer's often-noted peculiar sense of humour.

Humour, and above all ingenuity, are the hallmark of Berkeley's crime fiction. While many of his contemporaries concentrated on finding ever more improbable means of dispatching victims and ever more implausible means of establishing an alibi, Berkeley focused on turning established

v

conventions of the crime and mystery genre upside down. Thus the explanation of the locked room in Berkeley's first Sheringham mystery, *The Layton Court Mystery* (1925), is absurdly straight-forward. In another novel, the official detective is right while the amateur sleuth is wrong. In another, the last person known to have seen the victim alive *is*, after all, the murderer. Above all, facts uncovered by any of Berkeley's detectives are almost always capable of more than one explanation and the first deduc-tions they draw are rarely entirely correct. In this respect, Berkeley clearly took some of his inspiration from certain histor-ical crimes, particularly those whose solution has never been clear-cut and where the facts, such as there are, routinely offer more than one possible explanation. *The Silk Stocking Murders* (1928) is one such title, inspired by the murder in 1925 of a young woman in London by a one-legged man; *The Wychford Poisoning Case*, which has also been reissued in this Detective Club series, is another.

In all, Roger Sheringham appears in ten novel-length mysteries—one of which Berkeley dedicated to himself—and Sheringham is also mentioned in passing in two other novels, *The Piccadilly Murder* (1929) and *Trial and Error* (1937). Perhaps the best-known of the Sheringham novels is *The Poisoned Chocolates Case* (1929) which, again, is based on a real-life crime. This was the attempt in November 1922 by a disgruntled horticulturist to murder the Commissioner of the Metropolitan Police Service, Brigadier-General Sir William Horwood, by sending him a package of Walnut Whips, laced with either arsenic or strychnine. The poisoning with which Cox's novel is concerned is investigated not only by the police but by Sheringham and the other members of 'The Crimes Circle', a private dining club of criminologists. Each member of the Circle advances a plausible explanation of the poisoning but one by one the solutions fall, including—to the reader's surprise—the solution proposed by Sheringham. Eventually the mystery is solved by Ambrose Chitterwick, an unassuming and

THE SILK STOCKING MURDERS

'THE DETECTIVE STORY CLUB is a clearing house for the best detective and mystery stories chosen for you by a select committee of experts. Only the most ingenious crime stories will be published under the THE DETECTIVE STORY CLUB imprint. A special distinguishing stamp appears on the wrapper and title page of every THE DETECTIVE STORY CLUB book—the Man with the Gun. Always look for the Man with the Gun when buying a Crime book.'

Wm. Collins Sons & Co. Ltd., 1929

Now the Man with the Gun is back in this series of COLLINS CRIME CLUB reprints, and with him the chance to experience the classic books that influenced the Golden Age of crime fiction.

THE DETECTIVE STORY CLUB

FURTHER TITLES IN PREPARATION

THE
SILK STOCKING
MURDERS

A STORY OF CRIME
BY
ANTHONY BERKELEY

WITH AN INTRODUCTION BY
TONY MEDAWAR

COLLINS
CRIME
CLUB

COLLINS CRIME CLUB
An imprint of HarperCollins*Publishers*
1 London Bridge Street
London SE1 9GF
www.harpercollins.co.uk

This edition 2017

First published in Great Britain by
W. Collins Sons & Co. Ltd 1928

A catalogue record for this book is available from the British Library

ISBN 978-0-00-821639-9

Typeset in Bulmer MT Std by
Palimpsest Book Production Ltd, Falkirk, Stirlingshire
Printed and bound in Great Britain by Clays Ltd, St Ives plc

aspergic amateur sleuth whose hobbies include philately and horticulture—tweaking the nose of anyone who remembered that it was a horticulturist who made the attempt to poison Sir William Horwood. As well as being a superb puzzle, with multiple solutions, *The Poisoned Chocolates Case* is fascinating for the links between the fictional 'Crimes Circle' and the Detection Club, which Berkeley had founded as a dining club for crime writers in 1929—the same year that *The Poisoned Chocolates Case* was published. The Detection Club, at least initially, comprised 'authors of detective stories which rely more upon genuine detective merit than upon melodramatic thrills', though that definition has been significantly stretched more than once over the nearly 90 years of the Club's existence. Over the years, Cox would collaborate with members of the Detection Club on various fundraising ventures, including four round-robin mysteries beginning with *The Floating Admiral* (1931), whose entertaining sequel—*The Sinking Admiral*—was published by Collins Crime Club in 2016. And in 2016, playing Berkeley in a posthumous game of detective chess, Martin Edwards, the current President of the Detection Club, proposed a wholly plausible additional solution to the *Poisoned Chocolates* mystery in a British Library reprint.

But Berkeley eventually tired of playing games with detective stories and, though Sheringham would go on to appear in a few recently discovered wartime propaganda pieces, some shorter fiction and even a radio play, the last novel in which he appeared was published in 1934, less than ten years after his debut in *The Layton Court Mystery*. But Berkeley did not abandon crime fiction altogether. On the contrary, he decided to take crime fiction in what was then a radically new direction. For this new approach, Berkeley decided to use the name of one of his mother's ancestors, a smuggler called Francis Iles. And, for three years, the real identity of Francis Iles was kept a secret. With *Malice Aforethought*, the first Iles novel, Berkeley broke the mould. At a stroke, he broadened the range—and respectability—of crime and detective fiction. Though the novel in part derives from an early short story and, while it could also be regarded as a variant of the inverted mystery popularised by Richard Austin Freeman's Dr Thorndyke stories, *Malice Aforethought* is a much more complex proposition. For the first time Berkeley achieved what he had tried to do many times before: he focused on psychology. In *Malice Aforethought* it is the psychology of the murderer; and in the second Iles title, *Before the Fact*, it is the psychology of the victim. Characteristically, both are based on real-life crimes.

In all, three novels were published as by Francis Iles, with the third—*As for the Woman* (1939)—less successful than it might have been had it been presented as non-genre fiction, perhaps under yet another pseudonym. While a fourth 'Francis Iles' title was planned and even announced, Berkeley had published his last novel.

A few short stories appeared from time to time and, in the late 1950s, he completed two volumes of limericks, which were published under his own name. Berkeley also wrote some radio plays for the BBC, including one that, though credited to Anthony Berkeley, included two songs 'by Anthony B. Cox'— and was introduced on its original broadcast by none other than Francis Iles!

In all, Anthony Berkeley published 24 books in a little over 14 years. He was also a prolific contributor to periodicals under his various names, authoring over 300 stories, sketches and articles; and he also reviewed crime fiction and other books up until shortly before his death in 1971.

To Agatha Christie, Berkeley was 'Detection and crime at its wittiest—all his stories are amusing, intriguing and he is a master of the final twist, the surprise denouement.' Dorothy L. Sayers also admired Berkeley and has Harriet Vane, in the Lord Peter Wimsey novel *Have His Carcase* (1932), describe the 'twistiness' of what she calls the Roger Sheringham method—'You prove elaborately and in detail that A did the murder; then you give the story one final shake, twist it round a fresh corner, and find that the real murderer is B.' The last word can be left to the mystery novelist Christianna Brand, a friend and near neighbour of Berkeley's in London, who when reminiscing about the early years of the Detection Club commented: 'Sometimes I have thought he was really the cleverest of all of us.'

TONY MEDAWAR
September 2016

CONTENTS

CHAPTER I

ROGER SHERINGHAM halted before the little box just inside the entrance of *The Daily Courier's* enormous building behind Fleet Street. Its occupant, alert for unauthorised intruders endeavouring to slip past him, nodded kindly.

'Only one for you this morning, sir,' he said, and produced a letter.

With another nod, which he strove to make as condescending as the porter's (and failed), Roger passed into the lift and was hoisted smoothly into the upper regions. The letter in his hand, he made his way through mazy, stone-floored passages into the dark little room set apart for his own use. Roger Sheringham, whose real business in life was that of a best-selling novelist, had stipulated when he consented to join *The Daily Courier* as criminological expert and purveyor of chattily-written articles on murder, upon a room of his own. He only used it twice a week, but he had carried his point. That is what comes of being a personal friend of an editor.

Bestowing his consciously dilapidated hat in a corner, he threw his newspaper on the desk and slit open the letter.

Roger always enjoyed this twice-weekly moment. In spite of his long acquaintance with them, ranging over nearly ten years, he was still able to experience a faint thrill on receiving letters from complete strangers. Praise of his work arriving out of the unknown delighted him; abuse filled him with combative joy. He always answered each one with individual care. It would have warmed the hearts of those of his correspondents who prefaced their letters with diffident apologies for addressing him (and nine out of ten of them did so), to see the welcome

1

their efforts received. All authors are like this—and all authors are careful to tell their friends what a nuisance it is having to waste so much time in answering the letters of strangers, and how they wish people wouldn't do it. All authors, in fact, are— But that is enough about authors.

It goes without saying that since he had joined *The Daily Courier* Roger's weekly bag of strangers had increased very considerably. It was therefore not without a certain disappointment that he had received this solitary specimen from the porter's hands this morning. A little resentful, he drew it from its envelope. As he read, his resentment disappeared. A little pucker appeared between his eyebrows. The letter was an unusual one, decidedly.

It ran as follows:

> The Vicarage,
> Little Mitcham, Dorset.
>
> DEAR SIR,—You will, I hope, pardon my presumption in writing to you at all, but I trust that you will accept the excuse that my need is urgent. I have read your very interesting articles in *The Daily Courier* and, studying them between the lines, feel that you are a man who will not resent my present action, even though it may transfer a measure of responsibility to you which might seem irksome. I would have come up to London to see you in person, but that the expense of such a journey is, to one in my position, almost prohibitive.
>
> Briefly, then, I am a widower, of eight years' standing, with five daughters. The eldest, Anne, has taken upon her shoulders the duties of my dear wife, who died when Anne was sixteen; and she was, till ten months ago, ably seconded by the sister next to her in age, Janet. I need hardly explain to you that, on the stipend of a country parson, it has not been an easy task to feed, clothe and educate five growing girls. Janet, therefore,

who, I may add, has always been considered the beauty of the family, decided ten months ago to seek her fortune elsewhere. We did our best to dissuade her, but she is a high-spirited girl and, having made up her mind, refused to alter it. She also pointed out that not only would there be one less mouth to feed, but, should she be able to obtain employment of even a moderately lucrative nature, she would be able to make a modest, but undoubtedly helpful, contribution towards the household expenses.

Janet did carry out her intention and left us, going, presumably, to London. I write 'presumably' because she refused most firmly to give us her address, saying that not until she was securely established in her new life, whatever that should be, would she allow us even to communicate with her, in case we might persuade her, in the event of her not meeting with initial success, to give up and come home again. She did however write to us occasionally herself, and the postmark was always London, though the postal district varied with almost every letter. From these letters we gathered that, though remaining confident and cheerful, she had not yet succeeded in obtaining a post of the kind she desired. She had, however, she told us, found employment sufficiently remunerative to allow her to keep herself in comparative comfort, though she never mentioned the precise nature of the work in which she was engaged.

She had been in the habit of writing to us about once a week or so, but six weeks ago her letters ceased and we have not heard a word from her since. It may be that there is no cause for alarm, but alarm I do feel nevertheless. Janet is an affectionate girl and a good daughter, and I cannot believe that, knowing the distress it would cause us, she would willingly have omitted to let us hear from her in this way. I cannot help feeling that either her letters have been going astray or else the poor girl has met with an accident of some sort.

My reasons, sir, for troubling you with all this are as follows. I am perhaps an old-fashioned man, but I do not care to approach the police in the matter and have Janet traced when probably there is no more the matter than an old man's foolish fancies; and I am quite sure that, assuming these fancies to have no foundation, Janet would much resent the police poking their noses into her affairs. On the other hand, if there has been an accident, the fact is almost certain to be known at the offices of a paper such as *The Daily Courier*. I have therefore determined, after considerable reflection, to trespass upon your kindness, on which of course I have no claim at all, to the extent of asking you to make discreet enquiries of such of your colleagues as might be expected to know, and acquaint me with the result. In this way recourse to the police may still be avoided, and news given me of my poor girl without unpleasant publicity or officialism.

If you prefer to have nothing to do with my request, I beg of you to let me know and I will put the matter to the police at once. If, on the other hand, you are so kind as to humour an old man, any words of gratitude on my part become almost superfluous.—Yours truly,

A. E. MANNERS.

P.S.—I enclose a snapshot of Janet taken two years ago, the only one we have.

'The poor old bird!' Roger commented mentally, as he reached the end of this lengthy letter, written in a small, crabbed handwriting which was not too easy to decipher. 'But I wonder whether he realises that there are about eight thousand accidents in the streets of London every twelve months? This is going to be a pretty difficult little job.' He looked inside the envelope again and drew out the snapshot.

Amateur snapshots have a humorous name, but they are seldom really as bad as reputed. This one was a fair average specimen, and showed four girls sitting on a sea-shore, their ages apparently ranging from ten to something over twenty. Under one of them was written, in the same crabbed hand-writing, the word 'Janet'. Roger studied her. She was pretty, evidently, and in spite of the fact that her face was covered with a very cheerful smile, Roger thought that he could recognise her from the picture should he ever be fortunate enough to find her.

For as to whether he was going to look for her or not, there was no question. It had simply never occurred to Roger that he might, after all, not do so. Roger (whatever else he might be) was a man of quick sympathies, and that stilted letter through whose formal phrases tragedy peeped so plainly, had touched him more than a little. But for the fact that an article had to be written before lunch-time, he would have set about it that very moment, without the least idea of how he was going to prosecute the search.

As it was, however, circumstances prevented him from doing anything in the matter for another ninety minutes, and by that time his brain, working automatically as he wrote, had evolved a plan. He felt fairly certain that the girl was still in London, alive and flourishing, and had postponed writing home as the ties that bound her to Dorsetshire began to weaken; the old man's anxiety was no doubt ill-founded, but that did not mean that it must not be relieved. Besides, the quest would prove a pretty little exercise for those sleuth-like powers which Roger was so sure he possessed. Nevertheless, unharmed and merely unfilial as he did not doubt the girl to be, it was easier to begin operations from the other end. If she had had an accident she would be considerably easier to trace than if she had not, and by establishing first the negative fact, Roger would be able the sooner to reassure the vicar. And as the only real clue he had was the snapshot, he had better start from that.

Instead, therefore, of betaking himself to Piccadilly Circus in the blithe confidence that Janet Manners, like everybody else in London, would be certain to come along there sooner or later, he ran up two more flights of stairs in the same building, and, the snapshot in his hand, sought out the photographic department of *The Daily Courier's* illustrated sister, *The Daily Picture*.

'Hullo, Ben,' he greeted the serious, horn-bespectacled young man who presided over the studio and spent most of his days in photographing mannequins, who left him cold, in garments which left them cold. 'I suppose you've never had a photograph through your hands of this girl, have you? The one marked Janet.'

The bespectacled one scrutinised the snapshot with close attention. Every photograph that appeared in *The Daily Picture* passed, at one time or another, through his hands, and his memory was prodigious. 'She does look a bit familiar,' he admitted.

'She does, eh?' Roger cried, suddenly apprehensive. 'Good man. Rack your brains. I want her placed, badly.'

The other bent over the snapshot again. 'Can't you help me?' he asked. 'In what connection would I have come across her? Is she an actress, or a mannequin, or a titled beauty, or what?'

'She's not a titled beauty, I can tell you that; but she might have been either of the other two. I haven't the faintest notion what she is.'

'Why do you want to know if we've ever had a photograph of her through here, then?'

'Oh, it's just a personal matter,' Roger said evasively. 'Her people haven't heard from her for a week or two and they're beginning to think she's been run over by a bus or something like that. You know how fussy the parents of that sort of girl are.'

The other shook his head and handed back the snapshot. 'No, I'm sorry, but I can't place her. I'm sure I've seen her face before, but you're too vague. If you could tell me, now, that she *had* been run over by a bus, or had some other accident, or been something (anything to provide a peg for my memory to hang on) I might have been able to—wait a minute, though!' He snatched the photograph back and studied it afresh. Roger looked on tensely.

'I've got it!' the bespectacled one proclaimed in triumph. 'It was the word "accident" that gave me the clue. Have you ever noticed what a curious thing memory is, Sheringham? Present it with a blank surface, and it simply slides helplessly across it; but give it just the slightest little peg to grip on, and—'

'Who is the girl?' Roger interrupted.

The other blinked at him. 'Oh, the girl. Yes. She was a chorus-girl in one of the big revues (I'm sorry, I forget which) and her name was Unity Something-or-other. She—good gracious, you really don't know?'

Roger shook his head. 'No. What?'

'She was a friend of yours?' the other persisted.

'No, I've never met her in my life. Why?'

'Well, you see, she hanged herself four or five weeks ago with her own stocking.'

Roger stared at him. 'The deuce she did!' he said blankly. 'Hell!'

They looked at each other.

'Look here,' said the photographer, 'I can't be certain it's the same girl, you know. Besides, this one seems to be called Janet. But I tell you what: there was a photo of Unity Something published in *The Picture* at the time, a professional one. You could look that up.'

'Yes,' said Roger, his thoughts on the letter he would have to write to Dorset if all this were true.

'And now I come to think of it, I seem to remember something rather queer about the case. It was ordinary enough in most ways, but I believe they had some difficulty in identifying the girl. No relatives came forward, or something like that.'

'Oh?'

'*The Picture* didn't pay much attention to it, beyond publishing her photo; rather out of our line, of course. But I expect *The Courier* had a report of the inquest. Anyhow, don't take it for certain that I'm right; it's quite possible that I'm not. Go down and look up the files.'

'Yes,' said Roger glumly, turning on his heel.

'I will.'

CHAPTER II

ACUTELY disappointed, and not a little shocked, Roger made his way downstairs. His thoughts were centred mainly upon that pathetic household in Dorsetshire, to whom his letter must bring such tragedy; but Roger, like most of us, while able to feel for other people strongly enough, was at heart an egoist, and it was this side of his nature which prompted the sensation of disappointment of which he was conscious. It was, he could not help feeling, most unfortunate that just when his help had been solicited as that of an able criminologist, the problem should be whisked out of his hands in this uncompromising way.

The truth was that Roger had been longing for an opportunity to put his detective capabilities into action once more. The letter had acted as a spur to his desires, coming as it did from one who evidently held the greatest respect for his powers in this direction. Roger himself had the greatest respect for his detective powers; but he could not disguise from himself the fact that others were obtuse enough to hold dissimilar views. Inspector Moresby, for instance. For the last nine months, ever since they had parted at Ludmouth after the Vane case, Inspector Moresby had rankled in Roger's mind to a very considerable extent.

And those nine months had been, from the criminologist's point of view, deadly dull ones. Not an interesting murder had been committed, not even an actress had been deprived of her jewels. Without going so far as to question whether his detective powers might be getting actually rusty, Roger had been very, very anxiously seeking an opportunity to put them into action once more. And now that the chance had come, it had as swiftly disappeared.

He began gloomily to turn back the pages of *The Daily Picture* file.

It was not long before he found what he wanted. In an issue of just over five weeks ago there was, tucked neatly into a corner of the back page, a portrait of a young girl; the heading above it stated curtly: 'Hanged Herself With Own Silk Stocking'. The letterpress below was hardly less brief. 'Miss Unity Ransome, stated to be an actress, who hanged herself with her own silk stocking at her flat in Sutherland Avenue last Tuesday.'

Roger pored over the picture. Like amateur snapshots, the pictures in an illustrated paper are considered fair game for the humorist. Whenever a painstaking humorist has to mention them he prefixes one of two epithets, 'blurred' or 'smudgy'. Yet the pictures in the illustrated dailies of today are neither blurred nor smudgy. They were once, it is true, perhaps so late as ten years ago, when the art of picture-printing for daily newspapers was an infant; nowadays they are astonishingly clear. One does wish sometimes that even humorists would move with the times. Roger had no difficulty in deciding that the two faces before him were of the same girl.

He turned to *The Daily Courier* of the same date.

There he found, unobtrusive on a page lined with advertisements, a laconic account of the inquest. Miss Unity Ransome, it seemed, had been a chorus-girl in one of the less important London revues. There was evidence that this was her first engagement on the stage, and she had obtained it, in spite of her inexperience, on the strength of her good looks and air of happy vivacity. Prior to this engagement, nothing was known about her. She shared a tiny flat in Sutherland Avenue with another girl in the same company, but they had met at the theatre for the first time. This girl, Moira Carruthers, had testified that she knew less than nothing about her friend's antecedents. Unity Ransome not only volunteered no information concerning herself, but actively discouraged questions on that subject. 'A regular oyster,' was Miss Carruthers' happy description.

This reticence the coroner had not been unwilling to emphasise, for on the face of it there appeared no reason for suicide. Miss Carruthers had stated emphatically that, so far as she knew, Unity had never contemplated such a thing. She had appeared to be perfectly happy, and even delighted at having obtained an engagement in London. Her salary, though not large, had quite sufficed for her needs. Pressed on this point, Miss Carruthers had admitted that her friend had more than once expressed a wish that she had been able to earn more, and that quickly; but, as Miss Carruthers pointed out, 'Unity was what you might call a real lady, and perhaps she'd been accustomed to having things a bit better style than most of us.' At all events, she had not complained unduly.

The police had made perfunctory efforts to trace her, Roger gathered, and attempts had been made, besides the publication of her professional portrait, to get into touch with any former friends or relations, but without success. To this also the Coroner called attention. In his concluding remarks, he hinted very delicately that the probability seemed to be that she had quarrelled with her family, left home (but not necessarily in disgrace, the Coroner was careful to add with emphasis, thereby showing quite plainly that this was precisely what he thought), and endeavoured to make a career for herself on the stage; and though she might appear to have met with unexpected success in this direction, who could say what remorse and unhappiness might not burden the life of a young girl cut off thus from all the comforts to which, it would seem, she had been accustomed? Or, again, she might have been an orphan, left penniless, and overcome by a loneliness which she felt, rightly or wrongly, to be unbearable. In other words, the Coroner was extremely sorry for the girl, but he wanted to get home to his lunch and the usual straightforward verdict was the best way of doing so.

He got his wish. Indeed, there was little likelihood of anything else, for Unity Ransome had simplified matters by leaving a little note behind her. The note ran briefly as follows: 'I am sick and tired of it all, and going to end it the only way.' It was not signed, but there was plenty of evidence that it was in her writing. A verdict of 'Suicide during Temporary Insanity' was inevitable.

Quite illegally Roger cut the little paragraph out of the file and put it away in his pocket-book. Then he went upstairs again and sought out the news-editor, with whom he usually lunched.

For some reason Roger did not say anything to the news-editor about his activities of the morning. News-editors, though excellent people in private life and devoted to their wives, are conscienceless, unfeeling bandits when it comes to news. Roger's reticence was instinctive, but had he troubled to search for its cause he would certainly have found it in the fact that the Dorsetshire Vicarage would have enough to bear during the next few days without a pitiless and lurid publicity being added to the sum of their troubles. That, at any rate, he could spare them.

It was still with the secret of Unity Ransome's identity undisclosed, then, that he returned later to *The Courier's* offices and, having obtained from the bespectacled one a copy of the photograph which had appeared in *The Daily Picture,* prepared to write to Mr Manners and ask him, as gently as possible, whether he recognised his daughter in the portrait of the girl who had committed suicide in the Sutherland Avenue flat.

Yet, seated definitely at the task, his pen in his hands, the paper spread out in front of him, Roger found himself quite unable to make a beginning. The paper remained blank, the pen executed a series of neat but meaningless squiggles round the edges of the blotting-pad, and Roger's brain buzzed busily. It was not the difficulty of the job which prevented him from forming even the initial 'Dear Sir' of the letter; it was something quite different.

'Hang it!' burst out Roger suddenly aloud, hitting the desk in front of him a blow with his fist. 'Hang it, it isn't *natural!*'

It was an old cry of his, and in the past it had led to important things. His own spoken words made Roger prick up his own ears. He threw the pen absently from him, drew out his pipe and settled down in his chair.

Ten minutes later he struck the match he had been holding during that period in his hand. Five minutes later he struck another. Three minutes after that he applied the third match to his pipe.

'Now am I,' communed Roger with himself, crossing his legs afresh and drawing deeply at his now lighted pipe, 'am I getting a bee in my bonnet—am I getting hag-ridden by an idea—am I all that, or *is* there something funny in this business? I'm inclined (yes, most decidedly I'm inclined) to think there is. Let us, therefore, tabulate our results in the approved manner and see where they lead us.'

Picking up the pen again, he began to cover the blank sheet at last.

'Assuming that Janet Manners = Unity Ransome:

(1) Janet was not only a dutiful but an affectionate daughter. She was at pains to write cheerful letters home every week. She went out of her way not to distress her father in any manner, even concealing from him the fact that she had found work on the stage, because he probably would not like it. Is it not, then, almost inconceivable that she should have deliberately taken her own life without at least preparing him towards not hearing from her for a considerable time? The only explanation is that she acted on a sudden, panic-stricken impulse.

(2) So far as one can see, Janet had no possible reason for suicide. She had been unusually lucky in getting good work. Her object was firstly to keep herself and so save

expense at home, and secondly to contribute to the Vicarage household upkeep. She had achieved the first, and she was on her way to achieving the second. Not only had she no reason for killing herself, but she had every reason not to do so. In short, on the facts as known, the only explanation for Janet's suicide is that she suddenly went raving mad. This is in accord with the panic-stricken impulse, and both show that all the facts are not known.

(3) We know that Janet did commit suicide, because she tells us so herself. But in what a very stereotyped formula! Would a girl who had the initiative to leave a country parsonage and go on the stage express herself, in a note of such importance, in such a very hackneyed way? And what was she "sick and tired" of? Again, this can only mean that we do not know all the facts.

(4) Why did Janet not sign that note? The omission is more than significant; it is unnatural. To sign such a note as that, or at the least to initial it, is almost a *sine qua non*. There seems no obvious explanation of this, except, possibly, frantic panic.

(5) What do we know of Janet? That she was a young woman of considerable character and determination. Young women of considerable determination do not commit suicide. Moreover, allowing for a father's prejudice, her photograph shows clearly that Janet was not a suicide type. Once more one is driven to the conclusion that events of enormous importance have not yet come to light.

(6) Janet hanged herself with her own stockings. In the name of goodness, why? Had she nothing more suitable? In fact, Janet's method of suicide is more than strange; it is unnatural. A girl bent on suicide would adopt hanging as a very last resource. Men hang themselves; girls don't. Yet Janet did. Why?

(7) Is Roger Sheringham seeing visions? No, he isn't. Then what is he going to do about it?— Jolly well find out what had really been happening to that poor kid!'

Roger put down his pen and read through what he had written.

'Results tabulated,' he murmured. 'And where do they lead us, eh? Why, to Miss Moira Carruthers, to be sure.'

He put on his hat and hurried out.

CHAPTER III

IT was with no definite plan in his mind, or even suspicion, that Roger jumped into a taxi and caused himself to be conveyed to Sutherland Avenue. All he knew was that here was mystery; and where mystery was, there was something in his blood that raised Roger's curiosity to such a point that nothing less than complete elucidation could lower it. The affairs of Janet Manners had, he acknowledged readily, nothing whatever to do with himself, and it was very probable that their owner, had she been alive, would very much have resented the poking of his nose into them. He appeased his conscience (or what served him on these occasions for a conscience) by pretending that his real object in making the journey was to acquire positive proof that Unity Ransome really was Janet Manners before he wrote to Dorsetshire. He did not deceive himself for a moment.

His taxi stopped before one of those tall, depressed-looking buildings which line Sutherland Avenue, and a tiny brass plate on the door-post informed him that Miss Carruthers lived on the fourth floor. There was no lift, and Roger trudged up, to find, with better luck than he deserved, that Miss Carruthers was at home. Indeed, she popped out of a room at him as he reached the top of the stairs, for the flat had no front-door of its own.

Chorus-girls (or chorus ladies, as they call themselves nowadays) are divided into three types, the pert, the pretty and the proud, and of these the last are quite the most fell of all created beings. Roger was relieved to see that Miss Carruthers, with her very golden hair and her round, babyish face, was quite definitely of the pretty type, and therefore not to be feared.

'Oh!' said Miss Carruthers prettily, and looked at him in dainty alarm. Strange men on her stairs were, it was to be gathered, one of the most terrifying phenomena in Miss Carruthers' helpless young life.

'Good afternoon,' said Roger, suiting his smile to his company. 'I'm so sorry to bother you, but could you spare me a few minutes, Miss Carruthers?'

'Oh!' fluttered Miss Carruthers again. 'Was it—was it very important?'

'I am connected with *The Daily Courier*,' said Roger.

'Come inside,' said Miss Carruthers.

They passed into a sitting-room, the furniture of which was only too evidently supplied with the room. Roger was ensconced in a worn armchair, Miss Carruthers perched charmingly on the arm of an ancient couch. 'Yes?' sighed Miss Carruthers.

Roger came to the point at once. 'It's about Miss Ransome,' he said bluntly.

'Oh!' said Miss Carruthers, valiantly concealing her disappointment.

'I'm making a few enquiries, on behalf of *The Courier*,' Roger went on, toying delicately with the truth. 'We're not altogether satisfied, you know.' He looked extremely portentous.

Miss Carruthers' large eyes became larger still. 'What not with?' she asked, her recent disappointment going the same way as her grammar.

'Everything,' returned Roger largely. He crossed his legs and thought what he should be dissatisfied with first of all. 'What was her reason for committing suicide at all?' he demanded; after all, he was more dissatisfied with that than anything else.

'Well, reely!' said Miss Carruthers. And then she began to talk.

Roger, listening intently, was conscious that he was hearing an often-told tale, but it lost none of its interest on that account. He let her tell it in her own way.

Uny, said Miss Carruthers ('Uny'! mentally ejaculated Roger, and shuddered), had absolutely no reason in the world for going and doing a thing like that. None whatsoever! She'd had a slice of real luck in stepping into a London show straight away; she was always bright and cheerful ('well, as happy as the day is long, you might say,' affirmed Miss Carruthers); everybody liked her at the theatre; and what is more, she was marked out by common consent as one who would go far; it was generally admitted that the next small speaking part that was going, Uny would click for. And why she should want to go and do a thing like that—!

In fact, Miss Carruthers could hardly believe it when she came in that afternoon and saw her. Hanging on the hook on the bedroom door, she was, with her stocking round her neck, and looking—well, it very nearly turned Miss Carruthers up just to see her. *Horrible!* She wouldn't describe it, not for worlds; it made her feel really ill just to think of it.—And here Miss Carruthers embarked on a minute description of her unhappy friend's appearance, in which protruding eyeballs, blue lips and bitten tongue figured with highly unpleasant prominence.

Still, Miss Carruthers was by no means such a little fool as it apparently pleased her to suggest. Instead of screaming and running uselessly out into the street as, Roger reflected, three-quarters of the women he knew would have done, she had the sense to hoist Janet somehow up on to her shoulders and unhook the stocking. But by that time it was too late; she was dead. 'Only just, though,' wailed Miss Carruthers, with real tears in her eyes. 'The doctor said if I'd come back a quarter of an hour earlier I could have saved her. Wasn't that just hell?'

Wholeheartedly Roger agreed that it was. 'But how very curious that she should have done it just when you might have been expected back at any minute,' he remarked. 'It couldn't be,' he added, stroking his chin thoughtfully, 'that she *expected* to be saved, could it?'

Miss Carruthers shook her golden head. 'Oh, no I'd told

her I wasn't coming back here, you see. I was going to tea with a boy, and I said to Uny not to expect me; I'd go straight on to the theatre. Well, now you know as much about it as I do, Mr—Mr—'

'Sheringham.'

'Mr Sheringham. And what do you imagine she wanted to go and do it for? Oh, *poor* old Uny! I tell you, Mr Sheringham, I can hardly bear to stay in the place now. I wouldn't, if I could only get decent digs somewhere else, which I can't.'

Roger looked at the little person sympathetically. The tears were streaming unashamedly down her cheeks, and it was quite plain that, however artificial she might be in other respects, her feeling for her dead friend was genuine enough. He spoke on impulse.

'What do I imagine she did it for? I don't! But I tell you what I do imagine, Miss Carruthers, and that is that there's a good deal more at the back of this than either you or I suspect.'

'What—what do you mean?'

Roger pulled his pipe out of his pocket. 'Do you mind if I smoke?' he asked, gaining a few seconds. He had to take a swift decision. Should he or should he not take this fluffy little creature into his confidence? Would she be a help or a hindrance? Was she a complete little fool who had had a single sensible moment, or was her apparent empty-headedness a pose adopted for the benefit of the other sex? Most of the men with whom she would come in contact, Roger was painfully aware, do prefer their women to be empty-headed. He compromised: he would take her just so far as he could into his own confidence without betraying that of others.

'I mean,' he said carefully, as he filled his pipe, 'that so far as I've been able to gather, Miss Ransome was *not* the sort of girl to commit suicide—'

'That she wasn't!' interjected Miss Carruthers, almost violently.

'—and that as she did so, she was driven into it by forces

which, to say the least, must have been overwhelming. And I mean to make it my business to find out what those forces were.'

'Oh! Oh, yes. You mean—?'

'For the moment,' said Roger firmly, 'nothing more than that.'

They looked at each other for a moment in silence. Then Miss Carruthers said an unexpected thing.

'You belong to *The Courier*?' she asked, in a hesitating voice. 'You're doing this for them? You're going to publish everything you find out, whether—whether Uny would have liked it or not?'

Roger found himself liking her more and more. 'No!' he said frankly. 'I am connected with *The Courier*, but I'm not on it. I'm going to do this off my own bat, and I give you my word that nothing shall be published at all that doesn't reflect to the credit of Miss Ransome—and perhaps not even then. You mean, of course, that you wouldn't help me, except on those terms?'

Miss Carruthers nodded. 'I've got a duty to Uny, and I'm not going to have any mud slung at her, whether she deserves it or not. But if you'll promise that, I'll help you all I can. Because believe me, Mr Sheringham,' added Miss Carruthers passionately, 'if there's some damned skunk of a man at the bottom of this (as I've thought more than once there might be), I'd give everything I've got in the world to see him served as he served poor old Uny.'

'That's all right, then,' Roger said easily. The worst of the theatre, he reflected, is that it does make its participants so dramatic; and drama in private life is worse than immorality. 'We'll shake hands on that bargain.'

'Look here,' said Miss Carruthers, doffing her emotional robe as swiftly as she had donned it, 'look here, I tell you what. You wait here and smoke while I make us a cup of tea, and then we'll talk as much as you like. And I have got one or two things to tell you,' she added darkly, 'that you might like to hear.'

Roger agreed with alacrity. He had often noticed that there is nothing like tea to loosen a woman's tongue; not even alcohol.

In a surprisingly short time for so helpless-looking a person, Miss Carruthers returned with the tea-tray, which Roger took from her at the door. They settled down, Miss Carruthers poured out, and Roger at last felt that the time was ripe to embark on the series of questions which he had really come to ask.

Miss Carruthers answered readily enough, leaning back in her chair with a cigarette between lips which even now must occasionally pout. Indeed, she answered too readily. Nevertheless, from the mass of her verbiage Roger was able to pick a few new facts.

In the main her replies bore out the brief account of her evidence at the inquest, though at very much greater length, and Miss Carruthers dwelt upon her theory that her friend was 'a cut above the rest of us, as you might say. A real lady, instead of only a perfect one.' To Roger's carefully worded queries as to any indication of Unity Ransome's real identity, Miss Carruthers was at first vague. Then she produced, in a haphazard way, the most important point she had yet contributed.

'All I can say,' said Miss Carruthers, 'is that her name may have been Janet, or she might have had a friend called Janet, or something like that.'

'Ah!' said Roger, keeping his composure. 'And how do you know that?'

'It's in a prayer-book of hers. I only came across it the other day. Would you like to see it?'

'I would,' said Roger.

Obligingly Miss Carruthers ran off to fetch it. Returning, she opened the book at the fly-leaf and handed it to Roger. He read: 'To my dear Janet, on her Confirmation, 14th March 1920. "Blessed are the pure in heart."' The writing was small and crabbed.

'I see,' Roger said, and took a later opportunity of slipping the book into his pocket. Miss Carruthers had definitely established the main point, at any rate.

He directed his questions elsewhere. Like Miss Carruthers, Roger had been struck with the idea that there might be a man behind things. He dredged assiduously in his informant's mind for any clue as to his possible identity. But here Miss Carruthers was unable to help. Uny, it appeared, hadn't cared for boys. She never went out with one alone, and would seldom consent to make up a foursome. She said frankly that boys bored her stiff. So far as Miss Carruthers knew, not only had she no particular boy, but not even any gentlemen-friends.

'Humph!' said Roger, abandoning that line of enquiry.

They sat and smoked in silence for a moment.

'If you wanted to commit suicide, Miss Carruthers,' Roger remarked abruptly, 'would you hang yourself?'

Miss Carruthers shuddered delicately. 'I would *not*. It's the very last way I'd do it.'

'Then why did Miss Ransome?'

'Perhaps she didn't realise what she'd look like,' suggested Miss Carruthers, quite seriously.

'Humph!' said Roger, and they smoked again.

'And with one of the stockings she was wearing,' mused Miss Carruthers. 'Funny, wasn't it?'

Roger sat up. 'What's that? One of the stockings she was actually wearing?'

'Yes. Didn't you know?'

'No, I didn't see that mentioned. Do you mean,' asked Roger incredulously, 'that she actually took off one of the stockings she was wearing at the time, and hanged herself with it?'

Miss Carruthers nodded. 'That's right. A stocking on one leg, she had, and the other bare. I thought it was funny at the time. On that very door, it was; and you can still see the screw-mark the other side. The screw I took out, of course. I couldn't have borne to look at it every time I came into the room.'

'What screw?' asked Roger, at sea.

'Why, the screw on the other side of the door, that she fastened the loop to.'

'I don't know anything about this. I took it for granted that she'd done it on a clothes'-hook, or something like that.'

'Well, I wondered about that,' said Miss Carruthers, 'but I expect it was because the hook in the bedroom was too low. And a stocking'd give a good bit, wouldn't it?'

Roger was already out of his chair and examining the door. 'Tell me exactly how you found her, will you?' he said.

With many shudders, some of which may have been quite real, Miss Carruthers did so. Janet, it appeared, had been hanging on the inside of the sitting-room door, from a small hook on the other side, which had been screwed in at the right angle to withstand the strain. The stocking round her neck had been knotted together tightly at the extreme ends. As far as one could gather, she must have placed it like that loosely round her neck, then twisted the slack two or three times, and slipped a tiny loop on to the hook on the further side of the door, over the top. She had been standing on a chair to do this, and she must have kicked the chair violently away when her preparations were complete, with such force as to slam the door to, leaving herself suspended by the little hook that was now completely out of her reach, so that she could not rescue herself even had she wished. This was an obvious reconstruction on the two facts that Miss Carruthers had found the door shut when she arrived, and an overturned chair on the floor at least six feet away.

'Good God!' said Roger, shocked at this evidence of such cold-blooded determination on the part of the unfortunate girl to deprive herself of life. But he realised at once that this version did not square with his theory of panic-stricken impulse. Panic-stricken people do not waste time adjusting things to such a nicety, screwing in hooks at just the right height and leaving every trace of thoughtful deliberation; they simply throw themselves, as hurriedly as possible, out of the nearest window.

'Didn't the police think all this very odd?' he queried thoughtfully.

'No-o, I don't think they did. They seemed to take it all for granted. And after all, as Uny did kill herself, it doesn't matter much how, does it?'

Roger was forced to agree that it didn't. But when he took his leave a few minutes later, to write that letter to Dorsetshire which must now put things beyond all hope, he was more than ever convinced that there was very, very much more in all this than had so far met the eye. And he was more than ever determined to find out just exactly what it might be.

The thought of that happy, laughing kid of the snapshot being driven into panic-stricken suicide had inexpressibly shocked him before. The thought of her now, driven into a deadly slow suicide, prepared with such tragic method and care, was infinitely more horrible. Somebody, Roger was sure, had driven that poor child into killing herself; and that somebody, he was equally sure, was going to be made to pay for it.

CHAPTER IV

TWO DEATHS AND A JOURNEY

NEVERTHELESS, during the next few days the case against the unknown made little progress. Roger received a reply to his letter from Dorsetshire which served to inflame his anxiety to get to the bottom of the affair, but his efforts in that direction seemed to be beating upon an impassable barrier. Try as he might, he could not connect Unity Ransome with any man.

He tried the theatre. Of any girl who had been at all friendly with her he asked long strings of questions, the eager Miss Carruthers constantly at his elbow. Under her protecting wing he interviewed stage-doorkeepers, stage-managers, managers, producers, stars, their male equivalents, and everybody else he could think of, till he had acquired enough theatrical copy to last him the rest of his life. But all to no purpose. Nobody could remember having seen Unity Ransome with the same man more than once or twice; to nobody had she ever mentioned the name of a male acquaintance in anything but a joking way.

He cast his net further afield. Armed with half-a-dozen pictures of Janet, enlarged from the groups outside the theatre, he sought out the restaurant-managers, waiters, tea-shop waitresses and hotel-keepers, whose various establishments Janet might have patronised. Here and there she was recognised, but it never went beyond that. Roger was discouraged.

One fact however, although it had no bearing on the subject of his search, did emerge during this busy week. Miss Carruthers having firmly appointed herself his theatrical guide and dramatic friend, Roger got into the habit of dropping in every other day or so at tea-time to report his lack of progress. The little creature with her preposterous name (she had confided by this time

that her real one was Sally Briggs, 'and what the hell,' she asked
wistfully, 'is the use of that to me?') both amused and interested
him. It was a perpetual joy to him to watch how even in her
most real moments she could not help being consciously
dramatic: with genuine tears for her friend's fate streaming
down her cheeks she would yet hold them up for the admiration
of an invisible gallery. In fact, Roger reflected, watching her,
when she was at her most genuine, she was most artificial.

On one of these occasions he took advantage of her absence
in the kitchen to study with minute care the fatal door. What
he saw there upset him considerably. For it was obvious that,
however anxious she might have been beforehand, when it
actually came to the point Janet had not at all wanted to die.
At the bottom of the door, only a few inches off the ground,
was a maze of deep scratches in the paintwork, such as might
have been made by a pair of high heels trying desperately to
find some sort of foothold, however minute, by which to stave
off eternity.

Roger's imagination was a vivid one. He felt rather sick.

'But why,' he asked himself, frowning, 'didn't she grip the
stocking above her neck and pull on that, at any rate for a few
minutes? She could have been saved if she had. But I suppose
there wasn't enough of it to grip on.'

He turned his attention to the top of the door. There at the
sides, and some little way down as well, were other scratches,
fainter, but not to be mistaken. He walked out into the kitchen.

'Moira,' he said abruptly, 'what were Unity's nails like? Do
you happen to remember?'

'Yes,' said Miss Carruthers, with a little shiver. 'All broken
and filled with paint and stuff.'

'Ah!' said Roger.

'And she used to keep them *so* nice,' said Miss Carruthers.

London having thus proved blank, Roger determined to try
the country. He felt a little diffident about intruding upon the
grief-stricken family, and uncertain whether to acquaint the vicar

with his suspicions or not. In the end he decided not to do so until he had more evidence to support them; what he possessed already would merely add to the old man's distress without effecting anything helpful. He trusted to his usual luck to acquire the information he wanted (if it was to be acquired) by some other means.

Having made up his mind, Roger acted with his usual impulsiveness. If he were to go at all, he would go the next day. But the next day was a Friday, and Tuesdays and Fridays were the days on which he spent the morning at *The Courier* offices. Very well, then; he would write his article that evening, merely call in at *The Courier* building to leave it and collect his post, and so catch an early train down to Dorsetshire. Excellent.

To turn out two articles a week for several months on the subject of sudden death is not, after the sixth month or so, an easy task. Having exhausted most of the topics on which he had wanted to spread himself, Roger was beginning to find the search for fresh ones getting rather too arduous. And now that he was anxious to polish one off in a hurry, of course no subject would present itself. After nibbling the end of his fountain-pen for half-an-hour, Roger ran down into the street to buy an evening paper. When inspiration fails, a newspaper will sometimes work wonders.

This one certainly came up to expectations. On the front page, in gently leaded type to show that, while startling, it could hardly be considered important, were the following headlines:

LONDON FLAT TRAGEDY

GIRL HANGS HERSELF WITH OWN STOCKING
PATHETIC LETTER

Roger was able to write a very informative article indeed, all about mass-suggestion, neurotic types, predisposition to suicide and how it is stimulated by example, and the lack of originality in most of us. 'Within a few weeks of the first genius discovering

that he could end his life by lying with his head in a gas-oven,'
wrote Roger, 'more than a dozen had followed his lead.' And
he went on to prove that a novel method of ending life, whether
one's own or another's, acts in such a way upon a certain type
of mind that it constitutes a veritable stimulus to death. He
instanced Dr Palmer and Dr Dove, Patrick Mahon and Norman
Thorne, and, of course, the twin stocking tragedies. Altogether
the article was in Roger's best vein, and he was not a little
pleased with it.

The next day he set off for Dorsetshire.

In his morning paper (not *The Daily Courier*) which he had
been saving up to read in the train, was a rather fuller account
of the tragedy, though now relegated to an unimportant page.
Roger was quite gratified to observe that such details as were
given corresponded almost exactly with those of Janet's case;
its perpetrator evidently corresponded exactly to the type which
he had described so meticulously last night. Whatever he might
feel for Janet, Roger had no sympathy with this girl; she was
of the kind which is far better out of this world than in it. And
she had copied poor little Janet with a slavishness that was
really rather nauseating: the silk stocking tied in a single loop
and twisted over the door, the screwed hook on the further
side, the bare leg, the unsigned note—they were all there.

Her name was Elsie Benham, 'described as an actress', as
the paper cautiously put it. ('And of course we know what that
means,' Roger commented caustically. 'Why do they always
"describe themselves as actresses?" It's uncommonly tough on
the real ones.') She was known as a habituée of night-clubs
('That's more like it') and had been seen at one on the night
of the tragedy. She was alone, and a friend who spoke to her
mentioned that she seemed depressed. She left alone, at two
o'clock in the morning, and must have killed herself very soon
after reaching the flat which she shared with another friend
who is at the moment out of London ('Euphemism for week-
ending in Paris,' observed the sarcastic reader), for when she

was discovered yesterday afternoon by a man who possessed a key to the flat ('As I said') the doctor who was hurriedly summoned gave it as his opinion that she had been dead for at least twelve hours. 'Which is not a bad sentence, even for *this* rag,' thought Roger.

He skimmed through the rest of the report, tossed the newspaper aside and opened a novel.

It was not till two hours later, as he was idly watching the fields fly past the window, that two things struck Roger. The evening paper had exaggerated when it spoke of the pathetic 'letter' left by the dead girl. It was not a letter; it was merely a quotation. 'How wonderful is Death!' she had written on a blank piece of paper. 'Death and his brother Sleep.'

'How wonderful is Death.
Death and his brother Sleep,'

murmured Roger. 'It's curious that a lady "described as an actress" and known as a habituée of night-clubs should choose to quote Queen Mab on such an occasion. It's curious that she could quote Shelley at all. It's *very* curious that she would quote him correctly; I'd have taken a small bet that any lady "described as an actress" who might improbably have a nodding acquaintance with Shelley, would quote: "How *beautiful* is Death." Very curious; but not, apparently, impossible. Well, well, there must be more things in our night-clubs, Sheringham, than are dreamt of in your philosophy.'

He watched a few more fields slide past.

'And here's another funny thing,' thought Roger. 'All the papers this time feature the bare leg. But the bare leg wasn't mentioned before, in any of the accounts I read. When Moira told me, it was complete news to me. I wonder how this woman got hold of that. I suppose it must have been alluded to in some paper I never saw; though I certainly thought I'd studied them all at one time or another. Curious.'

He went on watching the fields, and set to wondering what he was going to say to Mr Manners. The nearer he got to Dorsetshire, the more impertinent his mission began to appear.

In the end he decided not to try the village inn at Little Mitcham, as had been his first intention, but to put up in the neighbouring town of Monckton Regis. This would look less intrusive. He could then, finding himself so near to Mr Manners, go over to Little Mitcham to pay his respects with perfect propriety.

This course he duly followed. Mr Manners welcomed him eagerly, carried him off at once to his study, and plied him with questions which Roger found a good deal of difficulty in answering tactfully. The old man seemed very depressed, as was only to be expected, but his grief was dignified and unembarrassing. Pressed with warmth to stay to luncheon and meet the rest of the family, Roger acceded after protest, quietening his conscience with the reflection that at such a time as this the presence of a stranger might be a blessing in disguise to the stricken household; at the least it would take their minds for a few hours off their loss.

The other four daughters were aged respectively twenty-four, seventeen, fourteen and twelve, and with the eldest, Anne, Roger found himself almost immediately on terms of good friendship. She was one of those capable girls whom the emergency seems so often to produce; and unlike most capable girls, she was good to look upon as well. Not so pretty as Janet had been, perhaps, but in a way more beautiful, and built in miniature; and her air of reposeful efficiency (not the assertive efficiency which most capable women possess) Roger found extremely attractive. Making his mind up with his usual rapidity during lunch, he sought an opportunity after the meal was over to take her aside, and, under pretext of admiring the garden in its garment of budding spring, proceeded to tell her the whole story.

If Anne was shocked, she scarcely showed it; if she was much upset, she concealed her feelings. She merely replied, gravely:

'I see. This is extraordinarily good of you, Mr Sheringham. And thank you for telling me; I much prefer to know. I quite agree with your conclusions, too, and I'll do anything to help you confirm them.'

'And you can?' Roger asked eagerly.

Anne shook her small head. She was small all over, delicately boned, with small, rather serious features set in a small, oval face. 'At the moment,' she confessed, 'I don't see that I can. Janet knew plenty of men round here, of course, and I can give you a list of the ones she knew best, but I'm quite sure that none of them could be at the bottom of it.'

'We could at any rate find out which of them had been in London since she went up there,' Roger said, loath to abandon the line on which all his hopes were now pinned.

'We could, of course,' Anne agreed. 'And we will, if you think we should. But I'm convinced, Mr Sheringham, that it isn't here that we must look for the cause of my sister's death. When she left here she hadn't a care in the world, I know. Janet and I—' Her voice faltered for a moment, but recovered immediately—'Janet and I were a good deal more than sisters; we were the most intimate of friends. If she'd been worried before she left here, I'm certain she would have told me.'

'Well,' said Roger, with more cheerfulness than he felt, 'we'll simply have to see what we can do; that's all.'

The upshot was that Roger spent a very pleasant weekend in Dorsetshire, saw a great deal of Anne, who, to his great delight, did not seem to have the faintest wish to discuss his books with him, and returned to London on the Monday apparently not an inch nearer his objective. 'Though a weekend in Dorsetshire in early April,' he told the lady in the office as he paid his hotel-bill, 'is a thing no man should be without.'

'Quate,' agreed the young lady.

Roger strolled down to the station. He had made a point of mentioning to Anne the time of his train, in case anything cropped up that she might want to communicate to him at the last moment. As he walked on to the platform, he looked up and down to see if she were there. She was not.

With a sense of disappointment which he could not remember having experienced for at least ten years, and of which he became instantly as near to being ashamed as Roger could concerning anything connected with himself, he made his way to the bookstall and bought a paper. Opening it a few minutes later, his eye at once caught certain headlines on the centre page. The headlines ran as follows:

ANOTHER SILK STOCKING TRAGEDY

SOCIETY BEAUTY HANGS HERSELF
LADY URSULA GRAEME'S SHOCKING FATE

'This,' said Roger, 'is becoming too much of a good thing.'

CHAPTER V

SEATED in the train, Roger began to peruse the account of Lady Ursula's death. Now that it had to deal with the daughter of an earl instead of an obscure habituée of night-clubs, the story had been allotted two full columns on the centre page, and every detail, relative or not, that could be hastily scraped together had been inserted. Briefly, the facts were as follows.

Lady Ursula had left her home in Eaton Square, where she lived with her widowed mother (the present Earl, her eldest brother, was in the Diplomatic Service abroad), shortly before eight. She dined with a party of friends at a dance-club in the West End, where she stayed, dancing and talking, till about eleven. She then began to complain of a headache and tried to induce one of the others to accompany her for a little run in her car; the rest of the party refused, however, as it was raining and the car was an open two-seater. Lady Ursula then left the club, saying that she would go for a run alone to blow her headache away, if no one would accompany her.

At half-past two in the morning a girl called Irene Macklane, an artist and a friend of Lady Ursula's, returned to her studio in Kensington from a party in a neighbouring studio and found Lady Ursula's car outside. She was not surprised at this, as Lady Ursula was in the habit of calling on her friends at the most unusual of times of the day and night. On going inside and calling, however, she could at first see no sign of her.

The studio had been made out of the remains of some old stables, and spanning its width in the centre was a large oak beam, some eight feet above the ground, in the middle of which, on the underside, was a large hook, from which Miss Macklane had hung an old-fashioned lantern. This lantern contained an electric light bulb which was connected by a flex to a light-point farther down the room. On turning the switch at the door, Miss Macklane was surprised to see the lantern light upon the floor some distance away from the beam instead of in its normal position. She lifted it up and was then horrified to see Lady Ursula hanging in its place from the hook in the beam.

The details of her death corresponded almost exactly with those of Janet's and the other woman's. An overturned table lay on the floor a few feet away, and Lady Ursula had made use of one of the stockings which she was wearing at the time; the leg from which she had taken it was bare, though the foot still wore its brocade slipper. A loop had been formed by tying the extreme ends of the stocking together, this had been passed over Lady Ursula's head, the slack twisted round three or four times, and a tiny loop at the end slipped over the hook. She had then apparently kicked the table away and met her death, like the other two, from slow asphyxiation.

The note she had left for Miss Macklane, however, was a little more explicit than those of the others, though its wording gave scope for conjecture. It ran:

> I'm so sorry to have to do this here, my dear, but there's simply nowhere else, and mother would have a fit if I did it at home. Don't be too terribly furious with me!
>
> U.

There followed a eulogistic account of Lady Ursula, 'by a friend,' expatiating on her originality, her lack of convention and her recent engagement to the wealthy son of a wealthy financier. Whether it was the engagement, or her determination at all costs to be original, that had led Lady Ursula to dispense with a life with which, as she was in the habit of informing her friends, she had for many years been bored stiff, the writer obviously found some difficulty in avoiding.

Roger put the paper across his knees and began absently to fill his pipe. This was, as he had commented, too much of a good thing. It was becoming a regular epidemic. Fantastic pictures floated across his mental vision of the thing becoming a society craze, and all the debutantes suspending themselves in rows by their own stockings. He pulled himself together.

The real trouble, of course, was that this did not square with the article he had written before leaving London. It upset things badly. For though the unknown habituée of night-clubs might have possessed the predisposition to suicide about which he had expatiated so glibly, he was quite sure that Lady Ursula Graeme did not. And from what he knew about the lady, even apart from the friend's article upon her, he was still more sure that, if by any strange chance she had decided to do away with herself, she would most certainly not imitate the method of an insignificant chorus-girl and a wretched little prostitute. If she were to imitate anybody it would be in the grand manner. She might cut an artery in a hot bath, for instance. But far more probably she would evolve some daringly unconventional method of suicide which should ensure her in death an even greater publicity than she had been able to attain in life. Lady Ursula, in short, would set the fashion in suicide, not follow it.

And that letter, too. It might be more explicit in its terms than the other two, but it was even more puzzling. Whatever one might think about them in other ways, one does give our aristocracy credit for good manners; and by no stretch of etiquette can it be considered good manners to suspend oneself by one's stocking in somebody else's studio. Indeed, it would be far more in keeping with the lady's character that she should have chosen a lamp-post. And would the dowager have no fit so long as her daughter did not suspend herself actually in Eaton Square?

It was all very curious. But it wasn't the least good arguing about it, Roger decided, turning to another page of the paper, for there was no getting away from the fact that Lady Ursula *had* done all these things which she couldn't possibly have done.

He proceeded to wade through the leading articles with some determination.

Lady Ursula's death provided, of course, a three-days' wonder. The inquest was fixed for Wednesday morning, and Roger made up his mind to attend it. He was anxious to see whether any of these little points which had struck his own attention, so small in themselves but so interesting in the aggregate, would strike that of anyone else.

Unfortunately Roger was not the only person who had conceived the idea of attending the inquest. On a conservative calculation, three thousand other people had done so as well. The other three thousand, however, had not also conceived the idea of obtaining a press-pass beforehand; so that in the end Roger, battered but more or less intact, was able to edge his way inside by the time the proceedings were not much more than half over. The first eye he caught was that of Chief Detective Inspector Moresby.

The Chief Inspector was wedged unobtrusively at the back of the court like any member of the public, and it was plain that he was not here in any official capacity. 'Then why in Hades,' thought Roger very tensely, as he wriggled gently towards him, 'is he here at all?' Chief Detective Inspectors do not attend inquests on fashionable suicides by way of killing time.

He grinned in friendly fashion as he saw Roger approaching (so friendly, indeed, that Roger winced slightly, remembering what must be inspiring most of the grin), but shook his head in reply to Roger's raised eyebrows of inquiry. Brought to a halt a few paces away, Roger had no option but to give up the idea of further progress for the moment. He devoted his attention to the proceedings.

A man was on the witness-stand, a tall, dark, good-looking man of a slightly Jewish cast of countenance, somewhere in the early thirties; and it did not need more than two or three questions and replies to show Roger that this was the fiancé to whom allusion had been made. Roger watched him with interest. If anybody ought to have known Lady Ursula, it should be this man. Would he give any indication that he considered anything curious in the case?

Regarding him closely, Roger found it difficult to say. He was evidently suffering deeply ('Poor devil!' thought Roger. 'And being made to stand up and show himself off before all of us like this, too!'), and yet there was a subtle suggestion of guardedness in his replies. Once or twice he seemed on the verge of making a comment which might be enlightening, but always he pulled himself up in time. He carried his loss with a dignity of sorrow which reminded Roger of Anne's bearing in the garden when he had first told her of his suspicions; but it was clear that there were points upon which he was completely puzzled, the main one being why his fiancée should have committed suicide at all.

'She never gave me the faintest indication,' he said in a low voice, in answer to some question of the Coroner's. 'She seemed perfectly happy, always.' He spoke rather like a small boy who has been whipped and sent to bed for something which for the life of him he can't understand to be a crime at all.

The Coroner was dealing with him as sympathetically as possible, but there were some questions that had to be asked. 'You have heard that she was in the habit of saying that she was bored stiff with life. Did she say that to you?'

'Often,' replied the other, with a wan imitation of a smile. 'She frequently said things like that. It was her pose. At least,' he added, so low that Roger could hardly hear, 'we thought it was her pose.'

'You were to have been married the month after next—in June?'

'Yes.'

The Coroner consulted a paper in his hand. 'Now, on the

night in question you went to a theatre, I understand, and afterwards to your club?'

'That is so.'

'You therefore did not see Lady Ursula at all that evening?'

'No.'

'So you cannot speak as to her state of mind after five o'clock, when you left her after tea?'

'No. But it was nearer half-past five when I left her.'

'Quite so. Now you have heard the other witnesses who spent the evening with her. Do you agree that she was in her usual health and spirits when you saw her at tea-time?'

'Absolutely.'

'She gave you no indication that anything might be on her mind?'

'None whatever.'

'Well, I won't keep you any longer, Mr Pleydell. I know how distressing this must be for you. I'll just ask you finally: can you tell us anything which might shed light on the reason why Lady Ursula should have taken her own life?'

'I'm afraid I can't,' said the other, in the same low, composed voice as that in which he had given all the rest of his evidence; and he added, with unexpected emotion: 'I wish to God I could!'

'He *does* think there's something funny about it,' was Roger's comment to himself, as Pleydell stepped down. 'Not merely why she should have done such a thing at all, but some of those other little points as well. I wonder—I *wonder* what Moresby's here for!'

During the next twenty minutes nothing of importance emerged. The Coroner was evidently trying to make the case as little painful for the Dowager Countess and Pleydell as possible, and since it was apparently so straightforward there was no point in spinning out the proceedings. The jury must have thought the same, for their verdict came pat: 'Suicide during temporary insanity caused by the unnatural conditions of modern life.' Which was a kind way of putting 'Lady Ursula's life.'

There was first the hush and then the little stir which always succeeds the delivery of a verdict, and the densely packed court began slowly to empty.

Roger saw to it that the emptying process brought him in contact with Moresby. Having already tested the strength of that gentleman's official reticence, he had not the faintest hope of expecting to crack it on this occasion; but there is never any harm in trying.

'Well, Mr Sheringham,' was the Chief Inspector's genial greeting as they were brought together at last. 'Well, I haven't seen you for a long time, sir.'

'Since last summer, no,' Roger agreed. 'And you'll oblige me by not talking about last summer over the drink we're now about to consume. Any other summer you like, but not last one.'

The Chief Inspector's grin widened, but he gave the necessary promise. They walked sedately towards a hostelry of Roger's choosing; not the nearest, because everybody else would be going there. The Chief Inspector knew perfectly well why he was being invited to have a drink; Roger knew that he knew; the Chief Inspector knew that Roger knew that he knew. It was all very amusing, and both of them were enjoying it.

Both of them knew, too, that it was up to Roger to open the proceedings if they were to be opened. But Roger did nothing of the kind. They drank up their beer, chatting happily about this, about that and about the other, but never about Coroner's inquests and Chief Detective Inspectors from Scotland Yard at them; they drank up some more beer, provided by Moresby, and then they embarked on yet more beer, provided again by Roger. Both Roger and the Chief Inspector liked beer.

At last Roger fired his broadside. It was a nice, unexpected broadside, and Roger had been meditating it at intervals for three glasses. In the middle of a conversation about sweet-peas and how to grow them, Roger remarked very casually:

'So *you* think Lady Ursula was murdered too, do you, Moresby?'

CHAPTER VI

DETECTIVE SHERINGHAM, OF SCOTLAND YARD

IT is given to few people in this world to see a Chief Inspector of Scotland Yard start violently; yet this was the result which rewarded Roger's broadside. With intense gratification he watched the Chief Inspectorial countenance shiver visibly, the Chief Inspectorial bulk tauten, and the Chief Inspectorial beer come within an inch of climbing over the side of the glass; and in that moment he felt that the past was avenged.

'Why, Mr Sheringham, sir,' said Chief Inspector Moresby, with a poor attempt at bland astonishment, 'whatever makes you say a thing like that?'

Roger did not reply at once. Now that he had got over the slight numbness that followed the success of his little ruse (he had hoped perhaps to make the Inspectorial eye-lid quiver slightly, but hardly more), he was filled with a genuine astonishment of no less dimensions than that which Moresby was so gallantly attempting to simulate. In attributing Lady Ursula's death to murder he had not so much been drawing a bow at a venture as deliberately making the wildest assertion he could think of, in order to shock the Inspector into giving away the much more insignificant cause of his presence at the inquest. But, perhaps for the first time in his life, the Chief Inspector had been caught napping and given himself away, horse, foot and artillery. The very fact that he had been on his guard had only contributed to his disaster, for he had been guarding his front and Roger had attacked him in the rear.

In the meantime Roger's brain, jerking out of the coma into which the Inspector's start had momentarily plunged it, was making up for lost time. It did not so much think as look swiftly over a rapid series of flashing pictures. And instantly that which had before been a mystery became plain. Roger could have kicked himself that it should have taken a starting Inspector to point out to him the obvious. Murder was the only possible explanation that fitted all those puzzling facts!

'Whew!' he said, in some awe.

The Chief Inspector was watching him uneasily. 'What an extraordinary idea, sir!' he observed, and laughed hollowly.

Roger drank up the rest of his beer, looked at his watch and grabbed the Chief Inspector's arm, all in one movement. 'Come on,' he said. 'Lunch time. You're lunching with me.' And without waiting for a reply he began marching out of the place.

The Chief Inspector, for once at a decided disadvantage, was left with no option but to follow him.

Quivering all over, Roger hailed a taxi and gave the man the address of his flat.

'Where are we going, Mr Sheringham?' asked the Chief Inspector, whose countenance bore none of the happily expectant look of those about to lunch at another's expense.

'To my rooms,' replied Roger, for once economical of words. 'We shan't be overheard there.'

The groan with which the Chief Inspector replied was not overheard either. It was of the spirit. But it was a very substantial spiritual groan.

In an extravagant impulse not many months ago Roger had walked into the Albany, fortified by a visit to his publisher's and the news of the sales of his latest novel, and demanded rooms there. A set being fortunately vacant at the moment, he had stepped straight into them. Thither he led the helpless Chief Inspector, now gently perspiring all over, thrust him into a chair, mixed him a short drink in spite of his protests in which the word 'beer' was prominent, and went off to see about lunch. During the interval between his return and the serving of the meal, he regaled his victim with a vivid account of the coffee-growing business in Brazil, in which he had a young cousin.

THE SILK STOCKING MURDERS

'Anthony Walton, his name is,' he remarked with nonchalance. 'I believe you met him once, didn't you?'

The Chief Inspector had not even the spirit left to forget his earlier promise and retort in kind.

Let it not be thought that Chief Inspector Moresby shows up in an unworthy light in this episode. Roger had him in a cleft stick, and Moresby knew it. When police inquiries are in progress that necessitate the most profound secrecy, the smallest whisper of their existence in the Press may be enough to destroy the patient work of weeks. The Press, which may be bullied on occasions with impunity, must on others be courted by the conscientious Scotland Yard man with more delicate caution than ever lover courted the shyest of mistresses. Roger knew all this only too well, and only too well Chief Inspector Moresby knew that he knew it. But this time the situation was not amusing at all.

In the orthodox manner Roger held up any discussion of the topic at issue until the coffee had been served and the cigarettes were alight, just as big business men always do in the novels that are written about them (in real life they get down to it with the *hors d'œuvres* and don't blether about, wasting valuable time). 'And now,' said Roger, when that stage had arrived, 'now, Moresby, my friend, for it!'

'For it?' repeated Chief Inspector Moresby, still game.

'Yes; don't play with me, Moresby. The boot's on the other foot now. And what are we going to do about it?'

The Chief Inspector tidily consumed the dregs in his coffee-cup. 'That,' he said carefully, 'depends what we're talking about, Mr Sheringham.'

'Very well,' Roger grinned unkindly. 'I'll put it more plainly. Do you want me to write an article for *The Courier* proving that Lady Ursula must have been murdered—and not only Lady Ursula, but Elsie Benham and Unity Ransome as well? Am I to call on the police to get busy and follow up my lead? It's an article I'm simply tingling to write, you know.'

'You are, sir? Why?'

'Because I've been following up the Ransome case since the day after the death,' said Roger with emphasis, but without truth.

In spite of himself, and the traditions of Scotland Yard concerning amateurs, the Chief Inspector was impressed. Nor did he take any trouble to hide it. 'You have, sir?' he said, not without admiration. 'Well, that was very smart of you. You tumbled to it even then that it was murder?'

'I did,' said Roger, without blenching. 'Ah, now we're getting on. You agree that it was murder, then?'

'If you must know,' said the harrassed Chief Inspector, seeing nothing else for it, 'I do.'

'But you didn't realise it as soon as I did?' pursued the unblushing Roger. 'You didn't realise it, in fact, till Lady Ursula's case came along?'

'It's only suspicion, even now,' replied Moresby, adroitly avoiding a direct answer.

Roger drew for a few moments at his cigarette. 'I'm sorry Scotland Yard's tumbled to the idea of murder,' he said, after a pause. 'I'd been looking on this as my own little affair, and I've been putting in some hard work on it too. And you needn't think I'm going to drop out just because you've stepped in. I'm determined to get to the bottom of the business (I've something like a personal interest in it, as it happens), with or without the police. And at present I'm far and away ahead of you.'

'How's that, Mr Sheringham?'

'Well, to take only one point, do you know Unity Ransome's real identity?'

'Not yet, we don't, no,' the Chief Inspector had to confess.

'Well, I do,' said Roger simply.

There was another pause.

'What's in your mind, Mr Sheringham?' Moresby broke it by asking. 'There's something, I can see.'

'There is,' Roger agreed. 'It's this: I want us to work together on this case. I wanted to at Ludworth last summer, but you wouldn't. Now I'm in a much stronger position. Because don't forget that I can help you very considerably as your assistant. I don't mind your looking on me as an assistant,' he added magnanimously.

'You could help me, could you, Mr Sheringham?' the Chief Inspector meditated. 'Now I wonder exactly how?'

'No, you don't,' Roger retorted. 'You know perfectly well. In the first place there's the material I've got together already. But far more than that, there's the question of the murderer. The circumstances of Lady Ursula's death make it quite obvious to me that the murderer is a man of good social position, or, at the least, somebody known to her (all Lady Ursula's friends weren't of good social position, I admit). Well, now, this is going to be a very difficult case, I think. We're dealing, I take it, with a homicidal maniac who is probably quite sane on all other subjects. There are only two ways of getting him: one is to catch him red-handed, and the other is to get into his confidence and attack him from behind (and we needn't have any sporting scruples in this case). Do you agree so far?'

'All that seems reasonable enough,' Moresby conceded.

'Quite so. Well, as to the first method, does one usually take homicidal maniacs of the sexual type red-handed? You people at the Yard ought to know, with your experience of Jack the Ripper. And I'm assuming that our man isn't quite such a dolt as Neil Cream, who almost invited the police to come and investigate him. Then only the second method remains. Well, now, Moresby, I don't want to be offensive, but are you the fellow to get into the confidence of such a man? Let's look at it quite reasonably. We narrow our suspicions down, say, to an old Etonian, who is a member of, perhaps, the Oxford and Cambridge Club. *Do* you think you could induce a man like that to confide anything further to you than the best thing for the three-thirty? You can't join his club, you see, and get at him that way, can you?'

'I see your point all right, Mr Sheringham,' Moresby smiled. 'Yes, there's a good deal in that. But of course we've got plenty of people at the Yard who could do all that. What about the Assistant Commissioner? He was at Eton himself.'

'Do you really imagine,' said Roger with fine scorn, 'that a man who has committed at least three murders is going to confide in the Assistant Commissioner of Scotland Yard? Don't pretend to be puerile, Moresby. You know well enough that nobody even remotely connected with Scotland Yard is going to be any good for that. It's just there where my position is so useful to you. I'm not connected with Scotland Yard. I'm known to the general public simply as a writer of fiction. Why, the man we're looking for has probably never seen even a copy of *The Courier* in his life.'

'Well, as I said, there's plenty of sense in all this, Mr Sheringham. And if I do refuse to take you on as an assistant, I suppose you mean you'll blow the gaff and do your best to queer our pitch?'

'I shall hold myself free to write what I choose about these cases,' Roger corrected with dignity.

'Um!' The Chief Inspector tapped absently on the table and appeared to be ruminating. 'I'm in charge of the investigation at present, of course. But we're not by any means certain yet that they are murders. There's a lot in that stuff you wrote in *The Courier* the other day about suggestion acting on a certain type of mind, you know.'

'Ah! So you read my articles, do you?' said Roger, childishly pleased. 'But Lady Ursula's wasn't that type of mind, you know. That's the whole point. Still, we'll go into that later. Are you or are you not going to take me on?'

'We're not allowed to do anything like that, not without permission, you know,' the Chief Inspector demurred.

'Yes, and I know equally well that you'll get the permission in this case for the asking,' Roger retorted, without modesty.

The Chief Inspector ruminated further. 'Well,' he said at

length, 'I'm not saying that you might not be able to help me, Mr Sheringham, in this particular case. Quite a lot. And certainly you're no fool,' he added kindly. 'I thought that at Ludmouth, though you were a bit too clever there. But it was really smart of you to tumble to murder in the Ransome case, before those others. I'll admit that it never occurred to us at all. Yes, very well, then, sir; we'll consider that settled. I'll apply for permission to take you in with us as soon as I get back to the Yard.'

'Good man!' Roger cried in high delight. 'We'll open a bottle of my precious '67 brandy to celebrate my official recognition.'

Over the reverent consumption of a couple of glasses of the '67, Roger made known to his new colleague the result of his researches into the case of Unity Ransome, first stipulating that her real identity should not be made public unless circumstances absolutely necessitated it; he was resolved to use any influence he had to save that unhappy family from further trouble. The Chief Inspector agreed readily enough and, now that it was no longer a case of rivalry but of collaboration, complimented his companion ungrudgingly on his astuteness. He had himself already paid a couple of visits to the Sutherland Avenue flat, but had made little progress from that end of the complicated case.

'What put Scotland Yard finally on the suspicion of murder?' Roger asked, having told all he knew.

'Something beyond your own knowledge, Mr Sheringham,' replied the Chief Inspector. 'On examining Lady Ursula's body, our surgeon reported that there were distinct signs of bruises at her wrists. I had a look at them myself, and though they were faint enough, I'm ready to swear to my belief that her hands had been tied together at some time. Well, she wouldn't have tied her own hands, would she?'

Roger nodded. 'And the other cases?'

'Nothing was noticed at the time, but we're taking steps to find out.'

'Exhumation? Yes. Well now, Moresby, let's hear your theory about it all.'

'Theory, sir? Well, I suppose we do have theories. But Scotland Yard works more on clues than theories. The French police, now, they work on theories; but they're allowed a good deal more latitude in their inquiries than we are. They go in a lot for bluff, too, which we can't use. All we can do is to follow up the pointers in a case, and see where they lead to.'

'Well, let's examine the pointers, then. What do you consider we've got to work on, so far?'

Inspector Moresby looked at his watch. 'Good gracious, sir,' he exclaimed, in artless surprise, 'I'd no idea it was as late as this. They'll be wondering whatever's happened to me. You'll have to excuse me, Mr Sheringham. I must get back to the Yard at once.'

Roger understood that not until official permission had actually come through would the Chief Inspector discuss the case with him further than to pick his brains. He smiled, well enough content with the result of his lunch-party.

CHAPTER VII

GETTING TO GRIPS WITH THE CASE

Soon after eight o'clock that same evening, in response to a telephoned hint from Roger, Chief Inspector Moresby again visited the Albany, official permission to discard his reticence at last duly obtained. Roger welcomed him with a choice of whisky or beer, pipe, tobacco or cigarettes, and they settled down in front of the fire, pipes alight and a pewter tankard at each elbow, to go into the case with real thoroughness.

'By the way, have you seen *The Evening Clarion*?' Moresby remarked first of all, pulling the paper in question from his pocket. 'You journalists do give us a lot of trouble, you know.' He handed it over, marking a certain paragraph with his thumb.

The paragraph was at the end of an account of the inquest on Lady Ursula that morning. Roger read: 'From the unobtrusive presence among the spectators at the back of the court of a certain highly placed official at Scotland Yard, it may be argued that the police are not altogether satisfied with the case as it stands at present. Certainly there seem to be many obscure points which require clearing up. It must not be supposed that the said official's interest in the proceedings necessarily means that Scotland Yard definitely suspects foul play, but it is not too much to assume that we have not yet heard the last of this tragic affair.'

'Very cleverly put,' was Roger's professional comment. 'Damn the fellow!' he added, unprofessionally.

'It's a nuisance,' agreed his companion. 'I've put a stop to any more, of course, and I daresay there's no harm done really; but that sort of thing's very annoying when you're doing all you can to keep your inquiries a close secret. Anyhow, there's one blessing; nobody's brought up the Monte Carlo business yet.'

'Monte Carlo? What's that?'

'Oh, didn't you know about that, Mr Sheringham?' asked the Chief Inspector, his eyes twinkling. 'I made sure *you* had that at your fingers'-ends. Why, a French girl—a *croquette,* or whatever they call 'em over there—'

'A *cocotte,*' Roger corrected without a smile. 'Described as an actress. Yes?'

'Well, a French *cocotte* was found dead in her bedroom in February in just the same way. She'd lost a good deal of money in the Casino, so of course they assumed she'd hanged herself. It was more or less hushed up (those things always are there) and I don't think it was even mentioned in the papers over here. We heard about it, unofficially.'

'Monte Carlo this February, eh?' Roger said thoughtfully. 'That ought to be a bit of a help.'

'It's about all we've got to go on,' said the Chief Inspector, rather dolefully. 'I mean, assuming that this is murder at all and that the same man's responsible for it. That, I should say, and the note.'

'The note? Oh, you mean the note Lady Ursula left. Yes, I'd realised of course that if it was murder, all those notes must have been written with quite a different meaning than the one everybody gave them later. The murderer's a clever man, Moresby, there's no getting away from it.'

'He is that, Mr Sheringham. But there's a bit more to be got out of Lady Ursula's than the others. If it *was* murder, then that note must have meant something quite different, as you say. But its importance to us is that it was creased. You can see it at the Yard any time.'

'I see,' Roger nodded. 'And it hadn't been left in an envelope, you mean. In other words, it must have been in another envelope at one time, and therefore was definitely not written on that occasion.'

'Or in somebody's pocket. The paper's a tiny bit rubbed at the creases as if it had been in a pocket. Well, Mr Sheringham, find the person to whom that note was written, and we've gone a long way towards solving the mystery. It's the only clue we've got, but I shouldn't be surprised if it isn't going to be the only one we shall want. Mark my words, sir, it's that note that's going to clear up this affair for us, if we can only find out who it was written to.'

'I shouldn't be surprised,' Roger replied non-committally. Privately, however, he did not feel so sure. He recognised that Scotland Yard was going to regard the letter as the Dominant Clue; but the method of the Dominant Clue, though often brilliantly successful (or rather, not so much brilliantly as pains-takingly) was liable to fall to the ground when the clue in question did not come up to scratch. By disregarding the side-issues in these latter cases Scotland Yard had many failures in its records which a less single-aimed method, such as the French with its inductive reasoning, would almost certainly have solved; and it was no palliative to point out that the reverse also was equally true, and that there are unsolved mysteries in the French annals which the more laborious method of Scotland Yard would probably have cleared up.

A really rogue-proof detective-service, Roger had long ago decided, should not stick to one method at all, but make use of them all; and he determined that the partnership between himself and Moresby should be such a service in miniature. Let Moresby pursue the Dominant Clue and call on the organ-ised resources of Scotland Yard to help him do so; he himself would look at the problem as a whole, from every possible side, and do his best to combine the amazing deductive powers of the Austrian criminological professors with the imaginative brilliance of the star French detectives. It is characteristic of Roger that he took this tremendous task on his shoulders with complete composure, between two pulls at his tankard.

The two settled down into a steady talk.

During the next half-hour Roger found himself much impressed with the common sense level-headedness of his colleague, whom he had been inclined to regard, in consequence of his preference for a Dominant Clue, as lacking in perception of the finesses of scientific criminology. He was also a little chagrined to find that Moresby's knowledge of criminal history was even more complete than his own.

As the discussion progressed Roger was not the only one to make discoveries. The Chief Inspector, too, hitherto disposed to regard Roger as a volatile-witted amateur intent only upon proving impossible theories of his own erection, now found himself considerably more impressed than he had anticipated by his companion's quick grasp of essentials and the vivid imagination he was able to bring to bear on the problem. If he had felt any misgivings about taking a leaf out of the story-books and admitting an amateur into his councils, they were not long in disappearing. By the end of half an hour the partnership was on a firm basis.

As if to mark the fact, Roger rose and replenished the tankards. The beer, it may be remarked, was a good sound XXXX, of a dark fruity colour, from a cask in the next room, Roger's study. Oh, all you young women, distrust a man who does not drink good sound fruity XXXX with zest as you would one of your own sex who did not care to powder her nose.

'Now it seems to me,' said Roger as he sat down again, 'that we've been talking too much at random. Let's take things under their proper heads, one at a time. First of all the deaths themselves. We've agreed that any other hypothesis but that of murder is putting too great a strain on coincidence, haven't we? Well, then, let's take a leaf out of the French notebook and reconstruct the crime.'

'Very well, Mr Sheringham, sir. I'd like to hear you do that.'

'Well, this is how I see it. The murderer first of all selected his victim with a good deal of care. She must fulfil certain conditions. For instance, she must above all be so far familiar with his appearance, at any rate, as to feel no alarm on seeing him. Then the opportunity would be chosen with equal cunning. It must be when she is alone and likely to remain so for at least half an hour. But all that's quite elementary.'

'There's never any harm in running over the elementary parts with the rest,' said the Chief Inspector, gazing into the fire.

'Well, having got the girl and the opportunity together, he proceeds to overpower her. I say that, because no girl is going to submit tamely to being hanged, still less is she going to take off one of her stockings and offer it for the purpose; and yet none of them show any obvious evidence of a struggle. Even the marks on Lady Ursula's wrists can't be called that. Well, now, how did he overpower them?'

'That's it,' observed Chief Inspector Moresby.

'He was devilish clever,' Roger continued, warming to his work. 'You try overpowering an ordinary, healthy girl and see whether there isn't going to be a deuce of a struggle. Of course there is. So it's an elementary deduction to say that he must be a strong, and probably very big man. And they didn't even cry out. Obviously, then, he must have stopped that first. I'm not so childish, by the way, as to suggest chloroform or anything fatuous like that; anybody but the writers of penny dreadfuls knows that chloroform doesn't act like that, to say nothing of the smell afterwards. No, what I do suggest is a woollen scarf thrown unexpectedly across her mouth from behind and drawn tight in the same instant. How's that?'

'I can't think of anything better, and that's a fact.'

'Well, a strong man could easily knot that at the back of her head, catch her wrists (her hands would be instinctively trying to pull at the stuff over her mouth) and twist them into the small of her back. I admit that it's more of a job to fasten them there, but a knowledge of ju-jitsu might help; he could put her, I mean, in such a position that she couldn't move without breaking an arm, hold both her wrists there with one hand and tie them together with the other. And as there are only the faintest bruises there, he would obviously have to fasten them with something that isn't going to cut the skin—one end of the same woollen scarf, for instance.' Roger paused and moistened his clay.

'Go on, Mr Sheringham,' urged Moresby politely.

'Well, then, of course, he'd got her where he wanted her. It wouldn't be difficult after that, I imagine, to remove one of her stockings; and then he could proceed with his preparations at leisure, screwing the hook in the door, arranging a chair to stand her on, and all the rest of it. And after he'd hanged her all he would have to do is to unfasten the scarf and untie her wrists and ankles.'

The Chief Inspector nodded. 'That's about what happened, no doubt of it.'

'Well, there's the reconstruction, and I don't see that it gives us anything fresh, except perhaps the woollen scarf, and that's only a guess. As to the man's psychology, that's obvious enough. He's mad, of course. His only possible motive, so far as one can see, is murder for love of killing. Homicidal mania, developed to hopeless insanity. The victim's own stocking, for instance. And I imagine it would have to be silk. Yes, that brain of his must be full of strange twists; the idea of hanging a girl with a lisle-thread stocking would probably shock him as much as it would you or me.'

'It's on Jack the Ripper lines, right enough,' commented the Chief Inspector.

'That's another heading: Criminological Parallels. There's Jack the Ripper, as you say, and Neil Cream, though he's rather different psychologically. I never could understand him not wanting to watch his victims die, could you? I should have imagined that was the whole object of that type of murderer. Can you think of any other similar cases besides those two?'

'Sexual murders, Mr Sheringham, or lust-murders, as the psychologists call them? Well, they're not very common in this country, are they? Most of the foreign ones are like Jack the

Ripper, too, aren't they? Stabbing, I mean. I suppose, taking 'em all round, the best-known are Andreas Bickel, Menesclou, Alton, Gruyo and Verzeni. Then there was an outbreak of stabbing murders in New York in July 1902, and another in Berlin, funnily enough, the same month. Then there was Wilhelm Damian, in Ludwigshafen in Germany, in 1901, and—'

'Great Scott, Moresby!' interrupted the astonished Roger. 'You must have been sitting up late since they made you a Chief Inspector. How on earth do you know all this?'

'It's my business, Mr Sheringham,' replied the Chief Inspector austerely, and drowned his smile in good XXXX.

'Well, what I meant,' Roger continued, in somewhat chastened tones, 'is, can we learn anything from these parallels?'

'I doubt it, sir, except that of all murderers these are the most difficult to catch; and it won't need any criminological parallels to teach us that, I'm afraid.'

'Well, let's go on to the next heading: Victims. What do they give us? The Monte Carlo woman—do you know anything about her?'

'Not yet. I've written over for all details. But if it was the same man, we get that he must have been in Monte Carlo at the time, of course.'

'Yes, that may help us a lot. What about getting hold of a list of all English visitors at Monte Carlo last February?'

'I've done that, Mr Sheringham,' replied the Chief Inspector with a tolerant smile; in matters of routine no amateur could teach him anything. 'And in Nice, Cannes and all the other Riviera places as well.'

'Good man,' said Roger, uncrushed. 'Well, then there's Janet Manners—or Unity Ransome, as I think we'd better go on calling her. The only thing I can see there is that he must have been known to her, and pretty well too for her to have taken him into her sitting-room when she was alone in the flat; that is, if I read her rightly. That may be a useful help to us.'

'That's true enough.'

'Elsie Benham, so far as I see, gives us nothing at all. He might have been known to her or he might not. In the second alternative she must have picked him up between the club and her flat off the Tottenham Court Road; in the first, he might have been waiting for her at the flat. The only hope is that the constable on the beat caught sight of them together.'

'And he didn't,' put in the Inspector. 'I've already ascertained that. But I'm having inquiries made as to anyone else having done so, though I don't think there's much hope.'

'And that leaves Lady Ursula. Well, you know, I can't see that there's much more there. When one comes to think of it, he needn't have known her at all. He could have introduced himself easily enough in the street as a friend of a friend of hers; a little thing like that wouldn't have worried Lady Ursula. Or he might have been a friend of the girl who owns the studio, and knocked in passing on seeing a light inside. I can't see that there's much more.'

'There's the note, Mr Sheringham,' the Chief Inspector reminded him. 'In my opinion that shows that the thing was premeditated, and the note was brought for the purpose.'

'But how could he have known that she was going to the studio? She never said anything about it to her friends. Probably she didn't know herself. She passed by on her way out of London and called in to see if the girl would go for a run with her.'

'That's possible, of course, but we mustn't lose sight of the notion that she had an assignation there, knowing her friend was going to be out, and all that talk about the run was to put the others off the scent. She'd guess well enough that none of them would go with her.'

'Humph!' said Roger, who was quite willing to lose sight of that notion, in which he did not believe for a moment. 'By the way,' he went on, as a memory occurred to him, 'I've a shrewd idea that that fellow she was engaged to—what's his name? Pleydell—has his suspicions. Did you notice him in the court this morning? Half a dozen times he seemed to me on the verge of saying something significant.'

'Yes, I thought he might have something in his mind. I was going to have a talk with him tomorrow morning.'

'It's a rotten position for him,' Roger said thoughtfully. 'And it'll be rottener still if he has got a suspicion that everything isn't as straightforward as it might be. To have one's fiancée commit suicide is bad enough, but to have her murdered. . .! Look here, Moresby, why not hold up your talk with him for a day or two?'

'Why, Mr Sheringham?'

'Well, it's rather a nice point. If he *has* got his suspicions, you see, would he let things stay as they are, to save her family any further scandal, or would he do his damnedest to get at the truth? In my opinion he'd want the truth. But he's not going to be quite sure at first what he wants. Well, if you descend on him before he's made up his mind, he might be driven into holding his tongue. A sort of counter-instinct, you know. And if he's got anything to tell us that would be a pity. On the other hand, if you leave him till he's quite clear about it, I shouldn't be at all surprised if he doesn't come to you; and in that case you'd get far more out of him than in any other way. This is all on the assumption that he *is* suspicious, of course, which may not be the case at all.'

The Chief Inspector consumed a little more beer. 'There's a good deal in that,' he admitted, wiping his mouth delicately on a large blue silk handkerchief. 'Yes, perhaps I was a little hasty, and that's the one thing we ought not to be. Very well, I'll give him three days and see if you're right. It'll be a feather in your cap if you are.'

Roger looked over the notes he had been taking of the conversation. 'Well, what it seems to amount to,' he said, 'is that we've got to look for a man who touches our circle at various points, including Monte Carlo last February. He's probably a hefty fellow, and a gentleman (or passing for one), and we can't necessarily expect anything abnormal in his mental make-up except on this one topic. If we narrow our search down to one man, I shall try to get him to talk on that topic (which won't be too easy to introduce, by the way), and if he gives himself away we can be pretty certain we're on the right track.'

'And then we've got to prove it against him,' added the Chief Inspector with gloom, 'and that's going to be the most difficult job of the lot. If you'd been at the Yard as long as I have, Mr Sheringham, you'd know that—Hullo, isn't that your telephone?'

Roger rose and went to the instrument in his study adjoining. In a moment he was back. 'For you, Moresby,' he said. 'Scotland Yard.'

Moresby went out of the room.

When he returned a few minutes later, his face bore an expression of rather reluctant admiration. 'That was a smart bit of psychological deduction you put in only a few minutes ago, Mr Sheringham,' he said.

'What do you mean?' Roger asked, agog.

The Chief Inspector stooped and plucked out a feather which was protruding from the cushion in his chair. 'Here you are, sir,' he said. 'Put it in your cap. Mr Pleydell's waiting at the Yard to see me at this minute. Care to come round too?'

'You bet I would,' said Roger, with fervour.

CHAPTER VIII

A VISITOR TO SCOTLAND YARD

PLEYDELL was in a waiting-room when Roger and the Chief Inspector arrived in Scotland Yard. There had been some discussion between the two on the way, as to whether Roger should appear at this first interview or not; and it had been decided that, as Pleydell would probably be still a little torn between reticence and the reverse, the presence of a third person might tend to tip the balance in favour of the former. In order that Roger should not, however, miss any of the conversation, he was to lurk behind a screen in a corner of the room.

Moresby had given instructions over the telephone that no hint should be given to Pleydell that the police were already taking an interest in his fiancée's death, so that whatever he had come to say should be completely spontaneous. It was therefore with eager anticipation that Roger retired into his corner, where he was pleased to find that, by applying an eye to a carefully cut aperture in the screen, he could watch the proceedings as well as hear them. A few moments later Pleydell was shown in.

Roger wondered at first whether their precautions had been unnecessary, for Pleydell seemed perfectly composed. 'Good evening,' he said, in reply to Moresby's greeting. 'I know nothing about the procedure here, but I wish to see somebody on a highly delicate matter.'

'That's right, sir,' Moresby assured him. 'You can say whatever you wish to me.'

Pleydell looked a little doubtful. 'I was thinking that perhaps the Assistant Commissioner . . .'

'Sir Paul is out of town this evening, sir,' Moresby replied untruthfully. 'At the moment I'm in charge. You can say anything you wish to me. Take a chair, won't you?'

Pleydell hesitated a moment, as if still not quite contented with a mere Chief Inspector, then seemed to accept the inevitable. As he turned to take the chair, Roger was not quite so sure of his composure; there were little lines at the corners of his mouth and eyes that might indicate mental strain. His self-control, however, was strong. Now that Roger could observe him more nearly than in the court, he saw that the Jewish blood in him was not just a strain, but filled his veins. Pleydell was evidently a pure Jew, tall, handsome and dignified as the Jews of unmixed race often are. Roger liked the look of him at once.

'Now, sir,' Moresby resumed when they were both seated, 'what did you want to see us about?' He spoke in easy, conversational tones, as if his visitor might have come, for all he knew, to sell him a drawing-room suite on the instalment system.

'My name is Pleydell,' said the other. 'I don't suppose that conveys anything to you, but I am—I *was*,' he corrected himself painfully, 'engaged to be married to Lady Ursula Graeme.'

The Chief Inspector's face took on the correct look of condolence. 'Oh, yes. A shocking business, that, sir. I needn't say how I sympathise with you.'

'Thank you.' Pleydell fidgeted for a moment in his chair. And then his composure and his self-control alike disappeared. 'Look here,' he blurted out abruptly, 'this is what I've come round for—I'm not satisfied about it!'

'Not satisfied, sir?' The Chief Inspector's voice was a model of polite surprise. 'Why, how do you mean?'

'I'm not satisfied about my fiancée's death. I'm sure that Lady Ursula would have been the last person in the world to kill herself like that, without any reason. It's—it's grotesque! I want you to look into it.'

The Chief Inspector drummed on the table with his knuckles. 'Look into it, sir?' he repeated. In cases such as this Chief

Inspector Moresby carried on most of his share of the conversation by echoing, in an interrogatory form, the last two or three words of his companion's last speech. It was a good method, for it saved him from sitting dumbly and it also saved him from contributing anything of his own to the conversation. Moreover, it is an excellent way of drawing out one's interlocutor.

'Yes.' Now that his outburst was over and Pleydell had got his chief trouble off his chest, his calm was returning. 'I'm convinced there's something behind all this, Inspector. My fiancée must have had some good reason for doing what she did. She must have been threatened or blackmailed, or—or something horrible. I want the police to find out what that reason was.'

'I see, sir.' Moresby continued to drum absently on his table. 'But that's really hardly a matter for us, is it?' he suggested.

'How do you mean?' Pleydell retorted, his voice indignant. 'I tell you, Lady Ursula must have been hounded into taking her life. She was driven into suicide. She must have been. And isn't that tantamount to murder? Supposing it was blackmail, for instance. That's a matter for you, isn't it?'

'Oh, quite, sir, if you put it like that. What I mean is, this is all too vague. It's only what you think, after all, isn't it? Now if you could give us some evidence, to support what you're saying—well, that might be a different matter.'

Roger smiled. He appreciated the Chief Inspector's method. By pretending to make light of his visitor's suspicions he was hoping to goad him into revelations concerning his fiancée which otherwise he might be most reluctant to make.

It seemed, however, as if Moresby's subtlety was not to be rewarded. 'Evidence?' said Pleydell, more calmly. 'That's difficult. I don't think I've got any evidence to give you. Lady Ursula never gave me the slightest hint that anything was amiss. In fact, the whole dreadful business is a complete mystery to me. All I know is that she wouldn't have done a thing like that without reason, and we don't know of any reason. Therefore that reason ought to be found. Surely it's up to you to unearth the evidence, not me.'

Roger reflected that, up to the present, Pleydell's suspicions almost exactly corresponded with his own concerning Janet Manners. Indeed, had not that chance bombshell flung vaguely in Moresby's direction blown away the cobwebs from his own brain in its bursting, they would probably be the suspicions that he still held. And what would Pleydell say when he found that it was not a case of hidden reasons for suicide at all, but of simple murder?

Roger studied him carefully through the little aperture. Under that normally composed, almost cold exterior, no doubt the fires of passion could burn as fiercely as anywhere else. More fiercely perhaps; for it is those who habitually keep a tight hand on their emotions, whose outburst, when it does occur, is far more violent than that of the normal individual. And after all, in this case the blood was Oriental in origin, however remote that origin might be. With the lust for vengeance which must sweep over him as he learnt the truth, Pleydell might prove a useful help in the investigation. Roger decided that he ought to be told that truth at once.

The Chief Inspector was ambling gently round the question at issue. 'But do you think the Countess would like Scotland Yard called in, sir?' he was asking. 'Now that everything's settled, wouldn't it be better to leave it like that, and not rake up what may turn out to be a nasty scandal?'

Pleydell flushed. 'I'm not necessarily "calling you in",' he replied. 'One only does that when there's something definite to call you in for, I suppose. I've merely come here, after considerable reflection, to report to you my personal opinion that there is something behind the scenes here which ought to be brought into the light. You may, of course, hint at "a nasty scandal" in connection with my fiancée; I prefer to look on her as the probable victim of a blackguardly conspiracy which has ended by driving her to take her own life. And in my opinion you people here ought to investigate the matter. That's all I've got to say.' He rose to his feet, picked up his hat and gloves and walked towards the door 'Good evening,' he added curtly.

Moresby rose too. 'One minute, sir. If you're not in a hurry, I wonder if you'd mind waiting a short time before you go. There may be something in what you say, and perhaps we ought to look into it. I'd like to mention it quickly to a colleague, and he might care to see you. In cases like this, you see, sir, we have to be very careful not to . . .' His voice droned away down the passage outside.

In a moment or two he was back. 'Well, Mr Sheringham? What do you make of all that?'

'He's thinking exactly as I did at first about Unity Ransome. Knows there's something very wrong, but can't just see what it is. We ought to tell him.'

The Chief Inspector looked dubious. 'Tell him it's murder?'

'Yes. He might be very useful. He's our chief lever for uncovering Lady Ursula's case, I should say.'

'Um! But I don't think we'll tell him straight out what we think, Mr Sheringham, if you don't mind. It's a thing we never do unless there's a very definite object to be gained, and there isn't here. But I've no objection to letting him know that we're already investigating the case.'

'Very well. And ask him if he can throw any light on that note of Lady Ursula's.'

'Of course. Well, I'll fetch him back.'

Returning, the Chief Inspector introduced Roger to Pleydell as 'Mr Sheringham, who is going to look into this case with me.'

Pleydell seized on the point immediately. 'Ah!' he said. 'So you are going to look into it?'

The Chief Inspector contrived to smile an apologetic smile in which there was no apology. 'I'm afraid I wasn't quite open with you just now, sir. You mustn't mind; we're very fond of our secrets here.' He winked maliciously at Roger. 'To tell you the truth, we're investigating this case already, in a quiet way. Have been for the last two days, in fact.'

'Ah!' Pleydell stroked his chin thoughtfully. 'So my coming wasn't such a surprise to you after all?'

'We wondered if you might,' Moresby agreed. 'Mr Sheringham was only saying a short time ago that he'd an idea that the same things that had struck us, might probably have struck you.'

Pleydell turned sharply to Roger, the ghost of a smile on his lips. 'They did, Mr Sheringham; very forcibly indeed. And I've been spending the last half-hour trying to induce the Chief Inspector to look into the case officially, without, as I thought, the least success.'

'Well, well,' said the culprit paternally, 'let's sit down and talk it over. Mr Sheringham'll tell you that official secrecy is rather a vice of mine. But now that the cat is out of the bag, so to speak, no doubt you can help us considerably.' As a metaphor applied to the circumstances of Lady Ursula's death, Roger could not help thinking this was an unfortunate one.

Roger and the Chief Inspector sat down on one side of the table, and Pleydell, removing his overcoat, took a chair opposite them. He was in evening kit, in which his tall, well-made form showed to advantage, unlike those of most of the financiers Roger had met. Moresby began by putting his questions, which the other answered as readily as he could, and Roger took the opportunity, while the familiar ground was being covered once more without anything fresh appearing to emerge from it, to study their visitor anew.

The term financier conjures up a slightly repulsive picture. It is unfortunate that financiers, in the abstract, should constitute an idea that is repulsive, but so it is. No doubt they will bear it. The ideal financier is short, stubby, with squat fingers, small eyes, no hair and a protruding stomach. Pleydell had none of these marks of the tribe; considered as a specimen of humanity he was pleasant to look on, with sharp clear features, dark brown eyes that were perhaps the slightest bit hard but only if one looked at them very searchingly, and plenty of black, crisp hair; considered as a financier, he was an Apollo. His age was somewhere between twenty-eight and thirty-five; it might have been either. Of course Roger had heard of him before the tragedy, as he had heard of Lady Ursula Graeme. Pleydell senior was of the financial rank that is known as 'the power behind the throne', meaning, in these days, the power behind the party; Pleydell junior had been spoken of for some years as more than a worthy successor, with several exploits of sheer genius on the financial battlefield already to his credit. Father and son were outstanding for another reason also; they were scrupulously honest, they were behind no shady deals, and they never crushed unless they were unnecessarily attacked.

Noting the lines of young Pleydell's jaw, the glint in his dark eyes and the tiny lines about the corners of his mouth, Roger summed up his impressions in a sentence: 'When that man does learn that she was murdered, he's not going to rest for a minute till he's seen the judge put on the black cap.' A not unpleasing little thrill ran through him. Though he was the other's junior by perhaps half a dozen years, he found himself looking at him just as, in his early 'teens, he had looked at his House football captain. It was not often that Roger suffered from an inferiority complex, but he came perilously near it at that moment.

Moresby, having hitherto been able to elicit nothing of very much help, was questioning Pleydell about the note Lady Ursula had left; warily, because he did not yet wish him to grasp their suspicions of murder. Roger understood that the Chief Inspector considered that more might be brought to light in these early stages if Pleydell remained in ignorance of that. Murder, especially where one's own fiancée is concerned, is apt to upset one's sense of proportion.

'No,' Pleydell said, 'I agree that the wording is curious, but I can't tell you anything else about it. It's in her handwriting, of course; otherwise I might have been tempted to suggest that it had nothing to do with the case at all.'

'You're sure of that, naturally?' Moresby asked. 'That it's in her handwriting, I mean. Quite sure?'

'Of course,' Pleydell replied, surprised. 'What else—oh, you mean, it might not have been left by her at all?'

'Something like that. Look at it this way. The wording's so curious that we might almost say that it was written on some other occasion altogether and got there by mistake, mightn't one? Well, can you give us any help on those lines? Ever seen it before, for instance, or heard of it?'

Pleydell looked puzzled. 'No, I can't say I have. But how should I? I mean, supposing it had been left there for Miss Macklane at some other time.'

'But it wasn't. I've ascertained that. You're quite sure you can't help us with that note, then?'

'Quite. Except that I agree with you that the wording is so remarkable that it might well refer to some different occasion altogether.'

The Chief Inspector studied the ceiling with some care. 'You and Lady Ursula were in Monte Carlo last February, weren't you?' he asked, apparently of a small fly.

'We were, yes,' said Pleydell, surprised again. Roger pricked up his ears. Moresby had not mentioned this fact to him, and he did not at first see its significance. The next moment he understood.

'Do you happen to remember what date you got there?' the Chief Inspector asked casually.

Roger listened intently. The French 'croquette', he remembered, had died on the 9th of February.

Pleydell was consulting a small engagement book. 'I got there on the 14th of February. But Lady Ursula went there earlier, at least a fortnight before me.' He flicked the pages. 'Yes, she left London on the 27th of January.'

'I wonder if it would be giving you too much trouble, Mr

Pleydell,' remarked the Chief Inspector, 'to make out a list some time for me of all Lady Ursula's men friends, or even acquaintances, who were already in Monte Carlo or the neighbourhood when you arrived.'

'I will, yes,' Pleydell said, looking considerably mystified, 'if you really want it. But what can that have—'

'I do want it,' beamed the Chief Inspector; and that was that.

Pleydell accepted his rebuff in good part, though it was plain that he had not an idea why he had been rebuffed at all, which is the most irritating kind of rebuff there is. 'When I arrived?' he said. 'Not the ones that came after myself. Lady Ursula, by the way, stayed on after I did. I left on the 3rd of March, and she was there for another fortnight or so.'

'Well, take the second week in February, Mr Pleydell,' said Moresby with apparent carelessness. 'The ones that were there when you arrived, or any you'd heard of who left during the preceding week. As full as you can make it. That will do well enough.'

A few minutes later it was intimated that Pleydell might leave and that the police could now be considered to have the matter in hand. Should anything further occur to him, he could always reach the Chief Inspector on the telephone.

'Well, we didn't get as much as I'd hoped,' Roger said, rather ruefully, when they were alone together.

'Except that about Monte Carlo,' Moresby pointed out. 'That's a bit of luck, you know, Mr Sheringham. He hadn't been engaged long then, and he'd be bound to have noticed all Lady Ursula's friends of his own sex, couldn't have better conditions for the observation we want; we might just as well have been there ourselves. Mark my words his memory won't slip a single man that Lady Ursula spoke to that fortnight.'

'Oh, and talking of lists, there's something I forgot to tell you,' said Roger, not without excitement, and went on to explain the one of Janet's Dorsetshire friends which he had obtained from Anne.

'Ah!' said Moresby significantly.

'In other words,' Roger pointed out unnecessarily, 'if by any luck one name figures on both lists, we've got our man!'

'We know who he is,' corrected the Chief Inspector, and left the rest unsaid.

CHAPTER IX

ROGER was thoughtful as he returned to the Albany that evening and mixed himself a nightcap before going to bed. This case was so different from his others that he was in danger of finding himself a little lost in it. With the others it had always happened that he had a multiplicity of motives and possible criminals, so that a solution had involved merely the narrowing down of the evidence till it pointed definitely to one of the suspects.

Here was the complete opposite. In place of several possible motives there was, in reason, no motive at all, except that of a sexual lust-murder planned by a twisted mentality; and in consequence the valuable pointer which an obvious motive affords, and which is in nine cases out of ten the thing which first directs the attention of the police towards the person ultimately proved guilty, simply did not exist at all. Moreover, in place of the large company of former suspects, was just blank nothingness. Nobody was suspect, everybody was suspect. The canvas Roger had to survey was so vast that it might be considered as infinite. The whole world was suspect.

He got into bed and tried to sleep, but his brain buzzed, revolving determinedly round the endless possibilities of the case. The note of optimism on which he had parted from Moresby had ceased to resound in his mind; the early hours of the night are no place for optimism. Before he had been in bed thirty minutes he had decided, once and for all, that there could not be the slightest possibility of the same name appearing on both Anne Manners' and Pleydell's lists. A lucky coincidence like that belonged only to fiction; things did not turn out that way in real life. No, he must give up that tenuous hope and find some other angle from which to attack the problem.

And the annoying thing was that, out of all the puzzles he had tackled, this was the one, the most baffling of the lot, that he was most anxious to solve; for if he did not contribute something of very real value to the partnership which he had succeeded in inaugurating, he was quite certain that neither Moresby nor the authorities at Scotland Yard would ever let him in on the inside of a really interesting case again. And Roger was extremely eager to be in on the inside of really interesting cases.

He kicked and turned. It was too much to hope that he could solve the case off his own bat, with Moresby there as well and all the resources of Scotland Yard behind him; but he did want to direct the lines of the chase along the right trail. Moresby, of course, was concentrating on Lady Ursula's note; and if by any chance he could find out to whom it had been written, the case was as good as solved. But how could he? Was it worth Roger's while to concentrate on the note too? Hardly. At following up a single outstanding clue Scotland Yard had no rival in the world; for an amateur to work on the same lines was simply a waste of time.

No, he would leave that to Moresby, and if, against all probability, Moresby was successful, then he deserved all the credit; in the meantime Roger would get to work in a different way, collecting all the infinitesimal data which Moresby was inclined to ignore, and trying to deduce something from them. And if *he* was successful he would not only deserve the credit but, so far as the authorities at Scotland Yard were concerned, would jolly well see that he got it! After Ludmouth, Roger was not at all inclined to stand modestly aside from a brilliantly successful solution, in the manner of the story-book sleuths, and present the blundering police-detective with all the credit.

He spent two and a half hours in examining all the infinitesimal data and was unable to draw a single further deduction from them. He then rose, swallowed three aspirins in a strong whisky-and-soda, and returned to bed. This time he got to sleep.

On paying a visit to Scotland Yard at eleven o'clock the next morning (it gave him an infantile thrill to pass the guardian of the door with a nod and be allowed to proceed unquestioned to Moresby's room), he found the Chief Inspector seated at his table, concentrating. In front of him lay the note. Roger smiled a secret smile. It was as if the prosaic Moresby were invoking its essence to rise up and proclaim its secret.

'Morning, Mr Sheringham,' he said, with an abstracted nod. 'Just take a look at this letter, will you? Notice anything queer about it?'

'Beyond what you pointed out, that it seems to have seen a little wear and tear, no.'

'Ah, but what about the paper it's written on?'

'I know nothing about papers,' Roger smiled, seating himself on the edge of the table. 'That sort of thing's your prerogative. It's no good giving me a bit of scrap paper like that and expecting me to be able to furnish its complete history from the time it was a Celanese vest, or whatever they do make that kind of paper from.'

There was a gleam of triumph illuminating the Chief Inspector's rather stolid face. 'Scrap paper, eh? But you see, Mr Sheringham, that's just what it isn't.'

'Oh?' said Roger politely. It was clear that Moresby considered it of the highest importance that this scrap of paper should not be scrap paper, but exactly why Roger was unable to see. 'I'll buy it,' he added. 'Explain the excitement.'

'Even we poor boobs at Scotland Yard can make a deduction or two occasionally,' Moresby grinned unkindly, 'even though we don't write clever articles about murderers' psychology for the newspapers. Just take a look at that piece of paper again, Mr Sheringham. Feel it in your hand. That isn't scrap paper; it's a bit of real expensive notepaper.'

'Ah!' said Roger, understanding.

'Yes, *and* it's been cut,' went on Moresby. '*And* there was a reason for the cutting. Now do you see what I mean?'

'I do. The address has been cut off. Good for you. It would be a printed address, ten to one, and you can—'

'*And* there was something cut off as well as the address,' interrupted the Chief Inspector, who was making no bones about enjoying his own perspicacity; it has been mentioned in a former chronicle that even Chief Inspectors are human. He paused deliberately.

'I told you I'd buy it,' Roger urged in humble tones.

'I'm surprised at you, Mr Sheringham,' the Chief Inspector mocked. 'I am really. I thought you were such a one for clever deductions. You don't see what I mean, even now? Well, well! Just think what you'd do if you were writing a note to a friend in a hurry like that; in his own rooms, too, as the wording of that note shows. Wouldn't you—'

'Write the friend's name at the top, and draw a line under it!' Roger exclaimed. 'Yes, of course I should. Moresby, you're a genius.'

'Well, you tumbled to it at last,' said the Chief Inspector, in distinctly disappointed tones. 'And I won't say it wasn't clever of you to think of that line,' he added handsomely, 'when you did get there. Just look at the right middle of the top edge— *there*.'

Roger examined the part of the paper indicated by Moresby's broad thumb. The extreme end of a pencilled line was distinctly discernible. He nodded. 'And the paper's been carefully cut with a knife,' he observed, turning it on edge.

The Chief Inspector leaned back in his chair. 'This is how I look at it, Mr Sheringham. If you study the creases in that paper, you'll see that the fold across the centre doesn't exactly bisect its length. Look, it's nearly an inch out. Well, to do that is all wrong; it—'

'It isn't natural,' Roger interjected.

'No, it isn't; it's almost an instinct to fold a piece of paper as nearly mathematically exact as possible. *Therefore* that paper was folded before the top was cut off. *Therefore* we can tell from that the exact size of the missing bit. *Therefore* we can tell also the exact size of the original sheet.'

'I get you,' said Roger.

Moresby pressed a bell on his table. 'This is where Scotland Yard has the pull over an outsider,' he said, and pulled a sheet of paper towards him.

When the messenger appeared in answer to the bell, Moresby sent him in search of Sergeant Burrows.

'Morning, Burrows,' he nodded a minute later, as a man with a particularly alert face entered the room. 'This is Mr Sheringham, who's attached to us for a time. Here's a job for you, Burrows. I want you to find out everything about the paper this note's written on. Take a look at it. I've noted down the description and watermark for you here, and the size of the original sheet; this one's been cut, you can see. Let me know who makes it, what stationers in London stock it, especially in the West End, and find out also the names of any clients who buy it, and still more, any who have an address printed on it as well. I've noted all that down for you too. That's going to take you some time, so put five men on to it. I want the full lists as soon as possible.'

'Very good, sir,' said Sergeant Burrows, and made a smart exit.

'Yes,' Roger agreed. 'That's where Scotland Yard has the pull.'

The Chief Inspector pulled out his pipe, and Roger offered his pouch. He was impressed. Moresby was going to play that note for all it was worth, and Roger could not help feeling that it was going to lead to discoveries in which he could claim no share.

'By the way,' he said, thinking it time that his own end of the investigations was brought a little more to the fore. 'By the way, here's that list of names I told you about, that Miss Manners made out for me.' He produced the list from his pocket and handed it across. 'That's a copy for you to keep. I've got the original.'

The Chief Inspector ran his eyes down the thirty-odd names as he filled his pipe. 'Um!' he commented. 'Seems to have moved in pretty good society at home. Lord This and Sir Somebody That and the Honourable The Other.'

'Her family was a pretty good one, and I expect they know most of the county set in those parts,' Roger answered carelessly. 'There are a lot of big houses in the neighbourhood, and the children would mix.'

'Seems funny none of those big pots did anything for her when she came up to London to get a job.'

'I don't suppose for a moment that she asked them. They probably didn't even know she was looking for work. The Manners may be poor, but they're probably devilish proud, if I know the type.'

'Not too proud to show herself off on the stage as a show-girl though?' Moresby suggested, applying a match to Roger's tobacco.

'What's that nowadays?' Roger retorted, a little irritably. 'Don't be so infernally Victorian, Moresby.' But the thought occurred to him that he would be very sorry to see Anne following in her younger sister's footsteps.

'Um!' grunted Moresby, and went on studying the list in silence.

Roger kicked his heels against the table-leg. He had a strong feeling that he ought to be out and doing something, but for the life of him he could not see what. Moresby seemed to be doing all that could be done at the moment. That infernal note. Was it going to take things out of his hands by providing the solution after all? Roger had an uneasy premonition that it was. Not without exasperation he picked it up and examined it again.

'Yes, this edge has been carefully cut with a sharp knife,' he announced. 'That argues premeditation, doesn't it?'

The Chief Inspector looked up from his list. 'Premeditation?' he echoed. 'Why, yes. That's what I said last night.'

'So you did. And I was inclined to query it. Well, I think the cutting clinches that, though I still don't think that the place was premeditated, although the crime was. I should say that whoever did kill Lady Ursula had had the intention of doing so for some days, and carried the note about with him for the purpose of using it whenever an opportunity presented itself. The meeting at the studio was simply a chance one.'

'That's likely enough,' Moresby agreed. 'In fact I wasn't too keen myself on the idea of an assignation at that studio. I just put it forward as a possibility we mustn't overlook. Well, that might help things. You mean, we could have a look round for someone with a good motive for killing Lady Ursula?'

'No, I don't,' Roger thumped the table crossly. 'That's just the devil of this case: motive doesn't help! We've *got* the motive for Lady Ursula's death. There it is—that note. When Lady Ursula dashed off that little note, she signed her own death-warrant, as the story-books say.'

'Ah!' said the Chief Inspector with interest. 'Yes, I hadn't looked at it that way. That's very ingenious, Mr Sheringham.'

'But very obvious,' Roger retorted, though not ill-pleased. 'This maniac is on the constant lookout for victims, you see. A girl whose death he can't twist into the appearance of suicide is no use to him. He's very fond of killing, but he's running no risks himself—so far as he knows. And devilish cunning he is at avoiding them! Of course, for his particular methods, suicide is the safest camouflage. Well, when that note of Lady Ursula's falls into his hands, she's simply a gift, isn't she? There's his next victim booked at once. All he's got to do is to wait for his opportunity, and in the meantime carry that note about with him everywhere so as not to miss it when it comes. Elementary, my dear Moresby.'

'But still leaving us pretty well where we were before, Mr Holmes. But you're right about motive in this case, Mr Sheringham, sir; it means we'll have nothing but circumstantial evidence about movements and that sort of thing to found our case on. In fact, however sure we may be one day of knowing between ourselves who the guilty party is, about all we'll ever be able to *prove* is opportunity. And what's the good of that?'

'Not much,' Roger confessed.

They looked at one another gloomily.

'Without, that is,' added the Chief Inspector, 'we have a bit of better luck next time.'

'Next time?' echoed Roger.

'Yes,' said the Chief Inspector matter-of-factly. 'The next girl that's murdered.'

'Oh!' said Roger.

The telephone-bell interrupted his unhappy musings. 'Yes?' Moresby answered it. 'Yes, this is Chief Inspector Moresby speaking.—Oh, yes. Good morning, sir.—You have? Good.—If you wouldn't mind, sir. Yes, as soon as you like.—Very well, sir.' He hung up the receiver. 'Pleydell,' he said. 'Coming round with that list.'

'Ah! Well, let's hope and pray we have a bit of luck there. I don't like sitting still like this while that brute may be planning to attack another girl at this very minute.'

'But what can we do, sir,' Moresby reasonably pointed out, 'not even knowing who he is yet?'

'Humph!' said Roger. There is nothing so irritating as reason, when it does not happen to fit in with desire. 'I suppose he *will* go for another girl?'

'Not a doubt of it, sir,' responded the Chief Inspector, with the greatest cheerfulness. 'Bound to; they always do. Especially at this sort of stage. He's just tickled to death now with the idea of killing, hasn't had time to cool off yet. They,' added the Chief Inspector with a judicial air, 'kill about a dozen before they get tired of it.'

'The deuce they do!' Roger said violently. 'But look here, you can't leave this maniac loose without warning the public against him. You must put these wretched girls on their guard, at least.'

'And put him on his guard, too? No, sir; that's no good. We'd never catch him that way, and he's too dangerous to be left without being caught, even if it does mean one more girl being killed before we get him. Her death may save a dozen others. But what we want to do is to get him first, and I'm going to push on my inquiries as fast as ever I can, now that I'm fairly certain that it is murder and a homicidal maniac that we're up against.'

Roger was unconvinced. He thought that a warning of some sort ought to be given, if only to unprotected girls, girls living alone, prostitutes and so on; he thought so strongly, and he said so with equal strength. The Chief Inspector remained adamant, and pointed out from a long experience that it never does any good to warn prostitutes of anything; they rarely pay the slightest attention. In the middle of their argument Pleydell was announced.

He greeted them with his usual grave, collected courtesy, which had an old-fashioned air in so young a man, and produced the list he had brought. Without even glancing at it, Moresby tossed it carelessly on to his desk and engaged Pleydell in a brief conversation, asking what his movements were going to be that day in case Moresby wanted to get hold of him suddenly. Pleydell outlined them roughly, and promised to ring up Scotland Yard and leave word should he change his plans to any extent during the day. He had seemed a little surprised at the request to do so, but had complied with the utmost readiness. Roger, watching him, saw that he had not yet arrived at the full truth concerning his fiancée's death.

He stayed about five minutes only, and immediately the door had closed behind him the two laid out the lists side by side and pored over them eagerly.

'Ah!' said Roger an instant later.

'Hullo!' exclaimed Moresby the next moment.

'Great jumping Jupiters!' shouted Roger within a second.

There was not merely one name that coincided on both lists, but three.

CHAPTER X

'AFTER all,' Roger was saying a few minutes later, 'it isn't such a coincidence as it seemed at first sight, you know. Half the Dorsetshire list are the sort of people who go to Monte Carlo in the season. Now one realises, it would have been even stranger if there hadn't been any name to coincide.'

'Well, it isn't what I was expecting,' said Moresby. 'Not three.'

'No, but it isn't any more odd than that I should know two of the three myself. It's a pretty small crowd, you know, the Ascot, Goodwood, Hurlingham, Monte Carlo lot; and if you get mixed up with them at all, it doesn't take long to run up against most of them. Not that I've had much to do with them myself, but I've met a few at various functions, and just as it happens Beverley is one of them. I don't know him at all well, of course. Personally, I'm afraid I can't stand the man.'

'Ah!' said the Chief Inspector interestedly. 'What's the matter with him, Mr Sheringham?'

'Oh, nothing. He's just precious. Very tall, very slim, very beautiful, very fair hair, very blue eyes, and insufferably conceited. He writes poetry. Not that I've any prejudice against poetry, Moresby, or even the people who write it (I used to try my hand at it myself, before I discovered that nature never intended me for a poet); but he calls his stuff poetry, and I don't.'

'What do you call it, then, Mr Sheringham?'

'Tripe. Also the fellow wears a beard, which no decent, self-respecting modern poet ought to do. In fact, Moresby, I won't disguise from you the fact that the man is a poisonous creature, although, I fear, hopelessly harmless. The one thing

I'd swear in his favour is that he couldn't kill a fellow-creature to save his own life. No, I wish he was our man, but he can't be, not possibly. He's a son of Lord Beverley, of course.'

'Um!' observed Chief Inspector Moresby. 'And this other one you know, Gerald Newsome?'

'Jerry Newsome? Oh, he used to be a great friend of mine. We were at school together, and then Oxford. Yes, I remember he came from Dorsetshire. Oh, Jerry's out of the question. A charming fellow, without a kink in his length or breadth. He got a half-blue for tennis, I remember. Smote a very vicious ball indeed.'

'Ah!' said Moresby, with an expressionless face. 'Strong sort of chap?'

'Very wiry, yes; not particularly big, but—Oh, I see. No, Moresby, I don't think you need worry about Jerry. He's even more out of the question than Beverley.'

'Then that seems to leave only George Dunning,' said the Chief Inspector, consulting the lists.

'Then George Dunning it is, whoever he may be,' replied Roger with complete conviction. 'We concentrate on George Dunning, Moresby.'

'Um!' said Chief Inspector Moresby, and reached for *Who's Who*.

Of the three suspects only Beverley figured in *Who's Who*, but beyond the fact that the poet had been educated at Eton and Christchurch, Oxford, and had published two volumes of verse and one of plays, that omniscient volume added little to their knowledge. As to Newsome, Roger had fallen out of touch with him of recent years, but had an idea that he had retired to look after his estate in Dorsetshire on the death of his father. A slip of paper despatched by Moresby to some unknown destination brought the information in a very short time that this was the case, and the place in question was found to be within ten miles of Little Monckton. The same slip also brought the information, a few minutes later, that George Dunning was a bachelor, about thirty years old, with a large private income, who occupied a flat in one of the expensive streets off Piccadilly; he was a member of several clubs, duly mentioned, had been educated at Rugby and Cambridge, and had played Rugger several times for the latter without, however, obtaining his blue.

'Hullo,' said Roger, studying this record with attention, 'he's a member of the Oxford and Cambridge, is he? I wonder if he ever goes there. I could scrape acquaintance with him, perhaps.'

'Do, if you can, Mr Sheringham,' approved Moresby. 'But don't give anything away, of course,' he added, not without a certain anxiety. 'He mustn't know we're on his track.'

Roger looked at his collaborator with dignity.

'And don't start trying to pump him till I give you the word,' added the Chief Inspector, unabashed by the look. 'I don't want him frightened. And remember, we haven't finished checking yet. There's the results of that notepaper inquiry to come in first, and that's pretty sure to knock two of 'em out.'

'Leaving George Dunning in,' Roger retorted. 'Very well, Moresby, I'll try to refrain from telling him everything about us the first time I meet him, and I think it's very good of you to trust me so far.'

Chief Inspector Moresby beamed paternally.

Leaving shortly after, Roger made his way to the Oxford and Cambridge Club for lunch, feeling that he could not get on Mr Dunning's trail too soon. As he walked briskly along he had not the least doubt that the murderer had been identified; now all that remained was proof. And in the collecting of proof Roger was glad not to be hampered by the restrictions set on the professional detective. He saw the glimmerings of one or two pretty little plans to that end which would certainly not have met with official approval.

On enquiring of the porter he learned that Mr Dunning was not in the club at the moment. Enquiring further, he was told that Mr Dunning did not come very often, not above two or three times a month. This was discouraging. However, Roger adhered to his scheme, feeling that after all it was quite time he did lunch at the Oxford and Cambridge, not having done so for at least a year, and soon found himself seated in the dining-room in solitary state. He chose a fillet steak and fried potatoes, with a pint of old beer, and looked round for a friendly face. Not one was in sight.

Nevertheless, Roger was not to lunch alone that day. Just as his steak was being set before him ten minutes later a voice hailed him, a little doubtfully, from behind his left shoulder. Spinning round he saw Pleydell standing by his chair and jumped up at once.

'You've saved me,' he said swiftly, grasping the opportunity before it could elude him. 'I was frightened to death that I'd got to eat my lunch in complete silence, a thing I abhor. If you're not meeting anyone, come and lunch with me, won't you?'

'I should be very glad,' returned Pleydell courteously, and took the opposite chair.

'You're Roger Sheringham, the novelist, aren't you?' he went on, when they were seated. 'I thought your face was familiar to me when I met you at Scotland Yard yesterday.'

'And I had a vague idea I'd seen you before, too,' Roger agreed. 'I remember now; it was here, of course, though I didn't know your name. Didn't we meet in a rubber of bridge about two years ago? I remember Frank Merriman was playing.'

'That's right,' Pleydell acquiesced with a smile. 'It's extraordinary how one meets fellows like that for a short time, without gathering their names or anything about them, and then perhaps doesn't see them again for years, isn't it?'

They exchanged a few conventional reminiscences, and Roger learnt that his guest had been at Cambridge but had had to leave early owing to the War. Having exhausted reminiscences the conversation hovered uneasily, while the minds of both were full of all the things that were not being said. Roger knew that the other must be wondering how he could tactfully find out how on earth such a person as Roger Sheringham could have come to be mixed up in a police inquiry into the circumstances of his own fiancée's tragic death; and Roger himself was wondering what in the world he was going to reply when the feeler was inevitably put forth.

Pleydell led up to it gradually. 'That Chief Inspector I saw at Scotland Yard,' he remarked, almost carelessly, after the conversation had stumbled, paused, tried desperately to plod on again, and finally halted. 'Moresby, his name was, wasn't it? Is he a sound sort of chap?'

'Oh, yes,' said Roger, with an equally casual air. 'Very sound, I think.'

'He didn't seem surprised to see me turn up yesterday evening,' hinted Pleydell.

'No,' Roger parried. 'We rather thought you might.'

'You're connected with Scotland Yard,' said Pleydell, framing his remark in the form of an assertion rather than a question. 'It must be extraordinarily interesting.'

'Yes, it is,' Roger agreed, accepting the implication, as indeed he could hardly help doing.

Pleydell looked him in the face. 'You're a man of sense,' he said abruptly. 'What do *you* think about my fiancée's death?'

This time Roger refused the advance. 'We thought it sufficiently strange to warrant a little investigation,' he replied colourlessly, trying to reestablish the impersonal note.

'It certainly is that,' Pleydell muttered. 'You think there's a man at the back of it?' he attacked again. 'At least, that seems the inference from the list Moresby wanted.'

'It's always possible, isn't it?' Roger fenced.

'Oh, why not be open with me, Sheringham?' Pleydell said swiftly in a low voice that nevertheless shook a little. 'Can't you see that the whole thing is torturing me beyond endurance? I shall go mad if it isn't cleared up soon.'

Roger was taken aback. An appeal to the emotions was the last thing he was expecting from the collected, self-contained

Pleydell. He realised something of what the man must be suffering to expose his innermost feelings to a complete stranger like himself, and guessed that perhaps no other person in the world had ever been granted such a view of the human fires that were hidden under that cool exterior—except, of course, Lady Ursula.

'You don't suppose I'd ever have brought myself to go to Scotland Yard and talk to a damned policeman about—about *her*,' Pleydell continued, crumbling the bread on his plate with shaking fingers, 'if I hadn't reached my own limit, do you? For heaven's sake tell me what they really think, and what they're going to do about it.'

Roger was alarmed. His earlier conviction, that once Pleydell learned the truth he would be ruthless in his vengeance, returned in doubled strength. Far more formidable because normally so self-controlled, once he reached his breaking-point the man would be dangerous. In his own interest he must be restrained.

And yet, if he stumbled on the truth by himself (as sooner or later he surely must), would he not be even more dangerous, because out of reach of control? Would it not be better to give him an idea of the truth now and bind him not to take individual action? If he really gave his word, Roger was inclined to think that he would abide by it. And in any case Moresby was going to break the news to him on the next day, as he must before putting the further questions that were necessary; it could hardly make any difference to forestall him by twenty-four hours, and it would give the poor devil a certain measure of relief; to know the worst is always better than to fear it.

Roger had to make up his mind in an instant, and he did so.

'What do *you* think about it first, Pleydell?' he asked, in a tone of voice different from the defensive one in which he had spoken hitherto.

Pleydell looked at him quickly, and the expression he read

in his host's face showed that he was to be fenced with no longer. 'I?' he said slowly. 'I hardly like to tell you what I think. You might call it too fantastic.'

'Then put it this way,' Roger said bluntly, now sure that the other's suspicions went nearer towards the truth than he had thought before. 'Put it this way: do you think Lady Ursula took her own life?'

Pleydell did not flinch. It was as if he had feared all the time the hint conveyed by Roger's question and so was not unprepared. 'Ah!' he said, scarcely above a whisper. 'So it *was* murder, was it?'

Roger was relieved. The man was taking it bravely, that Roger had expected; but it was not such a shock to him as it might have been had the idea been a new one. After all, Pleydell was no fool. It was a possibility that must have occurred to him.

'We don't know for certain,' he said, though in a voice that held out little hope. 'But coming after those others, you know.'

Pleydell nodded. Now that suspicion had been changed into certainty he had pulled himself together, and when he spoke it was in tones that were almost matter-of-fact. Roger marvelled again at his self-control.

'Yes,' he said. 'I was afraid of it as soon as I realised that. In fact, it was that which sent me to Scotland Yard. But when I got there I hardly liked to say so straight out. It *did* seem fantastic, somehow. Ursula, you know, and the idea of murder . . . Incongruous, to the point of absurdity.' He sighed. 'But I suppose murder always does seem fantastic when applied to somebody in one's own circle. Have you got any clues?'

'Precious few,' Roger said ruefully. 'We'll lay our hands on him sooner or later, I promise you; but it's not going to be an easy job. By the way, Pleydell . . .' He paused awkwardly.

Pleydell looked up. 'Yes?'

'Look here,' said Roger in some embarrassment, 'you mustn't forget the man's mad, of course.'

'Mad?'

'Yes. A sexual maniac. I mean, it isn't like an ordinary case of murder, where one can feel as rancorous as possible against the murderer. I don't know whether the law will hold this man responsible for his actions, but I very much doubt it.'

'Do you?' said Pleydell, with a certain dry grimness. 'But I think we'd better make sure of catching him, all the same.'

'Yes, yes, of course. But—'

'And I need hardly say,' Pleydell interrupted, as if hardly conscious that Roger was speaking at all, 'that if you want anything in the nature of funds to help you do so, you've only got to mention it to me. I'm a pretty rich man, but I'd give almost everything I've got to see that swine brought to the scaffold.'

'Oh, yes,' murmured Roger, acutely uncomfortable. 'Of course.'

'And any other way I can help . . .'

'Yes!' said Roger abruptly. 'There's one way you can help. Scotland Yard's got the matter in hand, and they're the best man-hunting machine in the world. I want you to remember just that. In other words, I want you to promise not to attempt anything off your own bat. You couldn't effect anything, and you might very easily queer our pitch.' It was remarkable how Roger, now that he was firmly established in an official status, seemed to have imbibed also the official ideas about enthusiastic amateurs and their well-intentioned industry.

Pleydell looked extremely unwilling to give any such undertaking.

'I've told you a lot more than I ought,' Roger urged, 'and I want you to reciprocate by giving me your word on this point. It's important, honestly.'

Pleydell appeared to be considering. 'Very well,' he said slowly. 'I'll give you my word on one condition, and that is that you keep me closely informed about how you get on and any discoveries you may make. Otherwise I shall hold myself free to employ private detectives, if I want, to supplement your efforts.'

'Oh, don't do that!' said the Scotland Yard man, with all the correct horror of such a notion. 'Yes, I'll keep you informed all right (unofficially, of course, and you must keep anything I tell you a close secret); but for heaven's sake don't go and let a lot of private detectives loose on us. Why, nobody outside Scotland Yard except yourself even guesses that we're looking into these cases at all. Our great hope is to capture the chap by complete surprise.'

'Very well, then,' said Pleydell briefly. 'That's a bargain. Tell me exactly how the case stands at present.'

As he complied, Roger felt that he had succeeded in turning what might have proved an awkward situation into a helpful one. Without doubt Pleydell, if handled properly and kept within bounds, could help the investigation to a very considerable extent.

Having given his guest a synopsis of the facts and the hopes entertained, he proceeded to his chief reason for asking Pleydell to lunch. 'So you see,' he concluded, 'that a good deal depends on these three men whose names are on both the lists. That is, on one of them, because in my private opinion both Newsome and Beverley are quite out of the running. By the way, I suppose you know nearly all of the men on your own list pretty well, don't you?'

'Most of them, more or less, yes. Well, I understand now what the Chief Inspector wanted that list for, which I must say puzzled me; but it's a great pity that I wasn't at Monte Carlo myself at the time of that girl's death. The fellow may have gone before I got there, you see.'

'It's possible, of course. But I don't think it's very likely. There's a gap of only five days, you see. Of course he may have got frightened and bolted at once, but we can easily find out who did leave during those five days. Personally, I think he would have stayed.'

Pleydell looked grave. 'All this is rather a shock to me, Sheringham. It never occurred to me that this brute could be actually one of our own friends.'

'It seems as if he must be. And you must remember that the fellow is quite probably sane enough in all other respects, except for this fatal kink. No doubt Jack the Ripper, whoever he was, was regarded in private life as a model citizen.'

'This is rather horrible,' Pleydell murmured.

'Well, anyhow,' Roger went on briskly, 'there are sure to be some people on your list whose careers I shall want to look into, and I think the best way of approaching them will be through you. Can you manage that for me?'

'Certainly, if they're men I know. I only wish you could give me something more difficult to do. I can tell you, Sheringham, I'm just itching to get my hands on that fellow.'

'Well,' said Roger, disregarding his companion's hands, 'I'd like to make a start with George Dunning. Do you know him?'

'Know George? Oh, yes. But it's evident that you don't.'

'Why?'

Pleydell glanced at his watch. 'You'll see. I'll take you round to his rooms directly we've finished lunch on some pretext or other, and leave you there. George will never smell a rat. But I warn you, Sheringham,' he added, with a slight smile, 'if you really suspect Dunning, you're making a hopeless mistake. George couldn't put a kink into his brain if he tried with curling-tongs.'

'Oh!' said Roger, somewhat dashed.

CHAPTER XI

AN INTERVIEW AND A MURDER

CIRCUMSTANCES which, applied to ourselves, can only bear one interpretation, find themselves carrying quite different ones when applied to other people. On finding Gerald Newsome's name on the list of suspects Roger had no hesitation in affirming, and thoroughly believing his affirmation, that he could not possibly be guilty because Roger knew he could not be; and he expected this statement to be accepted as authoritative. But when Pleydell, with equal certainty, pronounced that George Dunning could not possibly be guilty because he could not possibly be, Roger was able to set this down at once as mere personal prejudice.

Yet it must be admitted that, when confronted an hour later with the gentleman in question, Roger's heart did sink. Instead of the potentially sinister, secretly vicious creature whom his imagination had tricked him into anticipating, he found himself face to face with a large mountain of transparent guilelessness and innocent benevolence. If appearances counted for anything at all in this world, George Dunning could no more be a potential murderer in cold blood than could Roger himself. Less so, if anything, for whereas Roger was at least able to put himself in that murderer's place and obtain some faint understanding of the horrible enjoyment experienced by that warped brain, George Dunning was obviously incapable of putting himself in any other place but his own, and possibly not always even there.

Only one thing did strike Roger as mildly curious, and that was the evident lack of ease which Dunning seemed to experience in Pleydell's presence. Even that, however, was explained when Pleydell, having settled the excuse which had brought him, a matter of a mooted bachelor dinner-party which would now have to be cancelled owing to his mourning, somewhat abruptly took his departure without offering to take Roger as well.

Dunning turned to his unsought guest with something of the aspect of a bewildered but well-meaning ram faced with a new shepherd. It was obvious that though perfectly ready to be hospitable, he had not the least idea what to do with this Pleydell-imposed encumbrance.

His countenance cleared. 'Have a drink, eh?' he said, with relief.

'Well, thank you,' Roger agreed. A drink would at least serve him with an excuse for a twenty-minutes' stop.

'Great fellow, old Pleydell,' observed George Dunning, mixing the drinks with skill. 'You know him well?'

'Oh, fairly well, yes,' said Roger, his back to the fire. He looked round the very comfortable room, in which fishing-rods, an oar and other sporting trophies figured prominently. Like most bachelor rooms, it seemed typical of its owner. Women's rooms, like their figures, are rarely individual.

'Rotten, that business about poor old Ursula, eh?' pronounced Dunning, squirting soda. 'Say when. Makes one feel all thumbs with Pleydell, doesn't it? Don't know what the deuce to say to a feller whose fiancée's just hanged herself. Devilish awkward.'

'Devilish,' Roger agreed. 'When.'

Dunning approached him with a half-filled tumbler. 'Well, chin-chin,' said the suspect.

'Good luck,' said the man from Scotland Yard.

They settled themselves in chairs before the fire.

'You were at Rugby, weren't you?' said Roger conversationally. 'I wonder if you knew J. B. Fotherington?'

'The games-bird?' rejoined Dunning, with some approach to enthusiasm. 'Rather. I should jolly well say so. Why, he taught me to play Rugger.'

'Did he really? I knew him very well at Oxford. We had rooms on the same staircase.'

Confidence being thus established, Roger allowed it to be

increased by a judicious conversation upon sporting topics, in the course of which he allowed Mr Dunning to elicit the fact that he had once upon a time been awarded a half-blue for playing golf against Cambridge.

'And now you write books, eh?' pursued Mr Dunning, in the course of his artless questionnaire. 'Pleydell said you were the Sheringham who wrote novels, didn't he?'

Roger admitted modestly that he wrote novels.

'Dashed good too,' said Mr Dunning politely. 'I've read one or two. Jolly interesting. Look here, finish that up and have another.' Roger suspected that it was the half-blue rather than his art that had prompted the offer, but he accepted readily enough.

'Yes,' he said in a meditative voice when Dunning returned from the sideboard, 'I've been lunching with Pleydell. He seems very cut up.'

'Well, naturally,' pointed out Dunning, with reason.

'You knew Lady Ursula pretty well, didn't you?' Roger asked innocently.

'Oh, so-so, you know. Not so frightfully. Not my type, exactly.'

'No,' said Roger. Dunning's type, he knew without being told, would be small, fluffy, blue-eyed and extremely clinging; he shuddered slightly; it was not his own type. 'She was a very modern sort of person, wasn't she?'

'Oh, yes, fairly hectic. Awfully good sort and all that, of course, but a bit—well, hectic, you know. Not exactly loud, but—well, hectic.'

'I know,' said Roger gravely. 'Hectic. The kind that calls every man "my dear", whether she's known him ten minutes or ten years.'

'That's it, exactly.'

'One gathered that,' observed Roger to his glass, 'from that note she left.'

'Oh, yes; rather. Exactly like her, that note. Just the sort of thing she would leave. "Mother have a fit," eh? Jolly good.'

'But it was the sort of thing she would do?'

'What, hang herself? No, that I'm dashed if it was. I could hardly believe it at first. Last thing in the whole world Ursula would go and do, if you'd asked me.'

'So I'd gathered,' said Roger.

They sat in silence for a few minutes.

Suddenly Roger started. 'Oh, good Lord, I've just remembered a note I've got to get written in a frightful hurry. I must run round to my club and get it done at once.'

'Oh, rot,' said the hospitable Mr Dunning. 'No need to do that. Why not write it here?'

'That's very good of you,' Roger murmured. 'Thanks. I'd like to.'

A moment later he was seated at his host's writing table, a sheet of thick creamy notepaper before him as unlike the bluish-grey paper of Lady Ursula's note as he had feared. Neatly printed at the top was Mr Dunning's address. There was no possibility even that this was a new lot, hastily ordered.

Roger scribbled something on the sheet, put it into an envelope and thrust it into his pocket.

'My man can run out to the post with it for you,' Dunning suggested as Roger rose.

'Oh, no, thanks,' Roger replied carelessly. 'It's only a memorandum about some work, and I shall be passing the place. I can drop it in as now I go by.' He resumed his seat. To himself he was thinking: 'Well, there's not the slightest hope, but I'll try the last card. Though how on earth does one steer the conversation on to such matters with this simple creature?'

'I've just been reading Freud, Dunning,' he remarked, a little abruptly. 'Most interesting. Have you ever read him?'

'Good Lord, no,' replied that gentleman, shying violently.

Shortly afterwards Roger took his leave, with the full knowledge that whenever his name should be mentioned hereafter in Mr Dunning's presence, the formula would greet it: 'That chap? Oh, yes, not a bad fellow, really. Got a half-blue for golf, you know. But a bit of a bore in these days. Will talk a hell of a lot of rot about sex and all that sort of thing. Get a bit fed up with that sort of thing nowadays, don't you?'

But one thing was as certain as anything in this world not based upon evidence can be: Mr George Dunning could be wiped forthwith off the list of suspects.

So that left the Hon. Arnold Beverley and Gerald Newsome. And neither of them could possibly have done the thing.

Roger took a taxi and drove back to Scotland Yard, to report lack of progress. Moresby was out, and, somewhat disconsolately, Roger returned to his rooms, leaving a message that he should be rung up when the Chief Inspector returned, there to ruminate alone on the other possibilities presented by this annoying case.

An hour later he was still in the same quandary. George Dunning could not be the man, and Jerry Newsome could not be the man; therefore, if one of those three it was, it must be Arnold Beverley. And Arnold Beverley could not be the man. The only conclusion seemed to be that it was none of them, and the whole case must be begun afresh. Chief Inspector Moresby, looking in on chance before returning to Scotland Yard, found his distracted colleague on the verge of pressing for the preventive detention of every person on either list.

'Or would it be a woman, Moresby?' he asked despairingly, having given his account of the day's results. 'We've never considered that, have we?'

'Now, Mr Sheringham,' soothed the Chief Inspector, 'you mustn't get upset because results don't fall into your hands right away. I shouldn't be surprised if we don't get hold of anything really definite for another month. These things have to be done gradually, Mr Sheringham.'

'Blast gradually!' returned his collaborator rudely.

With imperturbability Moresby retailed his own activities since they parted. He had put men on to inquiring into the movements of the three suspects on and around the dates in question, and he had himself taken a hand in the investigation into the notepaper. The makers had been identified, and Moresby had been to see them and asked for a list of stationers, wholesale and retail, to whom it had been supplied. He remained confident of important results from this line of inquiry.

'It's our only clue, Mr Sheringham, to say *clue*,' he pointed out. 'We're bound to follow it up as hard as we can.'

'Of course,' said Roger thoughtfully, 'it's the Monte Carlo list that's the really important one. The fellow must have been in Monte Carlo then, and assuming that he knew Lady Ursula (of which the probabilities are in favour, to put it at its lowest), he ought to figure on that list. But he needn't be on the other one at all. There's no reason why Miss Manners should know the names of *all* her sister's male friends, however intimate the two were.'

'Yes, and as to that, even if he isn't on Mr Pleydell's list, he'll be on the one the French are getting out for us, of all English residents in and around Monte Carlo on February the ninth. That ought to be quite enough to check by, when we get our results from that notepaper'

'I suppose he *is* an Englishman?' queried Roger.

The Chief Inspector laughed. 'Oh, don't go suggesting things like that, Mr Sheringham. We've got all England to consider as it is before we lay our hands on him; don't go making it the whole world.'

'It is the whole world,' replied Mr Sheringham, with gloom. 'But at any rate don't forget that the Germans go in for this kind of murder more than any other nation. Except perhaps America.'

The Chief Inspector promised not to lose sight of that point.

They continued to debate, but nothing fresh seemed to emerge from the talk.

'Well,' said Moresby, rising, 'I must be getting back to the Yard. There may be a report or two in by now, though it's a bit early. Care to come round on the off-chance, Mr Sheringham?'

Roger glanced at his watch. 'Ten to four. Yes, I'll come round with you; and the British nation can stand me a cup of tea in your office. There's nothing like— Excuse me a minute, there's the telephone.' He crossed to the instrument. 'For you, Moresby,' he said, laying down the receiver. 'Scotland Yard. Well, let's hope something's turned up.'

Moresby spoke into the telephone. 'Hullo? Yes, Chief Inspector Moresby speaking. Oh, yes, sir.— Good gracious, sir, is that so?' He pulled out a notebook and pencil and began to jot down notes. 'Yes. Yes. Six Pelham Mansions, Gray's Inn Road? Yes. Inspector Tucker, yes. Very good, sir. And we'd better have Dr Pilkington, hadn't we? Superintendent Green will see to the rest. Very well, I'll meet you there in twenty minutes. Oh, and you don't mind if I bring Mr Sheringham along, do you? Seeing that he's been working with me on the other cases, I mean. Yes, exactly. Very well, sir. In twenty minutes.' He hung up the receiver.

Roger, who had hardly been able to contain himself in the background, gushed forth into a stream of questions.

The Chief Inspector nodded with a grave air. 'Yes, this is a nasty business, Mr Sheringham. There's been another girl murdered in just the same way, in one of those blocks of flats in the Gray's Inn Road. We're going round at once.'

Roger opened the door into the passage feeling, in spite of all sense, as if he were personally to blame for the death of this further victim.

The Chief Inspector, however, retained his professional outlook. 'It's only once in a lifetime that one meets with these mass murderers, you know, Mr Sheringham,' he said conversationally, as they put on their coats. 'It's a real experience. I'm glad they put me in charge of the other investigations.'

CHAPTER XII

To one who, like Roger, has never seen his country's crimi-nal-hunting machine in action, the spectacle of Scotland Yard's first concentration upon the scene of a murder is extraordinarily impressive. It is often said that the detection of crime has been reduced to a science, but it would perhaps give a clearer impres-sion to say that it has been expanded into a business, with its card-indexes, its heads of departments, its experts in various branches, and its smooth-running efficiency; the way in which it is organised is, in fact, far more closely related to that of a commercial enterprise than to the more rigid and less imagi-native efficiency of the Army or the other administrative governmental departments. If the murderer himself could catch a glimpse of the activity which prevails upon the spot he has recently left, all hopes he had fondly entertained of escaping arrest must abruptly disappear; he would watch the skilled and methodical pains that are taken to ensure his capture with a feeling of helpless despair.

When Roger and Moresby arrived the business was just getting into its stride. From the moment that an agitated girl had run out into Gray's Inn Road, clutched the arm of the first constable she could find, and gasped out that the friend who shared a flat with her had hanged herself on the sitting-room door while she herself was out at lunch—from that moment the machinery had been set in motion. The constable had hurriedly reported the news to a policeman on point duty within a few yards before accompanying the girl back to the flat, and he had got in touch with his station; the sergeant there had telephoned through to the Divisional Inspector, who had immediately communicated with Scotland Yard before jumping into a car and going round to the block in person. Scotland Yard had notified the Chief Inspector who had the other investigations in hand, luckily finding him at the first number they called, and had already rushed round the necessary experts; a superior officer or two, including perhaps the Assistant Commissioner himself, were following in a few minutes. The Divisional Surgeon was summoned, and constables sent off to guard the entrance to the flat and stand by for any further orders.

The constable who was the first on the scene had lifted the body down from the door on which it was hanging, having first been careful to form a mental picture of its exact position and appearance, and had laid it on a divan which filled one corner of the small room; otherwise nothing else had been touched. Everybody was anxiously excited. All stations had already been acquainted with the tentative conclusions reached by Headquarters in the other cases of this nature, and a warning had been issued that any further deaths in the same category were to be regarded *prima facie* as murder, evidence in the form of farewell letters to the contrary notwithstanding. Considerable anxiety therefore existed as to whether this case might provide a definite clue at last.

It seemed to Roger, as he entered the little sitting-room in Moresby's wake, that the confusion prevailing was such that any possible clues must be obliterated. It took him exactly thirty seconds to realise that exactly the opposite was the case: the small room was full of men, it was true, but there was no confusion; each had his own job and he was doing it quietly and methodically, and without getting in the way of anybody else. Roger, feeling exceedingly unimportant in the middle of all this scientific bustle, stepped unobtrusively into the nearest corner, where he might be more or less out of the way, and watched what was happening.

Moresby had joined the Divisional Inspector by the divan, and they were bending over the body; a photographer was setting up his camera near them; a fingerprint expert was closely examining all the shining or polished surfaces in the room; a constable, evidently used to the job, was making notes for the plan he was going to draw; in the bedroom adjoining another constable had even been sent off to look after the dead girl's friend, and was there administering what consolation he could.

The more Roger looked, the smaller he felt. It was not difficult, in the face of this sort of thing, to understand something of Scotland Yard's good-humoured scorn for the amateur detective.

From the conversation about him Roger gathered the main facts. The circumstances of the death were almost exactly the same as those of the others, Lady Ursula's excepted. The hook screwed into the further side of the door, the overturned chair, the silk stocking and bare leg, the way in which it had been arranged round the victim's neck, all were precisely the same. The only minute points of difference, so far as he could hear, were that the girl was dressed only in her underclothes and that the usual farewell notice instead of being written consisted of a printed line or two of poetry, apparently cut from a book, and was pinned on to her clothes at the breast with a brooch. A mauve silk wrapper lay across the back of an armchair.

Roger's lonely vigil did not last long. He had hardly had time to realise what was going on around him and take in these few facts before Moresby beckoned to him to join them by the divan, where he proceeded to introduce him to the Divisional Inspector, a soldierly-built figure with a carefully-waxed moustache.

'You take a look at her, Mr Sheringham,' said the Chief Inspector, 'and see if you can make anything fresh of her, because I'm blessed if I can.'

Roger had seen plenty of violent death during his service in France during the War, but dead men are different from dead girls, and girls dead through slow strangulation are different from any others. He shuddered in spite of his efforts to control himself as his gaze rested on the distorted face. She may have been pretty in life, but she certainly was not pretty in death. By her sides lay her hands, tightly clenched.

She was a small girl, not much more than five feet in height and slightly built, and she was dressed in her underclothes only, with a light-coloured silk stocking on one leg; the other stocking still lay, though now loosely, round her neck.

'Who was she?' Roger asked, in a low voice.

The Divisional Inspector answered him. 'Name of Dorothy Fielder, sir,' he said briskly. 'An actress, she was. Had one of the small parts in that play at The Princess's, *Her Husband's Wife*. The other girl, Zelma Deeping, she's in it too; understudying, I believe.'

'I see,' said Roger. He bent over the body and read the wording on the little piece of paper pinned to her breast:

> One more unfortunate
> Weary of breath,
> Rashly importunate,
> Gone to her death.

'Hood,' he said. '*The Bridge of Sighs*. Well, that's certainly a little more usual than *Queen Mab*, but I don't see how it's going to help.'

'Now you see the advantage of having a literary gentleman to help us, Tucker,' said Moresby jovially to the Divisional Inspector, who smiled politely. 'By a poet called Hood, is it, Mr Sheringham? Now, I wonder whether they'd be likely to have a volume of his works here. You might look in that bookcase, Tucker. And be careful of course, if there is one.'

Tucker nodded, and crossed the room.

The photographer came forward. 'The doctor'll be here any minute, Chief Inspector. Shall I take my photographs now?'

'Yes, Bland, you may as well. I shall want the usual, and you'd better take one or two close-ups of the face and neck.

Don't touch her till the doctor's finished, of course. And stand by when you're through; we may want some more later, if there's any bruises on the body.' Roger had already noticed that, though the two Inspectors had bent over the body and examined it as closely as possible, they had been careful not to touch it.

'This is pretty damnable, isn't it?' Roger muttered, as the photographer, who had focused his camera in advance, now proceeded to expose his plates.

'It is that, Mr Sheringham. But even now there doesn't seem any way of proving murder. It still *might* be suicide, you know.'

'It might, but it isn't,' snapped Roger, whose nerves were beginning to feel the strain.

'Well, Tucker tells me Superintendent Green (he's the Superintendent of this district; one of the Big Four you newspaper men are always talking about)—he may be coming. And I shouldn't be surprised if the Assistant Commissioner (it was him who spoke to me on the telephone) didn't turn up too. If these are murders, and I'm not saying you're not right about 'em, then we've got to get busy at the Yard. You don't know Sir Paul Graham, do you?'

'The Assistant Commissioner? No. He's new, isn't he? It was Sir Charles Merriman I came up against, over that Wychford business eighteen months ago. What's he like?'

'You'll like him, Mr Sheringham. A very nice gentleman. But of course he hasn't hardly shaken down yet. Hullo, here's the doctor. Afraid you'll have to excuse me, Mr Sheringham. Good afternoon, Dr Pilkington. Nasty business this, by the look of it.'

Roger turned away and saw Inspector Tucker approaching with a book held gingerly in one hand. 'Would this be the one, sir?' he asked.

Roger glanced at the title and nodded. 'Yes, that's the man. Let's see if that passage has been cut out of this copy.'

'One minute, sir, first, please.' Tucker beckoned to the fingerprint expert and held out the volume. 'Just take a look at this, Andrews, will you?'

Andrews took the book in a cautious grasp and examined it minutely. Sprinkling over one corner a little light-grey dust out of a receptacle like a pepper-pot, he scrutinised the result, then shook his head regretfully and gave the book back. 'Nothing, I'm afraid. Or anywhere else either, except the two girls'. Why, did he handle this?'

'Half a minute, and I'll tell you. Could you find the place, Mr Sheringham, sir?'

Roger glanced at the index and turned to a page. Nearly cut out of it were the lines in question. He pointed to the blank space in silence.

Andrews nodded and made a rueful grimace. 'That establishes that he worked in gloves, then, at any rate. And those'll be the scissors he cut it out with.' He gestured towards a small pair of nail-scissors lying on a side-table. 'I've examined them already and there's not a mark. No, I'm afraid there's nothing for me here.'

'You seem to be taking it for granted that there is a "he",' Roger remarked mildly. 'I thought Scotland Yard hadn't made up their minds on that point yet?'

Andrews regarded him with a smile of amusement, in which Tucker joined. Roger had an uncomfortable feeling that he must have made a fool of himself somehow, but could hardly see how. Andrews proceeded to enlighten him.

'There's no prints *at all* on that book, sir,' he pointed out gently. 'If the girl had cut it out herself she'd have been bound to leave her own prints. And so would anyone else. But somebody cut it out, didn't they? Therefore that somebody must have been wearing gloves.' He spoke as to a very small child, grappling with its ABC.

'Oh—um—yes,' Roger agreed. 'Well, anyhow, that certainly does clinch the fact of the extra "he", doesn't it?'

'It does that, sir,' said the Divisional Inspector grimly, and went over to report to Moresby, who was talking to the doctor as the latter bent over the body.

A minute later the door opened and three further men came in. Two of these Roger was able to identify as Detective Superintendent Green, whom he had met for a few minutes once before, and Sir Paul Graham; the other, he learned on enquiry of Andrews, was an Inspector who was an expert in strangulation cases. Roger gathered that Scotland Yard was now seriously perturbed about this unknown maniac and his gruesome work, whatever its representatives might pretend to himself.

He listened to the conversation which followed.

'Found anything, Moresby?' the Superintendent asked laconically, after a cursory glance at the body.

Moresby shook his head. 'I haven't been here long. Tucker tells me he had a look round before I came, but couldn't get hold of anything.'

'I'll look round myself,' remarked the Superintendent, who was a large man beginning to show signs of corpulence. Without more ado he dropped on his hands and knees. 'Haven't opened the hands yet, I see,' he grunted as he did so.

'Been waiting for the doctor,' Moresby replied. 'He's only just got here.'

Roger watched the large form of the Superintendent with interest. While Sir Paul joined the doctor and Moresby by the divan, he began to crawl with lumbering agility up and down the carpet, subjecting every square inch of it to a minute examination; and when the carpet was exhausted, he examined the boards round it with equal care, poking his head under tables and chairs, but never shifting any piece of furniture from its position. At the end of seven or eight minutes he arose and shook his head at Moresby. 'Not a sign,' he wheezed.

In the meantime the doctor had completed his first examination, flexing the limbs, moving the head between his hands, taking careful note of the skin round the neck and the condition of the features. He now proceeded to open the clenched fingers. Moresby and the Assistant Commissioner bent forward eagerly as he did so, only to draw back again the next moment with expressions of acute disappointment. The small hands were empty.

'There's not the least sign of a struggle even, that I can see,' muttered the doctor, examining the dead girl's nails. 'Look—nothing here at all.'

'Hell!' muttered Moresby under his breath. It is in the hands, as Roger knew, that the most valuable clue is usually to be discovered if any sort of a struggle has taken place.

'Well,' Moresby added, 'I'd like to know if there are any bruises on the body.'

'At once?' asked the doctor. 'I shall be examining her later on in any case, of course.'

'I'd like to know at once, I think, doctor. It's most important to find out if there are any signs of a struggle on the body.'

'All right,' said the doctor. 'I'll get her undressed. But I don't think there will be any such signs, judging by the hands.'

Superintendent Green who, his crawlings over, had joined the other three at the divan (Roger was holding himself a little uneasily aloof, not knowing quite what to do), turned round. 'All right, Canning,' he said to the photographer, 'you can wait in the hall; and you too, Andrews.' He gave similar directions to the plan-drawing constable and the other subordinates, who filed out. 'No need for a whole Sunday-school treat in here while the doctor's examining her, sir,' he grunted to the Assistant Commissioner, 'is there?' It was the first sign of feeling he had yet shown.

With practised hands the doctor proceeded to examine the body. 'I'll take the temperature first,' he said.

There was a dead silence for half a minute.

'No sign of any bruising on the front, was there, doctor?' said Moresby.

The doctor, who had been bending over the body, looked up. 'None that I saw, but I'll examine it more closely in a moment. Don't seem to be any here either. There was no struggle. Hullo, what's this, though?'

Conquering his reluctance, Roger drew nearer. The four were looking at two indistinct marks that lay transversally across the backs of the girl's thighs, about a third of the way down. They were very faint indentations, not discoloured, and each was about four to five inches long.

'Funny,' observed the doctor. 'What do you make of them, Superintendent? They must be recent. Made shortly before death, I should imagine, or they'd be discoloured. Too late for bruises, and too early for post-mortem staining.'

Superintendent Green looked puzzled. 'Looks as if she'd been hit smartly across the legs, almost, doesn't it? With a thin bit of cane, or something like that.'

The doctor frowned. 'Oh, no. That couldn't possibly have produced them. It must have been a steady pressure, and applied for some considerable time; otherwise they'd have flattened out by now. They're not much more than half an inch broad, you see. I should say she's been sitting for at least half an hour well forward on a chair that had a sharp metal edge raised an inch or so in the front.'

'What on earth would she want to do that for?' asked Moresby in perplexity.

'Don't ask me,' retorted the doctor. 'And I don't suppose for a moment she did. I'm only suggesting the kind of thing that could have made those marks.'

'Do you attach any importance to them, doctor?' asked the Assistant Commissioner.

'Not the least,' replied the doctor briskly. 'The cause of death is perfectly obvious, strangulation by hanging. Well, let's have a look at this thermometer.' He plucked it out and examined it. 'Humph!' was all he said.

'And the front, doctor?' suggested Moresby, who seemed anxious to have this point cleared up.

The doctor turned the body over and scrutinised the skin with close attention. 'Not a mark!' he announced finally. 'I'll carry out an autopsy, Sir Paul, if you like, but I don't see that there's anything to be learnt from it.'

'Better, I think,' murmured the Assistant Commissioner. 'And you see no signs of a struggle?'

'None at all. There can't have been a struggle. Even her wrists aren't bruised; nor her ankles. And she's been dead, I should say, about three hours. Not more than three and a half at the outside. What's the time now? Half-past four. As near as I can put it, she died between one-twenty and one-thirty-five; she was almost certainly alive at one o'clock, and she was almost certainly dead by a quarter-to-two. Rigor hasn't set in yet, you see. Well, that's all I can do here. You'll have the body moved to the mortuary later, I suppose.'

'You've finished, doctor?' said the Superintendent. 'Then will you turn her on her face again? I want those marks on her legs recorded.'

The doctor nodded and did so, spreading the flimsy little garment over her before making his preparations for departure.

Roger was staring at the still form. 'One o'clock!' he was thinking. 'At one o'clock, when she was alive, I was ordering Pleydell's steak; at one-thirty, when she was probably dying, I ordered another half-pint of beer; at two o'clock, when she was certainly dead, I was paying my bill.' It seemed somehow horribly callous and shocking that he and Pleydell should have been eating lunch while this unhappy girl was being done to death. Yet people must eat as well as die.

Roger told himself, without much conviction, that he was a sentimental fool.

CHAPTER XIII

A VERY DIFFICULT CASE

With the departure of the doctor the group round the divan broke up. The photographer was brought back and, while Moresby and Inspector Tucker conferred in low tones nearby, Superintendent Green gave his orders.

'See these marks?' he said, exposing the backs of the dead girl's thighs again, but keeping the rest of the body covered. 'I want as good a picture of them as you can get. Move the divan if the light's better for you from behind, but put it back again in the same place. You can go and get the plates developed after that; there are no other marks on the body.'

He joined Moresby and Tucker. 'As the doctor said, I don't suppose they're of any importance, those marks,' he observed, 'but we'd better have a record of them, just in case.'

'If he can get one,' agreed Moresby. 'Not an easy thing to photograph.' They went on talking.

Roger strolled across the room and examined the door. He had already noticed that there were no scratches on the lower part such as might have been made by a pair of high-heeled shoes, struggling desperately, as had been the case with Janet Manners; he now saw that there were no marks on the upper part either, which bore out the doctor's statement that nothing was to be learnt from the girl's nails. Evidently poor little Dorothy Fielder had died peacefully at any rate, which neither Janet nor (as he had heard since) Elsie Benham had done.

In front of the door, lying on its back with the top rail towards the doorway, was still the overturned chair. Roger looked at it closely, but could not see that anything was to be learnt from it. The chair was of the low-seated, high-backed *prie-dieu* type, with a moulded wooden rail at the top of the back; in fact, the seat was so low that Roger was a little surprised that it has proved adequate for its purpose. The surface was only about a foot above the castors, and unless the girl had been standing on it on tiptoes he would have expected the stocking to stretch far enough to enable her to get her toes on the ground. Then he remembered that the chair was, after all, merely part of the stage-setting for suicide and had no other importance. But it was curious, nevertheless, that the murderer, so very much on the spot in all other respects, should have chosen the one chair in the room which suited his purpose least.

He turned away, and saw the Assistant Commissioner approaching him.

'You're Sheringham, aren't you?' said Sir Paul pleasantly, holding out his hand. 'I must apologise for not speaking to you before, but things have been so busy. My predecessor told me about that brilliant piece of work of yours down at Wychford. Well, what do you feel about all this?'

'That I oughtn't to be here,' Roger replied promptly. 'I never felt so insignificant in my life.'

'Oh, we're all insignificant cogs in the same big wheel, if it comes to that,' laughed the other. He swept a glance round the room and his eyes grew grave again as they rested on the dead girl. 'This is really an appalling business, isn't it?' he said soberly. 'Assuming, I mean, that it really is murder. It's the first big case I've had since my appointment, of course, and candidly I don't like it at all. And there's going to be some fur flying when the papers get hold of it, of course, if we can't lay our hands on the man. Do you remember what they had to say about us at the time of Jack the Ripper?'

'Yes, but it wasn't Scotland Yard's fault. They had nothing to work on.'

'Nor have we now,' responded Sir Paul ruefully. 'We haven't unearthed a single fresh clue here yet. The man must be a criminal genius. Not a sign of a finger-print, even.'

'It's the devil,' muttered Roger.

'It certainly is,' agreed the Assistant Commissioner with gloom. 'And so is he.'

They watched the others for a few moments in silence. The room was getting emptier now. The photographer had gone, and so had the Divisional Inspector, to give orders to his men about keeping the approaches to the flat guarded and the removal of the body. The finger-print man had returned and continued to prowl, but his face had quite lost its hopeful expression. Moresby and the Superintendent were still conferring in a corner.

'And I was having lunch at my club when it happened,' Roger muttered. 'Hell! With Pleydell, by the way; Lady Ursula's fiancé, you remember.'

'Yes, I know him slightly. He'll be smelling a rat soon.'

'He's smelt it already.'

The Assistant Commissioner sighed. 'We can't keep it out of the papers much longer.'

They fell into silence again.

'And there are no signs of a struggle at all, this time,' Roger mused. 'It's curious.'

'None in the room, as you can see; and so far as the doctor could find, none on the body. He's going to carry out an autopsy, but I can't see how that can add anything to our knowledge. The cause of death is obvious enough, even to our lay eyes.'

'And no bruises at the wrists.'

'Apparently not even that, nor the ankles.'

Roger ruminated. 'Lady Ursula's wrists were faintly bruised, weren't they? Yes, I remember they were. And her ankles too?'

'Yes, very slightly. She'd evidently been bound, if that's what you mean.'

'And this girl hadn't? That's odd. Or with something that didn't mark, at any rate.'

'I don't suppose he used exactly the same methods every

time,' said the Assistant Commissioner. 'The other two girls' wrists weren't bruised, did you know?'

'No, I didn't. Moresby told me they were going to be examined.'

'Yes, I got the report this morning. No bruises on the bodies of either of them; in other words, apparently no struggle. Yes, Superintendent?'

Superintendent Green had approached. He nodded slightly to Roger as if to convey that though they were only just acquainted he knew enough about him not to resent his presence; but it was not a very cordial nod.

'I'm afraid this case isn't going to help us much, sir,' he said. 'Moresby and I can't find a blessed thing. This man knows his job all right, but it's none of our regulars, I'll swear.'

'No,' agreed Sir Paul. 'I never thought it was. Well, you and Moresby had better go over the ground again, just to make sure you've missed nothing. We've simply got to get this fellow somehow, you know, now that the absence of finger-prints on that book does seem to point definitely to his existence at last.'

The Superintendent seemed a trifle hurt; it was clear that he did not like the suggestion that he might have missed something. Roger was inclined to agree with him. The Superintendent looked as if he would miss very little.

'And the papers will be on to us now, I expect,' Sir Paul added unhappily. 'I wonder we haven't had any journalists nosing round here already.'

The Superintendent glanced at Roger as if not quite sure that one was not here already. 'What are we to tell them if they do come, sir?' he asked. 'We don't want to scare our bird by letting them tell him that we're on his tail.'

'No, certainly not. You'd better have a chit sent round to the various editors asking them not to comment on the case, I think. You can just say tactfully that Scotland Yard isn't altogether satisfied, but doesn't want any public interest roused pending their investigations. You know, the usual sort of thing.'

'Yes, sir. I'll see to it.'

'And by the way, Superintendent, what about another line of approach? This man's obviously mad, as Moresby says. I think you'd better have inquiries made as to any homicidal maniacs at large for the last couple of months.'

'Yes, sir, we can do that, of course,' admitted the Superintendent, a little condescendingly. 'But I think if you or I were to meet him, not knowing who he was, we'd no more guess he was mad than we should each other.'

'That's just what I've been saying all the time,' Roger put in.

'Is that so, Mr Sheringham?' said the Superintendent very politely but without the least interest, and turned back to Moresby.

The Assistant Commissioner smothered a smile; he knew his Superintendent Green. 'Well, Sheringham,' he said, 'we can't do much more here. Come along to my club and have a cup of tea. I'd like to have a chat with you about the case and hear what you think of it so far.'

'Thanks,' Roger replied. 'I'd like to.' Roger never refused an invitation to talk.

As they passed out on to the stone landing Sir Paul jerked his head backwards. 'There's that other girl, of course, but we'll let those two question her. It's their business and they'd do it better than us, and too many of us would probably confuse her; she's half hysterical as it is. But I don't anticipate the slightest information from her. Heigho! This really is a perfectly damnable case.'

They got into a taxi and were driven to Pall Mall.

Finding a secluded table in a corner of the big lounge, Sir Paul ordered tea and they settled down. Roger described how his suspicions had been first aroused, and detailed the various conclusions at which he had arrived. Sir Paul was an admirable listener. Roger went on to express his doubts as to the advisability of pinning everything to the clue of the notepaper. But here Sir Paul was not in agreement.

'After all,' he pointed out, exactly as Moresby had done, 'it's the only real clue we've got, you know. It must be followed up to the limit.'

'I've a feeling,' said Roger, 'that this case isn't going to be solved by your ordinary methods. The clue isn't strong enough. It was the same with Jack the Ripper, you remember. I always have thought that the French way of approach might have produced results there.'

'We've got to stick to our own ways,' returned Sir Paul. 'The British public would never stand for anything else. Look what a fuss there was not long ago about taking a suspect's finger-prints. The man had nothing to lose by it if he was innocent, and possibly plenty to gain; but the great British public thought it an infringement of their liberty, and the papers talked a lot of nonsense about un-English methods, so that now our hands are tied and we're not allowed to do even a small thing like that. No, Sheringham, it's no good telling me to change our ways, even to catch a murderer. The British public would rather have all its murderers uncaught than change anything in the means of catching them. Surely you ought to know that.' It was evidently a subject on which Sir Paul felt rather strongly.

'I suppose there is a good deal in that,' Roger had to admit.

'There's everything,' said Sir Paul, with feeling. 'Besides, you must remember that a British jury, too, isn't the same as a French jury. Only definite evidence carries any weight with a British jury. A Frenchman takes a pleasure in clever reasoning, but the Britisher doesn't care a hang for it. You can try to dazzle him with brilliant reasoning and the most cunning deductions, and prove your case on those lines, to the hilt; but unless it rests on a firm basis of solid facts, your British jury won't even blink. It's unanswerable facts that we've got to lay before our courts of law, not just cleverness.'

'Yes,' Roger had to agree. 'Moresby's always rubbing into me the difference between being sure of your man and proving your case against him sufficiently to satisfy the law. And he seems to think that when we have found our man, we're going to have a good deal of difficulty in proving things against him, in these cases.'

'I'll bet we are,' Sir Paul concurred gloomily. 'The beggar simply won't leave us anything to fasten our proof on to. Just look at this last case. Except for that one bit of negative evidence about the lack of finger-prints on the book, which may convince us but wouldn't necessarily convince a jury at all—except for that, there simply *isn't* anything to prove that it isn't suicide. We know it can't be suicide, but how on earth are we going to prove merely that it's murder at all, without even considering the case to be made out against any one man? Oh, we're up badly against it here.'

'We certainly are,' said Roger, and registered his silent conviction yet again that, as the case stood at present, ordinary police methods would never secure a conviction. And if that really were so, what was he going to do about it? The answer, to Roger, was obvious. Scotland Yard might be hampered; he, on the other hand, was not.

They dropped into a desultory discussion of the crime in its relation to criminology in general, of which Sir Paul, like Roger, was an eager student.

'It's almost perfect,' Sir Paul said, lighting a fresh cigarette. 'So far as one can see, there isn't a flaw. It's the almost perfect crime—and it takes a madman to do it. There's a nice comment on the professional criminal.'

'"Almost" perfect?' Roger echoed. 'Why not quite perfect?'

'Surely the quite perfect crime,' Sir Paul smiled, 'is the one that never gets suspected of being a crime at all.'

'The point is yours, yes. By the way, you've noticed, of course, how few of these lust-murderers ever do get found out.'

'Well, naturally; unless they deliberately give themselves away, like Neil Cream did, there's simply nothing to go on. No starting-point for inquiry at all. In other words, no motive that's going to lead anywhere. After all, it's motive that really puts a man in the dock in nine cases out of ten. Motive and opportunity together make a professional detective carol with joy; he knows he's got his man all right then.'

'I suppose it's because I'm an amateur,' Roger sighed, 'but I must say I do like quick results. It frets me to have to sit quiet while this brute murders half a dozen more unfortunate girls before we can get our hands on him, as no doubt he will.'

'But you must realise the immense amount of patient research work that a case of this sort requires, Sheringham, before an arrest can be made. Stupendous! Why, do you realise that it took Superintendent Neil nearly a whole year's hard work to establish his case against Smith, "the brides-in-the-bath man", as the newspapers christened him?'

Roger nodded. 'Yes, I know. But for all that, delay irks me horribly. I'm afraid I shouldn't have made a good professional detective at all. Look here, are you going back to Gray's Inn Road?'

'Meaning you're itching to get back there yourself?'

'Frankly, I am. They ought to be through with the examination of the other girl, and I'm very anxious to hear whether they've found out anything from her. And then there are all the other inquiries, whether anybody saw him come in or leave, and all that sort of thing. I suppose they've got all that in hand?'

'Oh, yes; Tucker will have seen to that. That's just routine-work, of course. Well, you get along if you want to, Sheringham. I can't come with you, I'm afraid; I must be getting back to the Yard myself.'

'And I say, Sir Paul,' Roger added very earnestly, 'I don't want to butt in or make a nuisance of myself, but if you *could* arrange for any information about these crimes that happens to come in, to be telephoned on to me at my flat, I should be most awfully grateful. Do you think it could be done?'

Sir Paul smiled. 'I think it might,' he said.

Roger's voluble thanks were cut short by a club attendant, who interposed to tell Sir Paul that he was wanted on the telephone. He excused himself, and Roger accompanied him as far as the hall, where they parted company, Roger to retrieve his hat and coat. He had conceived a shrewd suspicion that his removal from the flat was not accident but design, to leave the official portion of the investigation to perform its routine-work unoverlooked by its unofficial colleague. If that were so, he considered that the others had had quite enough time to themselves by now, and his return could not be resented. And even if it were, Roger would not be so overcome with grief as to hurry away at once.

He was just going down the steps outside the club when he heard his name called. Sir Paul was standing in the doorway, beckoning. Roger turned and ran back to join him.

'You've had some news!' he declared.

Sir Paul nodded. 'The first bit of luck yet,' he said, in a voice that could not be overheard by the porter. 'I thought you might like to know. Moresby's just telephoned through that he's been able to get hold of a really good description of the man we want.'

'Joy on earth and mercy mild!' exclaimed Roger in high delight, and fled off to catch a passing taxi.

CHAPTER XIV

DETECTIVE SHERINGHAM SHINES

MORESBY welcomed Roger kindly enough (if the Superintendent did look a little bleak) and told him what had happened. From the other girl, Zelma Deeping, they had been able to learn nothing. So far as she knew Dorothy Fielder had been expecting no visitor, nor could she even suggest who the visitor might have been; so many dozens of men, mostly connected with their profession, dropped in from time to time if they happened to be in the neighbourhood, that it was impossible to say who this one might have been.

Briefly, her information was merely negative. Dorothy had been expecting nobody, Dorothy was not engaged to anybody, Dorothy had no particularly favoured men-friends. Nor (and here Moresby looked significantly at Roger) had Zelma Deeping ever heard the names George Dunning or Gerald Newsome. She *had*, she thought, heard of Arnold Beverley, but in what connection she could not recall; at any rate, she was sure of never having met him. She had been cautioned to say nothing whatever of the afternoon's events, and been allowed to go, under police supervision, to the house of a married friend in Hampstead, where she would stay till the police had finished with her flat.

From the porter of the block of mansions, however, valuable information had been obtained. The porter lived in a small basement flat on the left of the entrance, his windows being half-above and half-below the level of the pavement, behind a narrow area. The approach to the entrance of the Mansions was by means of a flight of eight stone steps, which led into the hall and towards the staircase. This was the only possible way in to any flat in the block, except by climbing over the roofs.

It was the porter's fortunate habit to sit, when not actively portering, in the front room of his little flat in such a position that he could see anyone going up or coming down the flight of steps outside; and there he would read his newspaper, especially in the latter part of the mornings when his first duties were over, glancing up from time to time when anyone passed up or down the steps. He had got into the habit of doing this, because he could often tell, from the manner in which a stranger entered, whether his own services would be required; and from his position he was enabled to get a good view of all entrants, but could see only the backs of those departing unless they turned in the direction of his flat, when he was able to see their profiles as they passed. The porter was an old sergeant in the regular army and a member of the Veterans' Corps, and Moresby had considered him to be not only reliable, but unexpectedly intelligent.

The porter had given a list of the strangers whom he had seen enter the Mansions between shortly before twelve, when he ensconced himself in his chair, and one o'clock, when he was called away to his dinner. He would not guarantee its accuracy, but affirmed that his memory was not a bad one on the whole. Moresby, at any rate, seemed quite satisfied with it.

Just before twelve a girl had come in whom the porter had no difficulty in setting down as an actress; she had only been inside a few minutes. At about five minutes past twelve a youngish man, with the appearance of a good-class artisan had gone in, and the porter had not seen him leave. Just after him an elderly woman had entered and after her, at about a quarter-past twelve, an elderly man, wearing gold-rimmed glasses, a short beard and a top-hat and looking like a family solicitor; he had been inside about twenty minutes and had then picked up a taxi outside and driven off in it. During his stay another man had arrived, at about half-past twelve, and had come out ten minutes later with one of the girls who had a flat there. There were one or two other women visitors between twelve-thirty and one, and then, just before one o'clock, a gentleman had arrived who seemed in rather a hurry. He got out of a taxi outside, paid off the driver, and ran quickly up the steps; but not so quickly that the porter had been unable to get a good look at him.

He seemed to be between thirty and forty years old, was well-built and well-dressed, good-looking, with a small dark moustache, wearing a blue overcoat and a bowler hat and carrying a pair of wash-leather gloves, not particularly tall, but certainly not short, good average height in fact, and the porter had no doubt that he could recognise him if he saw him again. He had not seen him come out, for he had been called to his dinner a few minutes later.

'And that, Mr Sheringham,' said Moresby impressively, 'is our man.'

'Good egg!' quoth Roger.

They were in the little sitting-room of the flat. The girl's body had now been removed, and the injunction against disturbing the furniture lifted. No one was left on the premises but Moresby and the Superintendent; even Inspector Tucker had gone, to make out his report. Evidently it was expected that nothing further was to be learnt from the flat itself. A constable, however, still remained on guard at the front door.

Superintendent Green, who had been looking at Roger with a long, unwinking stare, took up the conversation. 'Yes, and now all that remains is for us to identify him, Mr Sheringham. Perhaps you'll tell us how we're going to do that?'

'Oh, that's routine-work, surely,' Roger smiled. 'I leave all that sort of thing to you.'

'Umph!' observed Superintendent Green, and turned away. He did not return Roger's smile. Not a very companionable man, Superintendent Green. But, as Roger perfectly well knew, a very clever detective; little though he looked like the popular idea of one.

Roger turned back to Moresby. 'What about the taxi he came in? You'll be able to trace it, of course?'

'Oh, yes, we should be able to get hold of the driver all right. He may help us, or he may not. He's our chief hope, though. But Mr Sheringham!'

'Hullo?'

To Roger's surprise Chief Inspector Moresby looked decidedly ill at ease. His manner was almost diffident. A diffident Chief Inspector is nearly a contradiction in terms, and Roger's surprise was not small. 'Yes?' he repeated, as Moresby seemed to have some difficulty in continuing.

'Well, I think I've got a pretty good idea who our man is,' said the Chief Inspector, almost with the effect of a small child blurting out a confession.

Roger took it that Moresby was apologising for having forestalled him with the solution—though certainly Moresby had not on former occasions shown any such nicety of feeling. 'What, already?' he replied genially, with the effect of saying: 'That's all right, my child; but don't do it again.' Perhaps he felt something of the sort, for he added quickly: 'That's uncommonly smart of you.'

'Yes, isn't it?' said Chief Inspector Moresby, with the greatest unhappiness.

Roger stared at him in astonishment. 'Well, who is the fellow, then?'

Roger's surprises were not yet over. With as guilty an air as if he had committed the murders himself, Moresby replied: 'Well, Mr Sheringham, do you mind if I don't tell you that just yet? Not till I've checked up on it, I mean. I will if you press me, of course, considering our agreement and everything; but I'd rather not at the moment, sir, honestly. You'll see why later, I'm afraid.'

'All right,' Roger said, mystified. 'I don't know what you're driving at, but don't tell me if you make such a point of it.' It had occurred to him that Sir Paul at any rate would not have these curious qualms about divulging such important news. 'But look here,' he added suddenly, 'if it's anything about publication, I should have thought you would have known me better by now than to—'

'No, Mr Sheringham,' the Chief Inspector interrupted hastily. 'No, it's nothing to do with publication. Nothing of that sort at all. Well, that's very good of you. We'll put it off till I've checked my results, then. That'll be much better.'

'And talking of checking,' Roger remarked, thinking it better to change the subject, 'I suppose you will make inquiries about the other men who came in during that hour? Just to be on the safe side, I mean.'

'Oh, yes,' agreed Moresby, wearing an air of almost comic relief. 'Yes, of course we do that. We don't leave any loop-holes, you know.'

'Loop-holes,' grunted the Superintendent, from the other side of the room. 'Seems to me the whole case is nothing but loop-holes, hung together with a couple of bits of string for evidence. How are we going to establish that he did the thing when we do catch him, eh? That's what I want to know.'

There was a little pause, during which all three evidently wondered the same thing.

'But with the porter's evidence,' hesitated Roger.

'What's to prevent him saying that he just ran up to take the girl out to lunch, couldn't get an answer, and ran down again?' demanded Superintendent Green. 'That'll be his story, of course; and we can't disprove it. Where's the porter's evidence then, Mr Sheringham, eh?'

'I see,' murmured Roger, abashed.

'What's even to prove that he had anything to do with this flat at all?' demanded the Superintendent, following up his advantage. 'There's not a blessed thing to connect him with it.

Not a fingerprint in the whole place. All the porter's evidence does is to prove that he had the opportunity, after the other girl had gone out; and what's the good of that?'

'Quite so,' agreed the humbled Mr Sheringham.

'Supposing he says he tried some other door and couldn't get an answer,' the Superintendent clinched the matter. 'The door of that girl the porter saw come out at about twelve-thirty. *We* can't say he didn't. All we can say is: "Yes, sir, perhaps. But, you see, we don't *think* you did, so there!"' The tone in which the Superintendent saw fit to present this piece of repartee on the part of Scotland Yard was ironical in the extreme. 'And that's a lot of use to us, Mr Sheringham, isn't it?'

'Yes,' said Roger hastily. 'I mean, no.—Er—what time did the other girl come out, Moresby—Zelma Deeping? You didn't mention that.'

'Oh, quite early,' replied the Chief Inspector, who, his recent diffidence apparently forgotten, had been watching the discomfiture of his colleague with an abashed grin. 'Not long after eleven, leaving this one in the flat alone. Said she had some shopping to do before keeping a lunch appointment at one.'

'I see. And we've only got the porter's observation from twelve o'clock. That leaves a margin of about an hour, doesn't it?'

'You mean, if anybody came between eleven and twelve, but didn't kill the girl till a couple of hours later?' Moresby said tolerantly. 'Well, it's possible, of course; but I don't think we need worry about that.'

'I was just thinking that the defending counsel would worry about it,' Roger pointed out mildly.

'Oh, it does leave the loop-hole; there's no doubt about that. But then, as the Superintendent says, the whole case is full of loop-holes.'

The Superintendent, still prowling about with an enormous magnifying-glass, grunted in the distance, as if to emphasise the multiplicity of loop-holes.

A thought occurred to Roger. 'What about the family solicitor, with the beard and the gold-rimmed spectacles?'

'Well, what about him, Mr Sheringham?'

'I mean, he sounds much more like the type we're after than
the athletic-looking, handsome man you've picked out. Have
you checked up on him yet? Does anybody in the Mansions
own to a bearded solicitor in a top-hat?'

'No, we haven't started that end yet. Tucker will get on to
that as soon as he's free. But anyhow, Mr Sheringham,' Moresby
pointed out patiently, 'it's no good you saying that the other
one doesn't sound like the type we're after. We've got to go on
facts, not types. The old gentleman couldn't have done it,
because he was out of the place just after half-past twelve and
the murder wasn't committed till one o'clock at the very
earliest, probably half-past. No, it lies between the artisan-chap
and the other, with the odds heavily on the other, because I've
no doubt Tucker will be able to find out all about the artisan
tomorrow.'

'I suppose it does,' Roger agreed, with a reluctance which
rather surprised himself. 'But it doesn't seem right, somehow.'

'It'll be right enough when we catch him,' said Moresby, with
happy optimism.

'Well,' came a grumbling voice from the other side of the
room, 'if you two've done arguing, I'm going to get back to the
Yard. And you'd better come with me, Moresby. I want to see
how those photos 've come out.'

'There doesn't seem much more we can do here,' said
Moresby. 'You'll keep the man on at the door, I suppose?'

'Oh, yes. We won't let anyone in yet awhile. You never know.
Well, this has been a waste of my time, I'm afraid. Are you
coming, Mr Sheringham?' Roger was evidently not to be allowed
to investigate without supervision.

Roger jerked his mind off finger-prints, their prevalence in
fiction, and their irritating absence in real life. 'Yes,' he said. 'I
may as well go to— Wait a minute! I believe I've got an idea!'

The two detectives looked at him without enthusiasm. Roger's ideas, it would appear, left them cold.

'You have, Mr Sheringham?' said Moresby, but more by way of making conversation than anything else.

'Yes. You were saying there were no fingerprints to connect this man with the flat, Superintendent. I take your word for it that there aren't any inside, but have you thought of looking outside?'

'And where,' queried the Superintendent heavily, 'might a man be expected to make any fingerprints that are going to be any use to us *outside* the flat, Mr Sheringham?'

'On the bell-push, Superintendent,' said Roger sweetly. He thought the Superintendent deserved that much.

'Well, that's a good idea, now,' said Moresby handsomely.

The Superintendent bestowed a sour look on him. It was the Superintendent's rule, one rather gathered, never to praise the ideas of amateurs to their faces. Praise is not good for amateurs, clearly considered the Superintendent.

Nevertheless, he consented to look at the bell-push.

'He ought to have been the last person to push it,' Roger explained happily, as they trooped out into the hall. 'Miss Deeping wouldn't; she'd use her key, of course. And the door's been open ever since then, more or less. Besides, you remember the porter said that our man was *carrying* a pair of wash-leather gloves, not wearing them. There is a chance that he didn't put them on till he got inside.'

On the landing the Superintendent bent down and examined the bell-push through his magnifying-glass. 'Humph!' he grunted, and produced a little tin of black powder. Pouring some of the powder into the palm of his hand, he blew it very gently at the bell-push, then blew away the superfluous powder. On the white porcelain stood out in clear, black relief the imprint of the middle portion of the ball of a thumb, the important papillary ridges standing out distinctly. He bent again and scrutinised it for a long minute.

'Not either of the girls', he announced at last, with no sign of emotion. 'This may be one to you, Mr Sheringham. Moresby, see that this isn't disturbed and have a photograph taken of it as soon as possible, will you?'

Roger looked as demure as he could and said nothing.

CHAPTER XV

MR SHERINGHAM DIVERGES

THAT evening Roger suffered badly from reaction.

It seemed inexpressibly tame to remain at home alone, thinking over the events of that momentous day; and yet to go out for mere amusement, to a theatre or a concert, would be sheer anti-climax. He badly wanted to talk over the case with somebody, but had not the face to inflict himself further on Moresby or anybody else at Scotland Yard; especially since, from being something like a joint-partner on equal terms, he had now shrunk to a mere excrescence on the great organisation which had at last taken the affair definitely in hand. Roger rather resented being looked upon as an excrescence.

He toyed with the idea of a visit to the little creature who had shared Janet's flat, Moira Carruthers. It was some days now since he had seen her, and after what she had done for him in the early stages of the case he did not wish to appear neglectful of her now that it had passed out of her orbit. Then he remembered that she would be at the theatre and gave up that idea, not without relief. Was there nobody else with whom he could discuss things, and not have to be too guarded in what he said?

Of course there was! He jumped out of his chair, grabbed the telephone-book and looked up Pleydell's number.

Luckily Pleydell was at home. To Roger's carefully worded query as to whether he would care to come round to the Albany and talk over a matter of some importance which had arisen since they lunched together, Pleydell replied with some emphasis in the affirmative, adding that he would be round within twenty minutes. Roger understood the emphasis. The evening papers had been discreet, but one and all they had reported the new tragedy, though Scotland Yard's interest in it had not, of course, been mentioned.

Roger filled in the time till Pleydell's arrival by adding the developments of the day to the rough diary he had been keeping of the case, with everything that had been learned from the porter and Miss Deeping in such detail as there was. He also chronicled the discovery of one finger-print, and by whom.

Pleydell arrived punctually during the twentieth minute and at once began to question Roger as to the latest development. His perturbation, for so imperturbable a man, was obvious. He repeated his threats to call in the best private detectives that money could hire; he even talked of sending over to America for some of Pinkerton's men, reputed to be the best private detectives in the world. The account of the porter's evidence and the finding of the finger-print (on which he congratulated Roger with a warmth which was in strong contrast with Superintendent Green's official coolness) did something to soothe him, and Roger set himself to do the rest.

'Don't spoil the broth, Pleydell!' he urged. 'You promised you'd do nothing if I kept you in touch, and I'm doing that. We'll get to the bottom of it all right. Why, Moresby told me straight out that he's got a pretty shrewd notion already about the identity of the finger-print maker.'

'He has?' Pleydell said eagerly, pausing in the restless peram-bulations he was making up and down the room. 'Who does he think it is?'

'Well, he wouldn't actually tell me the name,' Roger said, not without a little embarrassment. It is difficult, after pointing out that you are hand-in-glove with Scotland Yard, to have to explain that the hand is not always in the glove. 'Wouldn't commit himself till he'd verified it, or some nonsense. I believe the Superintendent must have been at him about me. It's quite evident that *he* doesn't like the idea of me being mixed up officially with Scotland Yard.' Roger managed to convey the idea that there existed a good deal of jealousy at Scotland Yard of gifted amateurs.

'But he thinks he knows, eh?' said Pleydell, disregarding the gifted amateurs and the professional jealousy they have to suffer. 'Well, that's something. Good God, Sheringham, I wish they'd hurry up and get this man. I shan't have any peace till they do. This wretched girl this afternoon—I couldn't help feeling when I read about it in the paper that somehow *I* was responsible. I ought to have prevented it somehow; I knew this brute was loose and I hadn't managed to catch him.'

Roger nodded. 'I know. That's exactly how I felt. It's absurd, of course, but it seemed to me horribly callous to think that you and I must just have been tackling our jam omelettes when the poor girl was being killed. I remember saying as much to the Assistant Commissioner,' Roger was not actually hinting that though unlettered Superintendents might be cool with him, Assistant Commissioners fed eagerly out of his hand; but the words rolled smoothly off his tongue.

'The Assistant Commissioner? Oh, Sir Paul Graham, yes; he's the Assistant Commissioner now, isn't he? I know him slightly.'

'Yes, he said he'd met you. Now look here, Pleydell,' Roger said firmly, 'stop pacing up and down like a lion in a cage, help yourself to a whisky and soda, and sit down here by the fire. I want to talk to you, and I can't while you're rampaging up and down.'

'What do you want to talk about?'

'This case, of course. I always have to talk about these things to somebody,' Roger said frankly. 'It's a dreadful nuisance for my victims, of course, but it helps me a lot; it clarifies what ideas I may have as no amount of silent thinking can do.'

'Well, you can have the use of my vile body for your talking-stool till the small hours,' Pleydell said, with a faint smile, 'and the more you talk, the better I'll be pleased. I'll help myself to that whisky and soda and sit down at once, to show I'm in earnest.' He did so.

Roger refilled his pipe and lit it with some deliberation. He wanted to collect his ideas.

'This is what I want to get off my chest,' he began, 'and you can see why the police, not excepting my excellent friend Chief Inspector Moresby, can't qualify for the role of confidant in this particular matter. I've got a feeling in my bones that Scotland Yard's working on the wrong lines!'

'You have?' said Pleydell, with the interest proper to a Watson.

'Yes. I've been saying so all the time about that notepaper clue they've been pinning their faith to, and I feel it in this new case just as strongly. In my opinion this is *not* the kind of crime that's going to be solved by the ordinary police methods of this country. It has a psychological basis which, I'm quite convinced, can only be uncovered by the application of imaginative psychological methods.'

'I'm inclined to agree with you there,' said Pleydell.

Roger thought for a moment. 'Take this fingerprint, for instance. What's the good even of a finger-print if they can't find the finger that fits it? There'll be no specimen of that print in their records, as there probably would be if it was a case of burglary that we were considering. The only use of it is to check their conclusions when they've found their man; it isn't going to help them to find him. And the porter's description of the fellow with the blue overcoat and the wash-leather gloves might apply to several thousand young men in London alone. No, the more I think of it, the more sure I am that this latest crime isn't going to help us in the least towards finding our man. Which means that the police will be thrown back more or less into the state they were before, and will go on concentrating on that notepaper clue for their results. And they may get them that way, of course,' Roger was ready to admit, 'but I very much doubt it.'

'Well?'

'Well, if that's the case, it seems to me that Scotland Yard and I are going to diverge hence-forward in our lines of investigation. I don't consider myself bound to follow them in the least. If I think they're on the wrong track, I shall break off it into one of my own making.'

'Quite right.'

'And,' said Roger, 'I want you to help me.' He shot a glance at the other.

'With pleasure,' Pleydell said quietly. 'It's very good of you, and I welcome the opportunity. You know I'm as anxious as you to lay this devil by the heels. And,' he added soberly, 'I've a good deal more personal interest in doing so.'

Roger nodded. This had not been an impulsive offer. He had considered its feasibility before ever telephoning to Pleydell. What was in his mind was that no harm could possibly come of its acceptance (he never doubted that it would be accepted) and the probabilities were that it would lead to a great deal of good. Pleydell was a very clever man, and no doubt a shrewd judge of the human animal, and his co-operation could not fail to be helpful on these counts alone. But above that, by being drawn into the official net he would be effectually prevented from acting as a possibly disturbing free-lance; and Roger was very anxious that a superfluity of cooks should not spoil this particular broth.

'It's this way, too,' he added, smoking thoughtfully. 'The Scotland Yard machine is excellent as a criminal-hunting organisation; none better. But it's just this very kind of case that puts grit in its bearings. The ordinary murderer, you see, isn't a criminal at all in one sense; I mean, he very often hasn't got a criminal mind. I'm not referring to the burglar who loses his head when trapped and shoots in panic; I just mean the usual, unpremeditated murderer—for of course the great majority of murders are unpremeditated.'

'So I suppose,' Pleydell murmured.

'Well, if you examine the records of successfully detected murders in this country,' Roger continued, now firmly mounted on his hobby-horse, 'you will see that the criminal already known to the police who turns murderer, is nearly always caught; once he gets on the records of Scotland Yard his chances of getting away with a murder are almost nil. In murders of that type our detective service probably has a better record than any other. The thoroughness of the entries are astonishing; not merely the physical characteristics, but the pyschological idio-syncrasies as well—Bill Jones likes a bit of raspberry jam out of the larder when he's finished a burglary; Alf Smith always enters a house through a trap-door in the roof; Joe Robinson kisses the maidservant whom he's held up with his revolver; that sort of thing. No wonder the criminal-murderer leaves half a dozen characteristic signs, quite apart from definite clues, by which the police can tell his identity at once.'

'Really?' said Pleydell, much interested. 'I had no idea the records were as thorough as that.'

'Yes,' said Roger, 'but when the police have to deal with the the other sort of murderer, the man about whom they know nothing in advance, you'll find that, unless he's left some very definite clue or there crops up some quite direct evidence, he simply isn't caught. That he nearly always is caught, by the way, simply means that he nearly always does leave such a clue or such evidence.'

'I suppose the average murderer is a bit of a fool,' nodded Pleydell. 'Otherwise he wouldn't be a murderer at all.'

'Quite so. In a word, if you examine the unsolved murder mysteries of the last fifty years, you'll find they are all in this last category; there was no direct evidence and no clue, or the one clue on which the police seized didn't lead to anything. Well, I ask you—if that notepaper clue doesn't turn up trumps, doesn't this case fall quite definitely into this category?'

'I should say so, decidedly.'

'Exactly. And the police are going to fall to the ground over it. In a word, if we want this man caught we've got to catch him ourselves.' Having reached his climax Roger relighted his pipe, which had gone out during this harangue, and proceeded to smoke in impressive silence.

They sat looking into the fire for a few minutes.

'I'm glad you've invited my co-operation, Sheringham,' Pleydell observed at last, 'because I've got an idea which I think is really worth considering. I wouldn't have bothered you with it otherwise; I should probably have followed it up myself. But now I'd like to hear what you think about it, though most probably there's nothing in it at all.'

'I'd very much like to hear it,' said Roger, with truth; any idea of Pleydell's was bound to be worth consideration.

'Well,' Pleydell said slowly, 'has it ever occurred to you that we might get at this man through his profession? If we could narrow him down to a doctor, for instance, and then look up the visitors' lists to the Riviera last February and pick out the doctors, we should have gone a very long way towards identifying our man.'

'We certainly should,' Roger agreed warmly. 'Why, do you mean that you know what he is?'

'Oh, no; nothing as definite as that. It has only suggested itself to me that he might possibly belong to a certain profession. I wonder if you'll see it if I put the facts to you in this way. Leaving the woman at Monte Carlo out of it, Unity Ransome was an actress, Dorothy Fielder was an actress, the night-club woman had been on the stage, I gathered; at any rate, she probably mixed with the shadier elements of the profession. Add to this that it seems most likely that the murderer was personally known to his victims—and doesn't it occur to you what he might have been?'

'An actor!' Roger cried promptly.

'Precisely.'

They smoked again in silence for a minute or two.

'This,' said Roger, 'is interesting.'

'So I thought,' Pleydell agreed modestly.

'We must follow this up.'

'I'm glad you say so. I was going to myself in any case. And as it happens, I'm in rather a good position to do so.'

'That's more than I am,' said Roger, thinking of Miss Carruthers, one of his few links with the theatrical world.

'Yes,' Pleydell explained, 'I'm financially interested in one or two productions, and so is my father. I could certainly get any introductions we might want, and possibly some useful inside information as well.'

'That's excellent. Well, the first thing to do is to get hold of the list of English visitors on the Riviera. I can get a copy of that from Moresby; but till it comes I don't see what we can do on these lines.'

'No, I'm afraid nothing, except perhaps make a few inquiries about the actor-friends of these girls.'

'I'll mention that to Moresby. The police can do that sort of thing far better than we ever could. Their inquiries cover all the possible ground, you know, and without missing a single person who might have information to give. They'll begin that in earnest now, I expect. Every single intimate friend of the murdered girls will be examined, and every single person as well whom they happen to mention, and then everyone whom *they* mention, and so on and so on till something does turn up. The patience of the police is amazing. Moresby tells me that sometimes they examine dozens of people, in a big and particularly difficult case perhaps even a hundred, before any vital information is elicited; but when they do get hold of a bit they're on to it like bulldogs.'

'You make it unpleasantly graphic,' Pleydell said, with a little smile. 'I hope I never murder anyone and have the pack of bulldogs on to me.'

'I've often thought that,' Roger concurred. 'It must be most disturbing to one's night's rest. The description of that man whom the porter saw, by the way, will be in the hands of every station in London and the country by now, I expect, sent out over the telephones as soon as the Superintendent got back to

Scotland Yard. The London railway termini are being watched for him; at every port they're on the *qui vive* for him, every policeman on every beat is keeping a sharp look-out for yellow wash-leather gloves and the rest, the hue and cry is in full throat. By Jove, I wouldn't like to be in that man's wash-leather gloves.'

'And you think he'll be caught?'

'That's different. I'm not at all sure about that. If he's got any sense at all, he won't be. The description's too vague; it applies to too many people. Alter one or two details, and you've got an entirely different man. No,' said Roger weightily, 'I do *not* think he'll be caught, on that description. But I wouldn't like to be in his gloves for all that!'

'And we've got his finger-prints,' Pleydell pointed out, with grim satisfaction, 'thanks to you.'

'That,' Roger agreed, 'is perfectly true.'

They sat on talking into the small hours, but the case remained unadvanced.

CHAPTER XVI

INDEED, so far as Roger was concerned, the case remained unadvanced for some days. In response to questions about his researches, Moresby became more and more reticent. From being amused Roger became hurt, from being hurt angry, and from being angry resigned, but in none of these states of mind could he induce Moresby to discuss the affair frankly with him as in the early stages. Roger thought he knew the reason, and blamed Superintendent Green with a good deal of bitterness. The divergence he had anticipated became a fact.

He was allowed to take a copy of the list of English visitors staying on the Riviera at the crucial date, however, when in due course this arrived, and he handed it over to Pleydell, who undertook to have the actors on it picked out by a competent authority. The latter informed him, moreover, that no friends of Lady Ursula seemed to figure in it who were not already on his own lists. Roger was also allowed to see the report from the French police on the Monte Carlo death, though he was subtly given to understand that this was no longer a right so much as a favour. In any case it did not help him in the least. The French police had had no doubt at the time of its being suicide, and apparently they thought so still; all the facts pointed to suicide, and they could see no cause to suspect anything else.

Certainly, if the case was to be considered as an isolated one, the French police had reason; as usual there were no signs of a struggle, no bruises either on the body or the wrists, and the farewell letter had been a good deal more explicit than the English ones, signed and, it seemed, perfectly convincing. A copy of it was attached, and Roger had to admit that, though a little vague, it might quite well have been genuine. In short, the French police not only still thought their own case one of suicide, but hinted with considerable delicacy that the English ones too might quite possibly (they were tactful enough not actually to write 'probably') turn out to be the same, and they added a few helpful remarks about neurotic women and suggestion.

'Which I did much better in my own article,' commented Roger disgustedly. 'Well, there certainly doesn't seem to be much help there.'

On the principle of returning good for evil, Roger mentioned to Moresby the theory that the wanted man might be an actor. Moresby received the suggestion with gratitude, but spoilt the effect by adding that such an idea had already occurred to Superintendent Green and himself.

'Then I suppose you're making your inquiries on those lines?' asked Roger.

'We're making inquiries on *all* lines, Mr Sheringham,' said the Chief Inspector politely, and went on to talk about the weather.

'Damn the weather,' said Roger, not at all politely, 'and you too, Moresby.'

On another occasion Roger tried to find out how the clue of the notepaper was progressing.

Moresby was as evasive as ever. 'We haven't got all the reports in yet, Mr Sheringham,' he said.

'Well, can I see the ones that are in?'

'Better wait till they're all in; then you can look at them all together, can't you?'

'Well, hang it, tell me if you've found out *anything* from it.'

'I've always said we should get results from that notepaper in the end, Mr Sheringham,' beamed Chief Inspector Moresby.

Roger went away in a naughty temper.

But his temper did not remove his powers of thought. Moresby *had* found out something, and something rather important too. And he very much did not want to share his information. Why not? There must be something more in all this than the whims and preferences of Superintendent Green.

He sought out Sir Paul and demanded to know why he was being shouldered out of the inquiry. Had Scotland Yard held out the sop of official recognition to him merely in order to pick his brains and, having discovered from him all they could, thrown him aside like a sucked orange? demanded Roger, not without warmth.

'Nothing of the kind,' replied Sir Paul, with manifest uneasiness. Oh, no; oh, dear, no; he mustn't think anything like that.

'Well, what am I to think, then?' Roger wanted to know.

Sir Paul hedged. The investigations were just reaching a very delicate stage; the official detectives had thought it best to keep things in their own hands just at present; the Home Office had enjoined particular secrecy for the moment; if Sheringham wouldn't mind keeping in the background for just a very few days . . .

Sheringham did mind, very much; but there was clearly nothing else for it. In the background, then, a distinctly fuming but undeniably helpless figure, Sheringham remained.

One morning, three days after his conversation to be precise, the telephone bell in the background rang. Answering it, Roger heard a feminine voice and groaned, for feminine voices on his telephone almost invariably meant invitations to dinners, dances or some other form of social torture, which Roger would give large sums of money to avoid; and that meant the manufacture on the instant of a credible excuse.

'Hullo!' said the feminine voice. 'Is that Mr Sheringham?'

'Yes,' groaned Roger.

'This is Anne Manners speaking,' said the voice.

Roger stopped groaning. 'Miss Manners? Good gracious, are you speaking from Dorsetshire?'

'No, from London; about half a mile away from you. Mr Sheringham, are you busy this morning?'

'Not in the least,' Roger replied promptly, and with perfect truth.

'Well, I'm very sorry to bother you, but I want to see you. In fact, I've come up to London especially to do so. Could you meet me somewhere, where we could have a cup of coffee perhaps, and talk?'

'I should be delighted,' said Roger. 'Where do you fancy?'

They arranged a place, in the restaurant of a big store near Piccadilly Circus (the choice was Anne's), and agreed to meet there in a quarter of an hour.

Roger was a firm bachelor. He knew very little about women in general, and cared less; his heroines were the weakest part of his books; the idea of meeting a girl in the restaurant of a big store held not a single thrill for him. But even Roger, when brought face to face with her fifteen minutes later, had to admit that Anne Manners was a pleasant person to meet, even in the restaurant of a store catering entirely for women. She was wearing a dark-grey tailored coat and skirt, and a close-fitting little grey felt hat without any ornamentation; in the enormous restaurant she looked smaller than ever. Roger discovered that he rather liked small women. They gave him a pleasing feeling of male superiority and capabilities of protection.

Not that Anne Manners appeared to need any protection at all. If anything, it was Roger who needed the protection; for, as soon as the waitress had brought them their coffee and biscuits, Anne proceeded to attack her companion with calm vigour.

'Why haven't you written to me about Janet, Mr Sheringham?' she demanded. 'You promised.'

Roger met the attack bravely. 'I know. I ought to have done.'

'You certainly ought,' Anne agreed with severity.

'But I was waiting till a few more details were cleared up,' Roger continued, a little lamely.

Anne pounced on this. 'Oh! So you have found out something, then?'

'A—a certain amount, yes,' Roger almost stammered. Really, this was going to be very difficult. What was he going to tell the poor child? Hardly the truth. At any rate, not yet.

'What?' fired Anne, point-blank.

'Oh, well, not very much, you know. Nothing quite definite. We haven't—I mean, I haven't been able to identify the man at the back of it yet.'

'There was a man at the back of it, then?'

'Oh, I think so. At least, it seems probable, doesn't it? That is to say—well, I always thought that the most likely explanation.' It was not often that Roger found himself ill at ease, and to some persons (one Alexander Grierson, for instance) the sight would have been an enjoyable one. If he had been present in the restaurant department of that store at this particular moment, Alec might have considered many old scores wiped out.

Anne looked her blethering *vis-à-vis* in the eyes. 'I'm not a child, Mr Sheringham,' she said, the knuckles of her small gloved hand beating an impatient tattoo on the table. 'Please don't play with me in this silly way. I want you to tell me straight out—was my sister murdered?'

Roger gaped at her. It was just by this same method that he had taken Moresby by surprise, but now that it had been used against himself he was equally taken aback. 'What—whatever makes you think that, Miss Manners?' he said, trying to gain time.

'By putting two and two together, of course,' Anne replied tartly. 'Besides, there's a certain amount of gossip, you know, on those lines.'

'Is there?' Roger frowned. 'Who told you so?' he asked, brought back to normal by this information.

'That girl, Moira Carruthers, who lived with Janet.'

'Ah! You've called there?'

'I'm living there,' Anne returned.

'You are? Good gracious! Why?'

Anne did not reply at once. Her knuckles continued their tattoo for a few moments, while she seemed to be making up her mind on what course to pursue. She drew a little quick breath.

'Look here, Mr Sheringham,' she said quietly, 'you're not playing fair with me. If anybody has a right to know the truth about my sister's death, I have; and I intend to discover it. I've come up to London and left things at home to Mary, although she's barely eighteen, for that very purpose. Please don't fence with me. I'm convinced that Janet was murdered. Was she?'

'Yes,' Roger replied simply. 'I'm afraid she must have been.'

The girl's small oval face whitened for an instant. 'Thank you,' she said, biting her lip.

Roger looked away while she recovered herself.

'I was sure of it,' she said after a short pause, 'but it's good of you to be frank with me. Do they know who—who killed her?'

'No, not yet. The police have it in hand, of course. I've been helping them as far as I could.'

'Then all those other girls were murdered, too?'

'I'm afraid so. Did you suspect all this before you left home, Miss Manners?'

'Oh, no. But I knew you were right when you said there must be something behind it all, and as I didn't hear from you I came up to see if I could find out what it was. Then Moira told me what they were saying at the theatre, and I felt I must ask you if it was true.'

'They're saying that at the theatre, are they?' Roger asked quickly.

'I think they're saying it everywhere, aren't they?' Anne replied, with a dreary little smile. 'Everywhere except in the newspapers, and some of those have hinted. Of course nobody at the theatre has said anything to me about it, but Moira told me because she thought I ought to know. She was very fond of Janet, in her own queer way, and she's almost as anxious as

I am that the horrible business should be cleared up and the—the murderer (if Janet was murdered) caught.'

'Yes,' Roger murmured, 'she's a good little soul—in her own queer way, as you say. She did her best to help me at the beginning, but nothing seemed to emerge from that line of inquiry.'

'Yes, she told me. And I think the others, or the management at any rate, have a pretty shrewd idea of what I'm after, because they let me join the chorus at once as soon as they heard I was Janet's sister. Luckily a girl wanted to leave to get married, so there was a vacancy; but she would have stayed on ordinarily till the end of the run. She guessed too, I'm sure.'

'But you're not in the chorus of *Thumbs Up!* are you?' asked Roger in astonishment and not a little dismay. Of all the girls in this world Anne Manners looked the least fitted to be a show-girl in a not very high-class revue.

Anne nodded. 'I'm stepping into Janet's shoes both on and off the stage, and there I stay till the devil who killed her is caught.'

'But—but why?'

'Because there's always the possibility that he might try to attack me too, you see; and then I should know who he was. That's my great hope. I want to catch him *myself*. Oh, Mr Sheringham, if I only could!' Her normally rather elfin face wore the rapt fierceness of a tigeress contemplating the tearing to bits of the hunter who had shot one of her cubs.

Roger respected her lust for vengeance. He had no use for the watery theory that man should not ensure his own revenge. He wanted vengeance on this brute himself, quite impersonally, on behalf of society in general, and he applauded the same sentiment in those who, like Anne and Pleydell, had a closer claim upon it. And both those two, in their own individual ways, seemed determined to achieve it. Well, if he could help them towards it, so much the better.

He spoke on impulse. 'Shall I tell you exactly how the case stands at present, so far as I know?'

'If you will, please,' said Anne, quietly, as if it was her right to know—as indeed, Roger thought, it was; hers and Pleydell's and anybody else's who was wearing mourning on account of it at the present moment. He had no qualms in telling her. By their own action the police had as good as absolved him from loyalty to them; he was going to work this case as a free-lance now, enlisting such recruits to help him as he, and he alone, considered suitable. He had already enlisted Pleydell; now he would enlist Anne Manners.

He gave her a brief account of the state of affairs to date and of the hopes, official and otherwise, for the future. She only interrupted once, when he came to mention the original three suspects whose names had been on both her own and Pleydell's lists. 'I know Mr Dunning, and Mr Newsome very slightly,' she said. 'It couldn't be either of them. And I've met Mr Beverley once or twice too; he's certainly not the man. No, it's none of those three.'

'Exactly what I said; we were on the wrong lines if the possibilities had been narrowed down to those three; they could none of them be the fellow, I'm convinced,' Roger agreed, and went on with his outline.

Anne sat for a few moments considering, when he had finished, her chin on her hands. Apparently there had been little in Roger's narrative that was unexpected to her, but she wished to assimilate the facts she had heard before relating them to her own course of action.

'My idea, when I joined Moira and secured Janet's place at the theatre,' she said slowly at last, 'was to set myself up as a kind of decoy. I wanted to make myself as like as possible to the sort of girl who seems to attract him. I shall go on with that idea.'

'But look here, Miss Manners,' Roger was beginning, 'you might be running into real danger. I don't see—'

'Except that now,' Anne continued, as if he had not spoken at all, 'I shall place myself at your disposal as well. Under your orders, if you like. I quite agree that Scotland Yard, tied as they are, are quite likely to fail in this case; but I think that a combination of you, Mr Pleydell and myself, not tied in any way, might have a chance of success. At any rate, it's worth trying.'

'But,' began Roger again.

'You'll be in charge, of course, as you've done this sort of thing before; Mr Pleydell will certainly agree to that. And I shall be on hand when required. There may be something in this idea about an actor, you see, and if you two are able to narrow your suspicions down to a few people, then you'll be able to make use of me for the final weeding-out.'

'But Miss Manners—hang it all—Anne!—I can't allow—'

'What I mean is that we must advertise the information, in an unobtrusive way, to all the people we suspect, that at certain times of the day (the late mornings and the afternoons, say) I shall be alone in our flat. Moira will go out ostentatiously every day. Then I shall simply sit in my parlour and wait for the fly. He won't be able to take me by surprise, you see, which must be his usual method, so it's no good talking to me about danger; there won't be any. And even if there were, what on earth does that matter? In any case there won't.'

'But the responsibility—'

'You'll be somewhere within call, you see. We can arrange a code of signals, or something like that. Well, now, Mr Sheringham, can you suggest a better plan than that? And do you agree to make use of me? Because if you don't, I shall simply do it on my own, and that will be much more dangerous.'

'You put me in a very difficult position, Anne,' said Roger, with some feeling.

'I mean to,' replied Anne serenely. 'Well, is it a bargain, and do I join your combination?'

'You jolly well do!' Roger cried, casting all scruples to the winds. 'Between the three of us we'll take a leaf out of the French notebooks and teach Scotland Yard a thing or two they never knew.'

CHAPTER XVII

AN UNOFFICIAL COMBINATION

BEFORE leaving her, Roger had arranged with Anne to meet again at tea-time when he would try to get hold of Pleydell so that the two lieutenants of the combination could be introduced; but fate, in the curious way it so often has on such occasions, forestalled him. Walking down Piccadilly soon after lunch with Pleydell, and having just that minute told him of this new development and ensured his presence at tea, Roger ran into Anne and Miss Carruthers coming straight towards them, and introduced Pleydell to the former then and there. And because Miss Carruthers was present, he could do no less than introduce Pleydell to her too.

'So pleased to meet you,' languished Miss Carruthers, with all the respectful deference due from a chorus-girl to an extremely rich young bachelor. 'So you're Mr Pleydell. Well, fancy that!'

'And you're Miss Carruthers,' responded Pleydell gallantly, 'I should have recognised you at once.'

'I say, would you really?' simpered Miss Carruthers, looking incredibly young and innocent.

'Hullo, do you two know each other already?' Roger asked.

'Well, not to say *know*, exactly,' murmured Miss Carruthers in lady-like accents. 'But I've often seen Mr Pleydell in front when we were rehearsing.'

Pleydell nodded. 'I told you I'd got theatrical interests,' he said to Roger. '*Thumbs Up!* is one of them. But, for heaven's sake, don't mention it beyond our four selves,' he added, smiling, 'or my reputation as a business-man would be

142

exploded for ever. No really good business-man ever touches the theatre, you know.'

'Well, I never knew you were *the* Mr Pleydell, and that's a fact,' fluttered Miss Carruthers.

'Nor does the stage-doorkeeper, nor the box-office manager, nor even the producer himself,' Pleydell laughed. 'I'm strictly incognito as soon as I step into a theatre, I can tell you. So now you see what a weighty secret you have in your keeping. If the newspapers got hold of the fact that I'd put money into a revue, I should be ruined in twenty-four hours.'

'Well, I never!' said Miss Carruthers, much impressed.

Roger had been confirming the tea-appointment with Anne during this exchange, and the four now split into two again and resumed their respective ways.

'And now,' said Pleydell, when they were safely out of earshot, 'you can see why Miss Anne stepped so easily into *Thumbs Up!* But I'm quite serious about keeping my theatrical interests a close secret, so don't mention it to anybody, even by way of a joke, there's a good fellow.'

'Certainly not,' Roger acquiesced promptly. 'Yes, I must admit I'd wondered how that came about. It sounded curious when she told me. And you'd gathered that she'd come up with that plan in mind?'

'Oh, dear, no; it never occurred to me. But I remembered your mentioning that the family were a bit hard-up, and I thought this girl might have come up to relieve the pressure at home, or even contribute her mite to it; so when I heard that a sister of Unity Ransome's had been asking for a job, I told them she was to have one. That's all.'

'Your word goes, so far as *Thumbs Up!* is concerned, then?'

'I've got a controlling interest in the rotten thing,' said Pleydell carelessly.

Roger, no less than Miss Carruthers, was impressed. If he himself had possessed a controlling interest in a London revue, even a minor one, he would certainly not have mentioned the fact with such unstudied carelessness. He bought Pleydell a drink in token of his respect. The respectful poor are always ready to buy the drinks of the careless rich.

But money has other uses beyond saving its possessor from having to buy his own drinks. Some of them were in evidence at the tea-table conference that same afternoon.

Seated round a secluded table in the most exclusive, and therefore the most expensive, hotel in London, the three discussed in low tones their plan of campaign, 'just like real conspirators', as Anne observed, with one of her unusual smiles. Roger had put forward for Pleydell's opinion the suggestions Anne had made regarding the part to be played by herself in the partnership together with his own qualms as to the wisdom of it, and after careful consideration Pleydell had pronounced favourably upon the proposal.

'I'm bound to say that I think it most unlikely to lead to any results,' he said, 'but if it did they would be so valuable as to justify our risking the waste of time involved. And I don't think that, if the proper precautions are taken, there is any real danger to Miss Manners.'

'None whatever,' Anne said briefly. 'I'm not an idiot.' She did not add that even if the danger were great she would not be in the least deterred, because that savoured of bragging; and bragging and braggarts constituted one of Anne's particular aversions.

'And of course,' Pleydell added in natural tones, 'I shall consider myself responsible for the precautions we do take; financially, I mean. Let us have that understood from the beginning, by the way; all matters of finance are my pigeons. Goodness knows it's small enough, but I feel that's going to be my chief use to you.'

Roger nodded, and Anne made no demur. She saw rightly that Pleydell's wealth was an inestimable asset to the combination, and that through it things became possible which to anyone else in their position, rashly challenging the official police, would have been out of the question. Besides, as she told Roger later, it seemed almost a kindness to let Pleydell spend as much money as he could on the pursuit of his fiancée's murderer; schooled and apparently unperturbed as he was, she could see something of the forces that were tearing him to bits inside and knew that he was on tenterhooks to do something, no matter what, that would achieve his end; and the spending of money is always a safety-valve, even to the very rich.

They proceeded to settle the details.

It was decided at once that the afternoons would be most convenient for the experiment, and the hours from two-thirty to half-past four were fixed. Every afternoon punctually at two-thirty Moira would leave the house as ostentatiously as possible, and Anne would stay, quite alone, in the sitting-room for two hours. At the end of that time she too would go out, for after four-thirty she would no longer be guarded.

The matter of her guarding was less easy to determine. The first consideration, of course, was that the murderer must have no suspicions of what was in hand; and the sight of Roger or Pleydell entering the house at about the time Miss Carruthers was leaving it would simply defeat their whole object. Nor would it prove very practicable if the guardian had to arrive so early that he would not be seen to enter if the house were watched.

In the end, Pleydell solved the problem in the grand manner. They would take a room in the house next door, or if there was no room available there, as near as possible, and there either Roger or Pleydell would lie in wait each afternoon during the crucial two hours. A bell was to be installed in this waiting-room, with its button under a rug in Anne's sitting-room so that she could press it with her foot without alarming her visitor, as soon as he disclosed his intentions. The watcher would then hurry down his stairs, change houses and run up the others (a performance estimated to take, at the outside, ninety seconds) and catch the man red-handed.

'Excellent,' Roger approved. 'But we must guard against a surprise attack as well. I suggest that Miss Manners presses the bell throughout the two hours at intervals of ten minutes to show that all is well—a short, sharp flick of the button. Then if we don't get that signal we shall know that something's wrong.'

'Yes, and to distinguish the ten-minutes' ring from the real danger-signal I could make the latter a long, steady pressure, couldn't I?' put in Anne, whose cheeks were flushing with excitement at the prospect of action at last.

'That is the idea, exactly,' Pleydell agreed. 'Well, I think that covers everything, doesn't it?'

'Yes, if things fall out right. But shall we be able to get a room at all in these days?' Roger wondered.

'You can leave that to me,' said Pleydell, with quiet confidence. 'I'll get a room all right.' And Roger had no doubt that he would.

'And supposing they won't let us fit up the bell-wire between the houses?' Anne suggested.

'They won't know,' Pleydell answered serenely. 'You can leave that to me too. I'll have all that done quite secretly. The wire could be taken along the roof, I imagine, or the outside wall.'

'And of course,' he added, by way of an afterthought, but so obvious that there was really no need for him to put it into words, 'of course if there *is* any trouble with the landlords, I'll have the two houses bought.'

Before such supreme omnipotence no further objections were raised.

'Now, how about advertising our trap to the various people we're setting it for?' said Roger. 'I suppose we must include George Dunning, though it seems quite unnecessary.'

'We must include everybody,' Pleydell said firmly, 'likely or unlikely.'

'Yes, I suppose we must really. Well, will you undertake Dunning? You knew him better than I do, of course. I'll put the hint to Jerry Newsome, though of all the impossible—

however! I wonder where he is, by the way? I haven't seen him since before the War. It'll be jolly to get into touch with Jerry again.'

'I think he's in London,' Anne put in. 'He only comes down to our part of the country in the middle of the summer for a few months, so far as I know.'

'Oh, well, I can easily find out his whereabouts. And that poisonous creature, Arnold Beverley; I wish you'd undertake him too, Pleydell.'

'I don't know him, I'm afraid.'

'I can manage him for you, Mr Sheringham,' Anne said, with a faint smile. 'I told you this morning that I'd only met him once or twice. That's quite true, because he's very careful whom he's seen about with in our neighbourhood (they're the great people of the district, of course, the Beverleys); but I fancy he might not be so particular in London. Anyhow, I'll send a line to him and say quite brazenly that I'm always in, alone, between two-thirty and four-thirty, shall I?'

'I wish you would,' said Roger fervently. 'I hardly know the man, but a little went a long way with me—about a mile out of his way every time I saw him in the distance ever after. And in any case, I don't quite see how I could introduce the fact that you're open to receive visitors during those hours if he wants to take advantage of it.'

'Very well. Of course if it comes out (and from what one hears of Mr Beverley such a thing is more than possible) my reputation's gone for ever; but I don't mind that.'

'I do, though,' said Roger. 'And especially as it's so completely unnecessary in Beverley's case. The man's been out of the running from the very beginning. I haven't even troubled to look him up or go into his movements or anything. If anybody on this earth since it flew off the sun has ever been incapable of murder of any sort, let alone this, Arnold Beverley is that man. Need we really worry about him, Pleydell, do you think?'

'We must worry about everybody,' Pleydell replied, with a

smile that was not without a certain grimness. 'And talking of that, I've got two more for you to worry over.'

'Two more suspects?' Roger asked eagerly.

Pleydell nodded. 'The only two actors on those Riviera lists. Here you are—Sir James Bannister and Billy Burton.'

Roger's face fell. 'Only those two? Oh, dear. Bannister might have played second murderer once on a time, but I'm sure he's far too important to play even first murderer nowadays. And Billy Burton—well, why not Charlie Chaplin?'

'Yet I've no doubt that both tragedians and comedians are quite human off the stage,' remarked Pleydell drily.

'But candidly, Pleydell, can you see either of those two in this particular role? And don't talk about humanity; there's nothing human about the brute we're after.'

'Candidly, I can't, no. But I don't pretend to be a psychologist. There may be hidden forces in one of them to impel him to do things that he may perhaps shudder over himself when his blood's run cold again—just as there are, I'm told, in all of us, though some control them better than others.'

'Well, I suppose they must be warned, like the others, but really—! However, if it comes to that, all five of our suspects to date seem to fail signally to qualify. If the murderer really *is* among them—'

'And he is,' Pleydell put in with quiet conviction. 'He must be. All the evidence points to it.'

'Well, if he is, he's going to turn out the most unexpected one of this century. Who's going to warn those two? I don't know either of them.'

'I think I can manage that for you. I know Bannister very slightly, and I can easily arrange to meet Burton.'

'Thanks. And I'll see what I can find out about their movements round the important dates. Which reminds me, I must go to Scotland Yard tomorrow and try to worry out of Moresby what he's discovered about the movements of the other three. And that artisan too . . . I'm not happy about him. I hope the police have been able to trace him. Have you considered, Pleydell, that though an actor fits the bill, so does an artisan? You let a plumber or a man from the electric light company or anybody like that into your house without either a qualm or an introduction. I wonder if we ought to follow that up?'

Pleydell shrugged his shoulders. 'How can we? There are probably several thousand plumbers alone in London, to say nothing of men from electric light companies and the rest. That sort of inquiry would be entirely beyond our scope.'

'I suppose it would,' Roger had to agree. 'But I'm not at all sure that it isn't there that the truth lies.'

Pleydell rose to his feet and made his excuses. He had over-stayed his time already, and had an important appointment in a short time.

Roger and Anne sat on for a few minutes after he had gone.

'I've never met a Jew I liked so much before,' Anne remarked.

'The real pure-blooded Jew, like Pleydell,' Roger told her, 'is one of the best fellows in the world. It's the hybrid Jew, the Russian and Polish and German variety, that's let the race down so badly.'

'And yet he seems as reserved and unimpassioned as an Englishman,' Anne mused. 'I should have thought that the pure-blooded Jew would have retained his Oriental emotion-alism almost unimpaired.'

Roger could have kissed her for the slightly pedantic way she spoke, which, after a surfeit of hostesses and modernly slangy young women, he found altogether charming.

'I suppose it's a matter of upbringing, and the sinister influence of the English public school,' he said lightly, thinking of one occasion at any rate when Pleydell had been neither reserved nor unimpassioned.

'And his money doesn't seem to have spoilt him a bit,' Anne concluded. 'That's very rare, isn't it?'

'Very,' Roger agreed, feeling absurdly jealous of the object of these encomiums. Yet what was he to Anne or Anne to him?

Then Anne discovered that she had only just time to get to Sutherland Avenue to fetch a clean handkerchief, or something equally unnecessary, if she was not to be late at the theatre. Roger's offer to buy her a dozen handkerchiefs for every quarter of an hour she would remain where she was now, was treated with the severity it deserved.

Roger paid the bill and they went.

Having put Anne into the tube which she insisted on patronising rather than a taxi at Roger's expense, that discarded novelist proceeded to his club to conduct a search for the present whereabouts of Gerald Newsome. By the time he had discovered the address in the London telephone directory, it was past seven, and, on calling the number, he learned that Newsome had just gone out and was not expected back till late. He left a message, arranging for lunch the next day, and went home to dine.

Feeling at a loose end after dinner, it occurred to him that he might just as well try Scotland Yard that evening as the next morning. Taking a chance, he rang up and was lucky enough to catch Moresby. By sheer tactlessness he forced the Chief Inspector into offering him a half-hearted invitation to go round.

Without more ado Roger went.

To his surprise Moresby greeted him with something of his old geniality. To Roger's request for information regarding the movements of the three original suspects on the important dates, Moresby replied at once that, though the reports were not yet complete, it seemed that anyone of the three might be the guilty man so far as movements went. None of the alibis for the period covering the death of Janet Manners were confirmed; at the time when Elsie Benham must have died all three were reported to be in bed (and all three, Roger remembered, were bachelors), and two of the three at any rate had no entirely convincing alibis for the Dorothy Fielder case; the report on the third was not yet in. So far as could be gathered from the Chief Inspector, the chances were still evenly balanced.

'Humph!' said Roger, distrusting the air of bland innocence with which this information had been given. There was something in the background somewhere, Roger was convinced, but he was equally convinced that the Chief Inspector was not going to divulge what it was.

He went on to ask about the artisan and the solicitor who had visited the Mansions within an hour of the murder.

There had been no difficulty in tracing the artisan, Moresby told him without hesitation, and gave details freely; Roger gathered that the police attached no importance to him. Nor did they to the solicitor-like old gentleman, who had, indeed, been out of the place at least half an hour before the murder was committed. The taxi which he picked up outside had been found, and the driver reported that he had set down his fare at Piccadilly Circus; the old gentleman had not been traced beyond that point. His business in the Mansions was still obscure, and nobody reported having received a visit from him or even knowing anything about him; but it was possible that he might have been to see Dorothy Fielder herself, who was of course alive at the time of the visit. In any case the police had not bothered very much about him, as he could not by any possibility be considered to have any connection with the murder.

'And the taxi that brought our real suspect—the man with the wash-leather gloves?' Roger asked.

'Oh, yes; we traced that easily enough,' replied the Chief Inspector glibly. 'It was picked up in—let me see now!—one of those streets off Piccadilly. Half-Moon Street, or one of those. But that,' said the Chief Inspector airily, 'doesn't help us much.'

'Doesn't it?' said Roger thoughtfully.

The Chief Inspector added a few remarks on the difficulty of tracing movements, even before the scent has had time to get cold.

'And that,' said Roger to himself, as he came away, 'is that. Now Moresby knows something, I'm absolutely sure, and something of tremendous importance at that. And he's particularly anxious that I shan't learn what it is. And, moreover, Moresby is convinced either that he's already solved the problem or else that he's just on the point of solving it; he wore every sign of "an arrest is imminent." Now what can it be that is making friend Moresby so insufferably pleased with himself?'

The answer to that question was to be sitting on Roger's breakfast-table when he arrived the next morning, in a purple silk dressing-gown and mauve silk pyjamas, to consume his eggs and bacon.

CHAPTER XVIII

THE letter which Roger leisurely opened the next morning, and began to read while pouring out his coffee with one hand, ran as follows:

DEAR ROGER,—What have you been doing with yourself all these years, and why the deuce have you never looked me up? It's no good asking me why I haven't looked you up either, because I got in first with that question. Congratters on your books and all that sort of thing, but what I want to know is what's the poor old public coming to when *you* can be a best-seller? Great Scott, when I think of . . . But I expect you're above all that sort of thing nowadays.

Well, in case you're wondering why I've broken our vow of silence, I'll tell you. I've seen the tosh you've been writing in *The Courier* on crime and so forth, and I wondered if you'd like to be in on a *cause célèbre* before the arrest, because as far as I can make out there's going to be one soon, and I'm going to be it.

Seriously, old lad, I appear to be in a bit of a mess. You may not credit it, but I really think the police are going to nab me on a charge of murder, of all unpleasant things. By a damned unfortunate coincidence I've got myself mixed up in this case the papers are all being so suspiciously quiet about (I expect you've heard rumours); a girl called Dorothy Fielder, who hanged herself with a stocking in her flat in Gray's Inn Road a week ago—the last of a batch to do the same, including Lady Ursula Graeme. But you're sure to know all about it.

Anyhow, the long and the short of it is that the police seem to think that she never did anything of the sort, but that I murdered her, if you please. Cheerful, isn't it? They haven't told me that in so many words, but it's obviously what they think. Anyhow, they've taken a state-ment from me, and taken my finger-prints, and interviewed me half a dozen times, and even taken samples of my notepaper! In fact they've asked such a lot about my movements since the beginning of February that I'm not at all sure they don't suspect me of doing in the whole lot of them.

Well, now, we all know what you did at Wychford, and even I, who know you for what you are, Roger Sheringham, must admit it was a pretty smart bit of work. What I mean is, do you feel inclined to take a hand in my little show and cheat the gallows of its prey? Because between you and me, Roger, I've never murdered anyone in my life. It may be old-fashioned of me, but there it is.

Anyhow, if you feel like it ring me up tomorrow morning when you've read this. I can tell you all the facts when I see you. Telephone number, Hyde 1266. I've seen my solicitor, of course, but I ask you, why are solicitors?

Yours *moriturus*,
JERRY NEWSOME.

'My God!' said Roger, and dived for the telephone.

'Is that you, Jerry?' he asked, when the connection had been made. 'Roger speaking. Are you dressed? You are? Then come round here at once. No, never mind about waiting for lunch. You wrote to me before you got my message last night, I suppose? Yes, our thoughts crossed. At once, by taxi, aeroplane or big gun, but *hurry*! Right!' He hung up the receiver.

'So *that's* why friend Moresby's been so reticent lately,' thought Roger, cramming eggs and bacon into his system at top speed. 'No wonder, as I'd given away that Jerry used to be a great friend of mine. Didn't want his bird warned. And it would have put me in a rotten position, certainly. But I'm free to do what I like now. Good Lord, was Jerry really the fellow with the wash-leather gloves? This *is* going to be a hell of a mess.'

Disposing of his breakfast in record time, Roger had just lighted the best pipe of the day when Gerald Newsome was shown in. He was a stocky, well-built man of Roger's own age, which was somewhere in the late thirties, still retaining the air of health and vigour of his athletic youth; his dark hair was getting a little thin on the temples, and his cheerful, alert face was red like a countryman's. He gripped Roger's hand in a way that made that gentleman wince.

'Well, Jerry,' said Roger, when the first greetings that had to bridge a fourteen-year gap had been exchanged. 'Well, you've gone and got yourself into a nice scrape, haven't you?'

Newsome's face fell. 'Roger,' he said frankly, 'it appears to me that I'm in a devil of a hole.'

'You are,' Roger agreed, no less frankly. 'There's only one worse, and that would be if you really had carried out those very interesting murders. You're quite sure you didn't, I suppose?'

'Quite,' Newsome grinned. 'I've got a rotten memory, I know, but it's not as bad as all that.'

'Well, sit down and tell me all about it. By the way, I must explain first that you've come to just about the right man, Jerry. As it happens, I've been in on the inside of this business from the very beginning.'

'The devil you have!' commented Mr Newsome.

They settled down, and Roger explained briefly the part he had played in the matter and how he was situated at the moment.

'This explains why they've been shutting me out, you see,' he concluded. 'And it's jolly lucky they did, because I can go right ahead now on any lines I like. And the line we'd better take first of all, I should think, is to prove that you're not the man they want.'

'You'll have your work cut out, then,' opined Newsome, with gloom. 'I was in the blessed building at the time, you see. That's the devil of it.'

'You *were* the man with the wash-leather gloves, then?'

'Yes, curse it; I was. And they seem to have got a finger-print of mine somewhere too.'

'Tell me exactly what happened,' said Roger.

Gerald Newsome began his account.

He had not very much to tell. He had known the dead girl, but only very slightly. Met her at a supper-party once, and exchanged a word or two in the street with her afterwards on two occasions. He was therefore surprised when she rang him up, on the morning of the murder, at about twelve-thirty, and hinted, not too delicately, that she would like to be taken out to lunch, to discuss "this exciting idea".'

'What exciting idea?' asked Roger.

'God knows! I'm telling you just what she said. I didn't know anything about an exciting idea in connection with Dorothy Fielder, but she seemed to take it for granted that I did; so I thought it up to me to be tactful and pretend. I said: "Oh, yes; rather." Or words to that effect.'

'Yes,' said Roger. 'Go on.'

'Well, she asked me to call for her punctually at one, so I said I would. And I did. I rang the bell three or four times, but couldn't get an answer. I hung about on the landing for ten minutes or so, but she didn't appear, so I thought she must have altered her arrangements in the haphazard way these stage-people do and no longer wanted to be taken out to lunch punctually at one. So I came away. And that's all.'

'You came away? At what time?'

'Oh, soon after one. About ten or a quarter-past, I suppose.'

'Leaving your finger-print neatly planted on the bell-push.'

'Oh, is that where it was?'

'Yes, and I found it, deuce take the thing. I wish I hadn't been so devilish clever. That's a nasty bit of evidence. You can't possibly deny being in the building that morning.'

'I don't want to. I told the police I was there when they asked me. Why shouldn't I?'

'Why, indeed,' said Roger. 'And did you pick up a taxi outside the building?'

'No, I walked along to Holborn and had some lunch in a restaurant there.'

'Well, that ought to be an alibi for you.'

'So I thought. But the police don't seem to agree. They don't say so, of course, but when I told them I got to the restaurant by about twenty-past one, at any rate not later than half-past, they said, "Yes, yes," in a soothing sort of way, which is only another way of remarking, "You're a liar." At least, that's how it struck me.'

'I'll look into that,' said Roger, and made a note.

'I didn't get served at once, it's true, and there was a big crowd there. It's one of these places that cater for the business-men in Kingsway. I suppose the waiter wouldn't swear to the time I came in. After all, I don't suppose he could. But the real trouble was that he couldn't pick me out in the identification parade.'

'Oh, Lord, have you had one of them?'

'I should say so. At the Gray's Inn Road police station. They lined me up with about seven other fellows, and the porter of the Mansions spotted me at once. So, though not so quickly, did the taxi-driver who drove me there. The waiter, of course, didn't.'

'Humph! I wonder why they haven't arrested you already. I suppose their case isn't complete yet. It's going to make a sensation when the facts do come out, and no doubt they're taking no chances. And they know you won't bolt.'

'It wouldn't be much good if I wanted to. I'm as good as arrested already; under a sort of open arrest. I'm followed wherever I go, and there's always a man outside my place. There'll be one outside here at this minute.'

'Well, good luck to him. Now, you made a statement, did you?'

'Yes, they had me up at Scotland Yard two or three times asking questions. I answered everything, of course; I thought the only thing to do was to tell the absolute truth immediately, always.'

'Quite the best,' Roger agreed.

'Well, after the last time they asked me if I'd have any objection to signing a statement embodying the various things I'd told them. I said not in the least. They presented me with a document, which I looked through and it seemed all right, so I signed it.'

'Um! And the document referred only to the Dorothy Fielder case?'

'No, that it didn't. It referred to the whole jolly lot. I'm sure they think I did them all, Roger.'

'Well, the fellow who killed Dorothy Fielder killed the others too; that's all right. But I don't see what they can have you on as regards the others. In fact, that's what must be holding them up. Oh, by the way, the notepaper: what happened about that?'

'Oh, they seemed most interested in that. Why, God knows. I use a sort of bluish-grey stuff, with my address in Clarges Street—'

'Not Princess Bond Superfine, is it?'

'Yes, I believe that is the name, or something like it. Why?'

Roger groaned. 'Merely another nasty coincidence for you. All right, go on. What else did they ask you about?'

Newsome flushed, and shifted uneasily in his chair. 'They asked me a hell of a lot of impertinent questions about Ursula Graeme,' he said gruffly.

'They would, yes, of course. And you knew nothing about the lady?'

'On the contrary,' said Newsome reluctantly. 'I knew her uncommonly well.'

Roger nearly jumped out of his chair. 'You did? Oh, Lord, Jerry, this gets worse and worse.'

'But why? I can't understand. Why on earth shouldn't I know Ursula well? That doesn't mean I killed her, does it?'

'No of course not. But—well, it's very awkward, that's all. Tell me how well you did know her and all about it.'

'All right, I suppose I may as well, by this stage. The police seem to know all about it anyhow. Well, to put it shortly, Ursula and I were rather close at one time. I believe there was the usual amount of chit-chat about us. Old hags spreading the glad news that we were going to get married, and all that sort of thing. Till Pleydell came along, of course.'

'Oh, my hat! And Pleydell cut you out?'

'Good Lord, no. That was all poppycock. We'd never thought of getting married for a moment. We went about a lot together, but that was all. Weren't in love with each other, or any rot like that. Nobody was more pleased than I was when Ursula got hooked up with a really decent fellow like Pleydell, for all he's got a bit of the Jew in him. For a man who doesn't know how much he can sign his name for, Pleydell's the nicest chap I know; though he is a bit cold for a high-spirited girl like Ursula was. No, that's just the whole point; I'd been telling her for months that she'd better hurry up and get engaged, or she'd lose her chances.'

'Very tactful of you,' Roger commented. 'Still, if you were on those terms with her I quite see there was nothing in the rumours. However, the police have undoubtedly got hold of those rumours, and they're going a long way to make things look uncommonly nasty for you, my son.'

'Oh, I shall come out of it all right,' said Newsome, but he spoke without too much conviction.

'Oh, yes,' Roger rejoined with great heartiness. 'We'll get you out of it all right. I was only thinking that we've got to get busy pretty quickly. Well, that's all about the last two cases. The one before that, Elsie Benham, "described as an actress," anyone might have done. Now what about the first one in this country? Haven't you got an alibi for the afternoon Unity Ransome was killed?'

'I don't know what I was doing that afternoon. How can I possibly remember? I'd just got back to London, about a week previously; that's all I know. Of course I can't get hold of an alibi.'

They went on talking. Roger put what other questions occurred to him, but the main ground had now been explored, and nothing further of importance cropped up. Newsome, in spite of his efforts to carry it off, evidently felt his position strongly, and Roger pressed him to stay to lunch and hear the result of a visit he proposed to pay at once to Scotland Yard; a change of scene, and companionship, he felt, was the best tonic he could prescribe.

Newsome accepted at once, and Roger retired to don garments more suitable to visiting Scotland Yard than the ones he was wearing at the moment.

Half an hour later he was demanding audience with Moresby.

The Chief Inspector received him with a somewhat shame-faced grin. 'I've been waiting in for you, Mr Sheringham,' he said. 'I've been expecting you any time during the last hour.'

'Yes. I suppose your sleuth telephoned through that he was now stationed at the Albany. Well, Chief Inspector Moresby, what have you got to say for yourself, eh?'

'I knew you'd find out sooner or later, Mr Sheringham,' said Moresby, with an effect of penitent impenitence, 'but we had to keep you in the dark as long as we could. We didn't want your friend warned, you see, and you could have got in our way a lot if you'd wanted to.'

'You're forgiven,' Roger said magnanimously 'I suppose it's no good telling you that you've got the wrong man, is it?'

Moresby shook his head. 'I was afraid you'd say that, Mr

Sheringham. And I only wish it was true, for he doesn't seem to fit the part a bit, as you've no doubt come to tell me.'

'Something like that,' Roger admitted.

'And you must allow that we're giving him every chance. We could have arrested him days ago on the evidence we've got, but we're straining all the rules to make dead certain before we do. *I* don't want him to be the guilty party, Mr Sheringham; don't think that. He's a nice fellow and a proper gentleman, and I must say it doesn't seem hardly possible. But look at the evidence! How can we help believing it on that?'

'Yes, I know. Well, you're showing better feeling than I gave you credit for, Moresby; and I'll reciprocate by admitting that the evidence is a facer. In fact, it's hell!' Roger perched himself on a corner of the Chief Inspector's table and swung a moody foot.

'I don't know how much you've gathered, Mr Sheringham,' went on the Chief Inspector, dropping into his chair, 'but I've no objections now the cat is out of the bag to telling you all we know. And if you can show us that your friend isn't guilty and another man is, why, nobody will be more pleased than we shall.'

'Moresby,' said Roger, 'this is highly unprofessional conduct. You don't seem to have read the story-books at all. No detective from Scotland Yard ever wants his selected victim to escape, you should know. Well, just run over the evidence, will you?'

Moresby complied, and his recital followed precisely the same lines as Roger had anticipated. In the absence of any other strange man in the building at the time Dorothy Fielder died, except the artisan whose alibi was complete, Newsome must be the murderer, both by a process of elimination and by the direct evidence of his connection with the flat in question given by the porter and the taxi-driver; the alibi he had attempted to set up had fallen completely to the ground; the waiter was not prepared to swear that he came in any earlier than a quarter to two, and the doctor had said that death might have taken place as early as one-fifteen. So far as the Fielder case was concerned, Newsome hadn't a leg to stand on.

The Graeme case was almost as conclusive, and here as well there was the important addition of a powerful motive. Lady Ursula had thrown Newsome over for another man; how many murders had been committed on account of that very thing? 'If I can't have her, then no man shall,' explained the Chief Inspector. 'That's the sort of idea.' Then the notepaper had been traced to Newsome, alone of all the three original suspects; and the police were in a position to prove that the very note supposed to be left by Lady Ursula had actually been written to Newsome himself the day before her death.

'Oh?' said Roger. 'I didn't know that. That's very interesting. How do you prove it?'

Well, admitted the Chief Inspector, the proof wasn't absolute, but it was as near as made no odds. Newsome's valet had stated that Lady Ursula had at one time often dropped in to tea and that sort of thing, but after her engagement her visits had been a good deal rarer. On the afternoon of the day before her death, however, she rang the bell and told the valet that her dog, a little white sealyham, had jumped out of her arms almost outside the door and run out into the road, where, besides being nearly killed half a dozen times, it had got smothered in mud, and she wanted to know if she could clean it up in the bathroom.

'I gathered,' said the Chief Inspector, 'that with Lady Ursula asking for permission to do something and saying she was jolly well going to do it, was about the same thing. Anyhow, she made short work of the valet's objections, if he raised any, and marched straight into the bathroom and gave the dog a bath. The valet did protest a bit when he saw what a mess she was making of the place, but she only laughed at him and said she'd leave a note for Newsome to explain that he hadn't been bathing a dog in his master's wash-basin himself.'

'Ah!' said Roger, who had been listening with deep interest. 'Well,' Moresby went on, 'she *did* leave the note. She left it in Newsome's sitting-room, and the valet saw it there himself. In fact he positively identifies the one we've got with the one she left. But Newsome swears he's never seen it before in his life. If it was left for him, he says, he never got it. Now, what do you make of that, Mr Sheringham?'

'I'm going to take it as an axiom that what Newsome says is true, Moresby,' Roger said seriously, 'and if the facts don't square with what he does say, then it's the facts that are at fault, not him. Which simply means that we don't know them all yet.'

'Um!' The Chief Inspector did his best not to look sceptical, for he was a kind man and he saw that Roger was seriously perturbed, but his effort was not very successful. 'Well, I hope you'll find out plenty more, Mr Sheringham,' he said politely.

'When are you going to arrest Newsome?' Roger asked bluntly.

'That depends. He's not going to run away, is he? You've taken on the responsibility now, Mr Sheringham, and you'll have to be answerable for him.'

'Very well; I agree to that. No, he won't run away.'

'Then I'll tell you what I'll do. We were going to arrest him today, but if you undertake that he'll hold himself at our disposal so to speak, and not on any account leave London, then I'll put it off till the day after tomorrow to give you a last chance, Mr Sheringham. That's the very best I can do, and that's stretching things a lot, you know.'

'Forty-eight hours to prove Jerry's innocence,' murmured Roger. 'My sacred hat! All right, Moresby. Thanks. That's a bargain.'

CHAPTER XIX

MR SHERINGHAM IS BUSY

ONE promise Moresby obtained from Roger before he left, and that was that Newsome's impending arrest should remain a profound secret between the two of them; he had no objection to Newsome himself being told as he must already have guessed so much and there was no object in secrecy, but beyond that it must not go. Roger bound himself to silence, although this meant that he would not be able to share his knowledge with his two lieutenants, and gave a similar promise on behalf of Newsome.

As he taxied back to the Albany he tried hard to grapple with the problem. If he was to establish Newsome's innocence in a paltry two days he had got to get to work without delay, but where was he to start? He could see no jumping-off place from which to attack in a new direction. The valet and the note, perhaps? That seemed the only new fact that had come to light.

His first action on arriving at his rooms was to ring up Pleydell. While keeping strictly to his promise, he told the latter that events of great importance might be expected at any minute, and it was essential that the arrangements made yesterday should be put in hand with the utmost speed. Pleydell replied that they had been in hand since yesterday, but that he would hurry them up so that the first sitting could be held that same afternoon; he had already warned the men that had been allotted to him. On Roger's surprised query as to how this could be done, as it was already past eleven o'clock, he said laconically that if he said it should be done, it would. Accepting this, Roger asked him if he would mind taking the sitting that afternoon, as he himself was going to be busy in another direction. Pleydell replied that he would, with pleasure.

'My aunt, that man doesn't let grass grow under his feet,' Roger commented as he hung up the receiver.

'Pleydell?' said Newsome. 'Whatever was all that about?'

Roger told him of the alliance that had been formed, and its plans.

'The Jerry Newsome Defence League, I think we ought to call it now,' he concluded. 'By the way, you mustn't tell anybody about it, or what we're going to do; especially not the police.'

'But good Lord, is there the slightest hope that you'll get any results?'

'Not the faintest, I should imagine,' Roger replied equably. 'If the man does turn up, he must be mentally deficient in all ways instead of only one; and I'm quite sure he's not that. But there *is* a tiny hope in the plan, and there's none in any other that I can see, so we're going to give it a trial at least.'

'I'd like to meet that girl again,' remarked Newsome. 'Anne Manners, by Jove! I wouldn't have believed it. She must be a well-plucked 'un.'

'She's got the smallest body and the biggest heart of any nice girl I've ever met,' affirmed Roger, with unwonted feeling. 'I'm jolly well going to make her the heroine of my next book.'

'The poor kid!' commented Mr Newsome, into whom not even impending arrest could apparently instil any respect for his boyhood's friend's literary talents. 'Whatever has she done to deserve that?'

Roger disregarded this ribaldry. 'Stop being funny, Jerry, and tell me this; did the police ask you about a note Lady Ursula was supposed to have left for you the day before she was killed?'

'Yes, they did say something about one. But they've got hold of the wrong end of the stick. I never had one from her. She called in to wash a dog or something equally mad, Johnson told me (that's my man), but—'

'Come on,' Roger interrupted. 'We've got no time to waste.'

'Where are we going?'

'To have a word with Johnson.'

They hurried off.

Johnson proved to be a small, dessicated man with protruding teeth, who was plainly devoted to his master, and just as plainly not at all devoted to the police. Before he had been speaking to him three minutes, Roger began to realise what a task they must have had to extract from him such information as they did.

Yet his story was simple enough. Lady Ursula had left such a note. He had seen it with his own eyes lying on the table when she went into Mr Newsome's bedroom to tidy herself after washing the dog (one gathered that the minor conventions meant nothing in Lady Ursula's life). Undoubtedly it was the same one that the police had got. Johnson had had no idea that his master had not received it, or he would not have said a word about it.

'It was lying flat on the table, then?' Roger asked. 'Not folded and put in an envelope?'

No, it was lying flat. Johnson would not have read it if he had known what it was, it went without saying, but seeing it lying there he had fancied it was something of Mr Newsome's and was going to tidy it away till he saw that it was Lady Ursula's note.

'What was written on the top?' Roger said. 'Was there a name or anything like that?'

'To the best of my knowledge the word "Jerry" was written on the top, sir,' replied Johnson, with a deprecatory air, as if apologising for having to allow his master's nickname to pass the barrier of his teeth.

'I see. Now, who came here between Lady Ursula's departure and Mr Newsome's return?'

'No one, sir,' Johnson replied with decision.

'No one? Then how did the note vanish?'

'I can't say, sir, I'm sure. I left it here, I know. I can only surmise that Mr Newsome overlooked it, and it was tidied away the next morning without my noticing it.'

'So that both of you overlooked it? No, that doesn't seem right. Now this is an important point, Johnson, so try and jog your memory. Are you certain you let nobody else in here that afternoon?'

'Quite certain, sir. You see, I went out myself shortly after Lady Ursula went. I remember distinctly. Mr Newsome was going to be out till late, and he had kindly said that I need not stay in if I cared to take a little air. I remained out till past six o'clock.'

'What doing?' Roger asked sharply.

Johnson looked hurt. 'I went to a cinematograph performance, sir,' he replied, with dignity.

Roger forebore to comment on Johnson's preference in air. 'Well, this seems a mystery,' he said. 'Somebody's got hold of that letter somehow, I'm convinced. Has the porter downstairs a pass-key to this flat?'

'No, sir. But since you raise the matter I might mention that one of our own keys appears to have been mislaid. There used to be three, and now there are only Mr Newsome's and my own. The spare one has been lost.'

'For how long?'

'Oh, for some months now. But perhaps it would be as well not to attach too much importance to that, sir.' Johnson's parched face again took on its deprecatory look. 'Mr Newsome sometimes does lose things, if he will forgive my mentioning it.'

'Johnson's trying to tell you politely that I lost the extra key myself,' Newsome laughed. 'It was my own key, and I had my pocket picked. I not only lost the key, but my pocket-book as well, with a nice little bundle of notes in it. There's nothing in that.'

Roger nodded. 'Thank you, Johnson. That's all.'

When they were alone he turned to Newsome. 'It's deuced

odd about that note. It can't have been overlooked by both of you. Is Johnson absolutely reliable?'

'Absolutely,' Newsome said emphatically. 'He's been with our family since he was a boy.'

'Well, he had one interesting thing to tell us,' Roger mused. 'The note was not in an envelope, you heard. Well, when we got it it *had* been folded.'

'Wouldn't the fellow who got hold of it have folded it?'

'He would, yes. But the interesting part is the way in which it was folded. Not that it helps us in the slightest, and I'm afraid it won't interest the police; as a matter of fact it's just a tiny point in your favour, but we won't bother about it now. I've got to run up to Maida Vale and warn Anne Manners to be ready for the sitting this afternoon.'

'I'll run up with you,' said Newsome promptly.

'Right you are,' Roger agreed. 'And your sleuth can run behind.'

They went out into the street and Newsome looked up and down it. 'Hullo,' he said. 'My sleuth doesn't seem to be here.'

Roger looked. Not a lounger, a passer-by or a loiterer was in sight. 'Well, that *is* sporting of Moresby,' Roger said warmly. 'I'll tell the world it is.'

Anne and Miss Carruthers received them kindly, and Newsome proceeded to renew his slight acquaintance with the former. Roger, however, had no time for light dalliance. He was not quite sure what he ought to do, but he knew it had got to be done at once. Newsome, on the other hand, could very well be left where he was for the time being. Apparently there was nothing more to be learnt from him, and his present surroundings might be even better for his morale than Roger's own flat.

On pretext of being shown out, Roger drew Anne out on to the landing with him, firmly shut the sitting-room door and told her that the sittings were to begin that very afternoon.

Anne's eyes sparkled. 'Oh, I am so glad,' she said. 'The men were in here so early this morning that I hoped we might be able to begin today. I told the landlord they were plumbers to see to the kitchen taps, and he seemed so relieved at not being expected to pay for them that he took it without a word. He lives on the ground floor.'

'And you're not a bit frightened, Anne?' Roger asked.

'I shan't have time to be frightened; I shall be too busy longing to catch him. But did I say you could call me "Anne"?'

'Didn't you?' Roger smiled. 'How forgetful of you, if you didn't. But I warn you, I always call my female accomplices by their Christian names. And all girls under the age of twenty-one, too.'

'Good morning, Mr Sheringham,' said Anne, and took a step towards the door.

'Oh, and by the way, Anne,' Roger said quickly, 'be kind to my excellent friend Jerry, won't you?'

'I'll be polite. But you're not forgetting that he's on our list of suspects, are you?'

'He's not, any longer. But you're not to tell anyone that, even Pleydell. It's a deadly secret. Between ourselves, Anne (and this is highly confidential), he's not our man, but the evidence looks very much as if he were.'

'Do you mean that the police are after him?' asked Anne, round-eyed.

'If they're not,' Roger replied evasively, 'they're failing in their duty. He's in a very ticklish position. I've told him of our plans, by the way.'

Anne looked doubtful. 'Was that wise, Mr Sheringham?'

'May I remind you, Anne Manners,' retorted Roger, with dignity, 'that *I* am in charge of this investigation? To your duty, girl. I shall be up at four-thirty to see if you're still alive. Till then, *au revoir*.'

As he ran down the steps outside Roger glanced at his watch. The time was just after half-past twelve. He would pay a flying visit to Gray's Inn Road before lunch.

It was in Roger's mind that, when it came down to hard

facts, the only way definitely of clearing Newsome was to find out who really had committed the murders; in face of the accumulation of evidence anything less than that would not meet the case. And besides, how was he to prove by any other means that Newsome could not be guilty? The facts at present showed almost conclusively that he was. Even in the case of Janet Manners the connection was there.

But if Gerald Newsome had not killed Dorothy Fielder, then who had? The artisan was cleared, the solicitor-like old gentleman was not on the premises. The only conclusion was that the real murderer must have arrived after the porter had gone to his lunch, past one o'clock. But as against this, there was the fact that Jerry had received no answer to his ring at one o'clock exactly.

Seated in his taxi, Roger tried to thrash out this particular point. Dorothy Fielder had asked, almost blatantly, to be taken out to lunch. Was it likely that she would not have answered his ring, knowing from the time that it must be he, if she were in a position to do so? Certainly not. Then she could not have been in a position to do so. Why not? Assuming that she had *not* changed her mind, the only answer seemed to be that she had been forcibly detained. But she could not have been forcibly detained, because the murderer could not have arrived before one o'clock; that was definitely established.

'Hell!' said Roger, and lit a cigarette.

But was it definitely established, though? There was that gap between eleven o'clock, when the other girl, Zelma Deeping, came out, and twelve o'clock when the porter began his observations. Could the murderer have arrived during that interval? In that case he must have been in the flat till after the girl's death at about one-thirty. Why, if that were the case, did he put off killing her so long? Was it because he knew that the porter would not be looking out between one and two and he would be able to escape unobserved? That, thought Roger, was a very interesting idea; it argued a close acquaintance on the murderer's part with conditions in the Mansions—in other words, close acquaintance with Miss Dorothy Fielder herself. How did this square with Pleydell's theory of an actor? Uncommonly well. But then one came up against Sir James Bannister and Billy Burton again, and neither the stately Sir James nor the lanky and elongated piece of humorous quicksilver, known to a hilarious public as Billy Burton, could possibly be the man they were after. Damn!

But was the field of actors so very limited? *Must* the murderer have been at Monte Carlo at the time of the first death? Couldn't (and here Roger sat up with a jerk) the truth be that the Monte Carlo death was a genuine suicide, which had so tickled the imagination of the super-sadistic murderer that he had felt impelled to go and do the same thing for himself? Now there *was* an idea.

It brought him to the front door of the Mansions.

Shelving further consideration for the moment of this new possibility, Roger sought out the porter.

'Good morning,' he said briskly. 'You remember me. I was here with the police last Thursday, regarding the death of Miss Fielder in flat No. 6.'

'Oh, yes, sir,' murmured the porter.

'There are one or two further points I want to learn from you,' Roger continued in a tone of authority. 'It seems obvious from what you tell us that the murderer must have arrived either after one o'clock or before twelve. Now is there any way of obtaining information as to the arrivals here between the time when Miss Deeping went out, soon after eleven, and twelve o'clock?'

The porter shook his head. 'No, sir. I'm afraid there isn't. Anybody might have come then, and none of us be any the wiser.'

'I see. That's a pity. Well, tell me this. Supposing the murderer entered the Mansions between eleven and twelve, but for some reason did not want to get into the flat till considerably later:

is there any place where he could have remained in hiding? A cupboard, say, or a box-room at the top—anything like that?'

Again the porter shook his head. 'No, sir. The stairs are quite bare, as you can see. There's no cupboards or anything like that. Without he'd been in one of the other flats, I don't see how he could have stayed out of sight inside the building.'

'Ah!' said Roger thoughtfully. 'Yes, it hadn't occurred to me that he might have been—Look here, I want a list of the names and professions of the other people who have flats in this block. Will you tell them to me while I write them down? No. 1, that's yours. No. 2?'

The porter proceeded to supply him with the information.

'You seem to have a lot of stage-folk here,' Roger commented, as the list proceeded.

'There's stage-folk *and* stage-folk,' said the porter darkly. 'I mean, there's them that say they're on the stage because they really are on the stage, and there's them that say they're on the stage because they've got to say something.'

'"Described as an actress," in other words. But you don't mean to say you've got any of that sort here?'

'Bound to have all sorts in a big place like this, sir,' said the porter, with an air of resignation. 'But isn't the landlord strict?'

'Well, he is, sir, yes. But it's not always too easy, you know. I mean, if it's a lady like No. 7, who only has . . . Well, what I mean, sir,' said the porter desperately, ceasing to make efforts to wrap up stark facts in a decent piece of circumlocution, and explained what he did mean.

'Dear, dear!' said Roger. 'I suppose it would be indiscreet to ask anything further?'

'I'm well enough paid to keep my mouth shut, sir,' replied the porter significantly.

Roger, who had no intention of paying him well enough to open it again, for information of a purely scandalous interest, smiled with equal significance and went on with his list.

CHAPTER XX

WHEN Roger arrived back at the Albany, ten minutes late for his lunch, he had the list in his pocket; but that did not say that he quite knew what to do with it. To investigate in person the circumstances of the twenty-odd people whose names appeared on it would take far more than the three short days he had at his disposal; yet he was not at all sure that such an investigation should not be undertaken. The case was so dark that any possible means of throwing light upon it must not be ignored; and improbable though it might seem, who knew whether the vital clue he was seeking did not lie inside that block of Mansions rather than outside it?

Over lunch he made up his mind. The police, no doubt, would know something about the other flat-holders, but the line of inquiry which they would have followed would not be the same as the one which Roger would want examined. He would therefore take the list round to a firm of inquiry-agents and put them on to it, no expense to be spared, a full report within thirty-six hours. He rang up Scotland Yard immediately after the meal, obtained the name of such a firm, conducted by an ex-C.I.D. Chief Inspector, and went round at once to put the matter in hand. He was assured that everything he wanted (and he mentioned particularly what he did want) could be obtained in the time.

His next move he had already planned. Obviously he must pay a call on Miss Zelma Deeping. Her temporary address he knew already. Once more he hailed a taxi (Roger felt that this was the most expensive case he had ever handled) and was driven to Hampstead.

Miss Deeping, whom he had not hitherto met, was a vivacious, dark-haired young woman of twenty-eight or thereabouts. Roger had no difficulty in getting her to talk. She told him frankly that she would talk to him for a year on end if it would help to catch the man who had murdered Dorothy. (Roger noticed that she used the word 'murder.' Evidently Miss Deeping had no doubts as to how her friend had met her death.)

Without beating about the bush, he proceeded to the questions he wanted to put.

'How was Miss Fielder dressed when you left her?'

'She wasn't,' replied Miss Deeping promptly. 'She was in the bath.'

'Oh! Then she might not have been fully dressed at all that morning?'

'No, I shouldn't say she was. She'd been having what we called one of our lazy mornings. We used to have them if we felt extra tired, or had a headache, or anything like that. The one who was going to be lazy would stay in bed, and the other would bring her breakfast; the lazy one would get up when she felt like it, have her bath, and be a perfect lady till lunch-time.' Zelma Deeping was trying to speak in a light voice, but her tones shook every now and then, and once she dabbed surreptitiously at her eyes.

'I see,' said Roger, who was terrified of her bursting into tears. He assumed a very matter-of-fact, brisk tone. 'You think it probable that she was wearing the underclothes she was found in, and just a wrapper over them (the one that was on a chair, I suppose), when she let her murderer in?'

'Yes,' agreed Miss Deeping, 'I suppose she must have been.' She spoke in a hesitating way.

'Why aren't you sure?' Roger asked quickly.

'Well, it doesn't sound a bit like Dorothy to let anyone in when she was in her wrapper. We weren't so very conventional, either of us, but once you go beyond a certain limit, if you happen to be on the stage, your reputation's gone, whether you've done anything to deserve it or not. Dorothy and I were always rather careful in that way. I don't mean we were so silly as not to give a man tea if either of us was alone in the flat; but I shouldn't have said Dorothy would have entertained a man in the morning in her wrapper.'

'What would she have done, then?'

'Either told him he couldn't come in, or else, if she knew him very well, pushed him into the sitting-room while she went to slip on a frock.'

'Supposing if it were a plumber, or a man to see about the electric-light—that sort of man?'

Miss Deeping smiled. 'Oh, well, that's different. I suppose it's silly, but it *is* different, you know. After all, one doesn't—what shall I say?—dally with a plumber, does one?'

'The point is well taken; yes, it is different. And supposing it had been an actor? She would have gone to slip on a frock?'

'Yes, I'm sure she would.'

'And yet she didn't,' Roger pointed out. 'Can you suggest any explanation, Miss Deeping? It seems to me quite an important point.'

Zelma Deeping considered. 'The only thing I can think of is that he took her by surprise as soon as she'd opened the door. Couldn't that be what happened?'

'Yes, quite well. Now, I've gathered that Miss Fielder didn't take much interest in men. That is so, isn't it?'

'No particular interest. She didn't flirt, if that's what you mean. We both had plenty of men friends. But they weren't any more than friends.'

'You're quite sure that Miss Fielder had not recently begun to have an affair with somebody?' Roger already knew that Dorothy Fielder's moral character had been all that the most zealous advocate of the purity of the British stage would have desired. But that did not say that she was not prepared to receive just one man in her wrapper.

Miss Deeping promptly extinguished this hope. 'No, I'm

sure she hadn't. She'd certainly have told me (we've lived together for over six years now), but she never said a word about one man more than any other.'

'Humph!' said Roger, disappointed; so far this interview had yielded nothing. He tried a new tack. 'Of course you're sure that when you went out you left Miss Fielder alone?'

'Quite sure,' agreed the girl, surprised. 'Why, I couldn't have overlooked anyone in the hall, could I?'

'No, I suppose not,' Roger admitted. 'Well, did you see anybody loitering on the stairs, or coming in as you went out, or generally behaving in a furtive manner?'

'No, I'm afraid I didn't.'

'That's a nuisance,' said Roger.

'Are you meaning that the murderer might have arrived as early as eleven o'clock?' asked Miss Deeping. 'Because if you think that, I'm quite sure you're wrong. Dorothy might have stayed a few minutes in her wrapper, if he'd come on really important business, but she certainly wouldn't have been with him like that for two hours. That I can tell you is out of the question, Mr Sheringham.'

'Is it? Then something is established. Now here's another thing I want to ask you about; had Miss Fielder ever mentioned the name of Newsome to you?'

Miss Deeping shook her dark head. 'The police asked me that too. No, I'm sure she didn't. At any rate, I haven't the least recollection of the name.'

'Not with regard to a supper-party once, and a casual meeting in the street once or twice afterwards?' Roger prompted.

'No, I'm sorry, I don't seem to remember it.'

'I'm very glad you don't. He's rather a friend of mine. Well, here's something else. Was she excited about anything that morning? Had she said anything about an interesting proposition that had been put up to her? Something to do with the stage, I should imagine?'

Miss Deeping looked bewildered. 'No, this is the first I've

heard of such a thing. No, certainly Dorothy wasn't excited at all; quite the opposite. And I know for a fact that she'd had nothing but a couple of bills by that morning's post.'

'There isn't another post, before half-past twelve?'

'There is, but it's at half-past ten. It had come before I went out. Dorothy got nothing by it at all.'

Roger paused for a moment. 'All this is important,' he said. 'You're sure of your answers?'

'About the excitement and the posts? Positive. Quite positive.'

'Good!' said Roger. 'Well, I think that about exhausts my questions this visit. May I come up here and see you again if I think of anything else that you can clear up?'

'Please do! I shall be in most of the time, except when I'm at the theatre of course. I'd do anything to help you, Mr Sheringham, really.'

She continued to press him to make use of her in any way possible till the front door had closed behind him.

'I like theatrical people, I think,' observed Roger to himself, as he walked quickly away.

It was now nearly half-past three, and he was not due in Sutherland Avenue for an hour. He turned in the direction of the Heath.

It was a fine, warm afternoon, and there is no time of the year, when the weather does happen to be fine and warm, to compare with the latter half of April—as the poet Browning has already hinted. Roger found a seat and settled down for half an hour's bask. While basking, he turned over in his mind the result of his late visit. There were several points that he felt deserved his close attention.

An hour later, punctually at half-past four, he was climbing the stairs towards Anne's flat, his heart a little inclined to thump. Had he and Pleydell been wise in allowing such a small person to take the risk? Supposing by any weird chance something *had*. . .

The sound of voices and laughter from the top floor relieved his anxiety. He tapped on the sitting-room door, and Anne's voice told him to enter. Standing in front of the fireplace smoking a pipe, and with every appearance of being thoroughly at home, was Newsome.

'Hullo, Jerry,' said Roger, with creditable mildness. 'You're very smartly back on the mark.'

'Back?' retorted that unabashed gentleman. 'I haven't been off it yet.'

Roger frowned. 'You haven't been here the whole afternoon?'

'I have, Roger. Don't look at me so fiercely. We forgot the time.'

'Don't let him tease you, Mr Sheringham,' Anne smiled. 'He hasn't been in this room. But I'm afraid he absolutely refused to leave the house. I couldn't do anything with him.'

'What about that tea you promised you'd give me, Anne?' Newsome cut in before Roger could speak. 'And you can get a cup for Roger too; I expect he'll only make a fuss if you don't.'

'And Mr Pleydell will probably look in, now it's the half-hour,' said Anne. 'Very well. Oh, don't look so cross, Mr Sheringham. Gerald was only pulling your leg.'

'"Gerald!"' quoted Roger nastily.

Anne blushed fiercely, but retained her dignity. 'Well, I've known *him* all my life—off and on,' she countered, and made a good exit.

Roger turned to Newsome. 'Jerry, would you mind telling me what you really have been doing?'

'Yes.' Newsome was looking more serious. 'Roger, I think you must have been out of your senses to let that kid sit here all alone waiting to be murdered like her sister was. I can't imagine what you were doing.' He went on to say more in the same style, a good deal more; and he became considerably warmer.

'But, my dear Jerry!' Roger tried to stem the tide. 'She was safe enough, with one of us next door all the time.'

'Next door!' snorted Mr Newsome. 'What the deuce is the

good of that?' He continued his monologue. The worst of the friends of one's youth is that they consider that they have the privilege of being so unpleasantly outspoken.

'All right, all right,' Roger interrupted in despair two minutes later. 'I deliberately tried to get the girl killed; I took advantage of her offer and telephoned to the murderer that there was another little job waiting for him; I'm not fit to be trusted to protect a Brussels sprout. We'll take all that for granted. Now will you please tell me what you've been doing?'

'Looking after Anne, of course. If you'd had the gumption of a wood-louse you'd have discovered, as I did, that there's a trap-door in the ceiling on the landing outside, which leads into a sort of cubby-hole in the roof. That was the place to lie in wait, of course. Not rig up a silly arrangement of bells, which ten to one'll go wrong when they're really needed. My dear chap!'

Roger tried to explain that the main object had been to escape the attention of any possible watcher with his eye on this particular house, but Newsome waved his words aside.

'You can watch over an alarm clock in Birmingham, if you like,' he said forcibly, 'but I'm going to skulk in that roof.'

Roger reflected that Newsome's presence would, after all, do no harm, for though he himself might be known to be connected with the police investigations, and Pleydell, of course, was already concerned in the case, there was no reason why the murderer should have any suspicion about Jerry. But one thing he must promise, and that was to arrive inside the house not less than an hour before the séances began.

'Oh, right-o,' Newsome grinned. 'I'm with you there. In fact, better make it two, I should say. There's nothing like being on the safe side, is there?'

A tap sounded on the door, to be followed the next instant by the appearance of Pleydell. His eyebrows rose a little as he saw Newsome.

'Hullo, Newsome,' he said, naturally enough, keeping any

surprise he might have felt out of his voice. 'I didn't expect to see you here.'

'I've just been hauling Roger over the coals for the way you two have been offering Miss Manners' neck to the knife,' Newsome replied good-temperedly. 'I might have expected it of Roger, but I didn't of you, Pleydell.'

'Jerry seems to have joined us as a new recruit,' Roger remarked, seeing Pleydell's bewilderment, and he explained the steps which the former proposed to take.

Pleydell assented with his usual courteousness, but Roger could see that he was not particularly pleased with the arrangement. Suggesting that Newsome should go and give Anne a hand with the tea (an idea which was at once taken up with the greatest enthusiasm), he made the opportunity to tell Pleydell privately that, between themselves, Newsome could be struck off the list of suspects henceforth.

Pleydell seemed a little dubious. 'Are you sure?' he asked. 'Can he prove his innocence? I admit that Newsome was a friend of mine,' he added pointedly, 'and personally I agree with you that he is quite incapable of being the man we want; but till this business is cleared up I have *no* friends.'

'Yes, yes,' said Roger, a little uncomfortably. 'That's the only attitude, of course. But I've been looking into Newsome's movements, and I think he's cleared all right.' This was untrue, and Roger knew it; moreover, he had an uncomfortable idea that Pleydell knew it too. Pleydell, Roger saw, was not an easy man to lie to.

'Definitely?' was all that Pleydell said, whatever he might have thought.

'In my opinion,' Roger replied, this time nearer to the truth.

Pleydell shrugged his shoulders perceptibly. 'Well, Sheringham, we agreed that you should be in charge of our independent inquiry, and I am the last to dispute your leadership. But to my mind nobody should be definitely considered innocent until somebody else has been definitely proved guilty.'

Which, thought Roger, as Anne tactfully put an end to a rather difficult situation by appearing with the tea-pot, is exactly what I was saying myself a few hours ago. How very awkward!

Pleydell had intimated plainly enough that he disapproved of the new addition to the partnership, inasmuch as the newcomer had stepped straight from the role of suspect into that of subordinate sleuth, but no hint of this appeared during tea. He was as gravely charming to Newsome himself as he was to Anne; though Roger, watching them with a somewhat uneasy amusement, thought he had never seen two men more totally dissimilar.

The conversation not unnaturally turned upon Anne's recent ordeal, which, now that it was over for the day, she was ready to admit that she had not enjoyed at all. 'It was much worse than I expected,' she said. 'I tried to read a book, but I simply couldn't. I had an unpleasant feeling that the horrible man was going to appear suddenly in the middle of the room and grab hold of me before I could reach that bell.'

'Yes, and what would you have felt like if I hadn't been actually in the same house?' Newsome asked, with what Roger privately considered a fatuous grin. The years, Roger felt sadly, had not improved Jerry Newsome. He had always been obvious, but now he was positively blatant.

'Exactly the same, I suppose,' said Anne, in a tone which would have been imputed to any other girl as nothing less than pert.

'I suppose you two have arranged some sort of signal on which you would drop down from the roof, like a *deus ex machina*, Newsome?' asked Pleydell. 'I mean, you don't intend to appear unless you're definitely needed?'

'Oh, no,' Anne answered quickly. 'He's promised most faithfully not to come out unless I scream.'

'And you promised just as faithfully to do that on the least sign of danger,' Newsome reminded her.

'Oh, I should,' said Anne, with some feeling. 'By the way,

Mr Sheringham, it may interest you to know that I had a productive afternoon, if not in the way we expected.'

'Oh? How was that?'

'I did some hard thinking. And I made one or two rather interesting discoveries. I began to put two and two together, in fact. Do you know, Mr Sheringham, I think you've been rather blind.'

'I've no doubt about it,' said Roger. 'But I'd be very grateful if you'd open my eyes.'

'I think I shall, in a day or two,' Anne replied serenely. 'I want to work out a nice little theory I'm beginning to form, and if certain things turn out to be as I suspect I rather fancy I may surprise you all.'

'I don't think anything else in this affair could surprise me,' said Pleydell, with a gloomy little smile.

'I think this will,' Anne replied sweetly.

'But Anne, we share ideas, you know,' Roger put in. 'All ideas go into the common pool.'

'Except this one,' Anne smiled. 'There are just one or two points I want to verify first. I shouldn't like you all to laugh at me, so I'm not going to be premature; but—let me see, you're my guardian tomorrow, aren't you? Well, if you come in and have tea at four-thirty, quite alone, I might be able to tell you by then.'

'Oh, I say, Anne,' objected Newsome, 'does that mean I don't get any tea tomorrow?'

'Not at all,' said Anne, still more sweetly. 'There are plenty of cheap tea-shops in the Kilburn High Road'

CHAPTER XXI

ANNE HAS A THEORY

It was now Thursday and, unless Roger could produce valid reason to the contrary, Newsome was to be arrested on Saturday afternoon. And so far Roger could produce no such reason whatever. He acknowledged frankly to himself as he returned with the suspected party to the Albany an hour or so later, that he was so far not even on the track of a reason. Certain curious facts had emerged in his conversation with Zelma Deeping, but that was really all the first day's efforts had to show.

He had carried Newsome back to dine with him because he badly wanted to talk about the case. Only by indefatigable discussion, he felt, could some new aspect of the business be brought into sight, or some fresh enlightenment be thrown on the case of Dorothy Fielder from the facts now at his disposal. And there certainly were possibilities of enlightenment, Roger felt, though at present the various issues were too confused in his mind to let him see clearly between them.

To Gerald Newsome, therefore, during cocktails, during dinner and afterwards, he talked with a will. And Newsome, whose neck after all might depend on this talk, bore it like a man.

'And so,' said Roger, as they sat over coffee, 'we might tabulate our conclusions as follows. The man can't have arrived between eleven and twelve, because Dorothy Fielder would not have stayed with him in her wrapper all that time. Therefore it would appear that he must have arrived after, say, a quarter-past one. But already we have Dorothy Fielder not answering your ring at one, from which we deduce that she must have been forcibly prevented; in other words, the murderer was already

183

in there with her. But her actions were unrestrained at any rate up till twelve-thirty, because she rang you up then and appeared perfectly normal. The conclusion would appear to be, then, that the murderer arrived between twelve-thirty and one o'clock.'

'But according to the porter's evidence, he didn't.'

'Precisely; and that's just what we must now consider. Is the porter right? He seems to have no doubt himself. Then are we wrong? I think we are. For consider this, Jerry. When the Zelma girl left, Dorothy had had no exciting news about propositions from you. When she rang you up, an hour and a half later, she had. Therefore somebody had communicated with her during that time, either by telephone or in person. That's plain enough.'

Newsome nodded. 'Yes, now you point it out.'

'Well, I'm inclined to favour the personal visit. The telephone is possible of course, but if this communication was made to her with the object that I imagine, she was put under restraint, so to speak, immediately she'd rung off after speaking to you.'

'The deuce she was! And what was the object, then?'

Roger looked curiously at his friend. 'Why, my Jerry,' he said softly, 'of course to throw suspicion on you.'

Newsome sat upright. 'Hell! But why?'

'Well, I think that's clear enough. The murderer knew that you were mixed up in the Lady Ursula case in a way which, if the police ever did look into it, would certainly cause a measure of alarm and despondency to your friends. And I take it that he was just taking the simple precaution of ensuring, by your presence at one o'clock on the doorstep, that should his pecca-dilloes ever come in for official investigation, the trail would lead straight to you.'

'Blast the fellow!' observed Mr Newsome uneasily. 'He seems to have succeeded, too.'

'And as soon as your footsteps resounded on the stairs again, he just got on with the job and proceeded to hang the lady at his leisure.'

'Well, but who was he?'

'That, I must say,' Roger had to admit, 'does completely baffle me. According to our evidence, it can't have been anyone. Bother that old solicitor! His time of arrival is exactly right, he sounds like the type, he'd be our man for a certainty—if only he hadn't most inconveniently gone away before the girl could have died. Well, we decided that the murderer must have arrived between twelve and one, so the only inference is that the porter *did* overlook him. And I don't believe he did for a minute!'

'This seems a bit of a muddle,' observed Mr Newsome sapiently.

Roger mused for a while in silence. 'Supposing he tied the girl up, went away to establish his alibi in full view of the porter, and came back after one-fifteen to finish her off. How's that? That fits the facts. And it means a knowledge of the Mansion's internal arrangements which, as I've already thought, would be interesting if it were true.'

'I believe you've hit on it,' said Newsome triumphantly. 'Roger, I do really. It was the solicitor. Now then, how the deuce are we going to get hold of him?'

'How, indeed? That's just as much of a problem as the other. And what's his connection with the other cases? So far as we know, none. No bearded solicitor crops up in any of the other cases to my knowledge.'

'No,' agreed Newsome. 'That certainly is a bit of a snag.'

'Nevertheless, the murderer must have been tolerably well known to Janet Manners, to Lady Ursula and to Dorothy Fielder. Can't we possibly find anyone whose orbit touched the case at those three points? Not, I'm afraid, in the time at our disposal.'

They lapsed into silence again. Roger had carried his conclusions a little further forward, but once again they seemed to have brought him into a blind alley.

'That damned old solicitor,' Roger murmured. 'He's our man right enough.'

Newsome remained respectfully silent.

'Let's try something else,' Roger went on after a minute or two. 'There's been something at the back of my mind all along concerning Dorothy Fielder. I've just remembered what it is: those indentations on the backs of her thighs.' He explained what had been pointed out to them by the doctor. 'He didn't seem to attach any importance to them, nor did the police. But I wonder . . .'

The audience was as expectantly attentive as the most exacting detective could require.

Roger reflected.

'They were made during life, of course, and the girl had been dead about three hours when we saw them. That means they must have been very much deeper at the time of death. Now what on earth could have caused dents so deep that their traces remained three hours after death? Steady pressure, the doctor said, applied for quite a considerable time. When the man tied her up, did he leave her with her legs pressing on some sharp-edged object, in such a position that most of her weight came on them? It's curious.'

'But look here,' Newsome ventured to interpose, 'about his tying her up and going away for a time; I thought you said some time ago that this girl hadn't been tied up, so far as they could tell? No marks on the wrists or ankles, and all that.'

Roger's face fell. 'By Jove, yes; I'd forgotten that. And no marks on the body either, except these two small dents. No signs of a struggle, in fact. And she wouldn't have let him tie her up without a struggle, would she?'

'Perhaps he chloroformed her?'

Roger told his companion in a few well-chosen words of the fatuity of this suggestion.

'Well, biffed her on the head, then, and put her out.'

'The doctor said nothing about a bruise,' Roger pointed out. 'He'd certainly have found it if there'd been one.'

'Then I give it up,' said Newsome.

Roger summed up his own convictions. 'If there was no

struggle and he didn't tie her up, then he laid her out in some other way; for of one thing, Jerry, I'm sure, and that is that when you rang that bell the girl was alive inside, but unconscious. We know she was alive, and I'm certain she was both in the flat and unconscious. But how on earth could he have managed it? It's no good suggesting morphia or anything like that. The doctor would have found out at the post-mortem if any drug had been used on her, and it hadn't. Great Scott, this man's a genius in his own line.'

And there, for that evening, they left it. For, as Roger remarked, they had now clarified the issues as much as possible and any further discussion would only addle them.

'I want to clear my mind of the whole thing and come back to it later on quite fresh,' he said. 'That's the way to get results. So what about a few shillings' worth of that rotten show where Anne is wasting her talents and friend Moira is enhancing hers?'

Newsome agreed with alacrity.

They went, and Roger spent an unhappy evening. Let it be enough to say that he had a respectful admiration for Anne, and to be compelled to watch her impersonate in turn a Hawaiian belle, a small girl of six, a private in a Scotch regiment, a powder-puff, a blue bird (species unknown), a lingerie manne-quin, an ornament on a wedding-cake and a Deauville bathing beauty, in company with Miss Carruthers and some twenty-two other mechanically smiling maidens, left him not merely cold, but frozen. He would have stalked out of the place as soon as the Scotch regiment appeared, had not Mr Newsome seemed to find these representations the last word in wit, beauty, art and dramatic genius.

However, if Roger wanted contrast with his recent preoccu-pations he had the consolation of knowing that he had certainly found it.

It was between two and three a.m. that inspiration had the habit of paying Roger a happy visit. In previous cases he had found that, after turning them over and over in his mind for a couple of hours after getting into bed, just when everything seemed so inextricably muddled that nothing could ever evolve out of the chaos, some illuminating ray would suddenly shoot across his mental vision. And so it was that night. Having decided that the only thing left to do was to get up, go to his study, read through six pages chosen at random from the *Encyclopædia Britannica*, swallow a strong whisky and then go back to bed again—having already lifted one arm out of the coverings to switch on the lamp by his bedside, there suddenly occurred to Roger in one single blinding flash exactly what that villainous old solicitor really had done, and precisely what those dents on Dorothy Fielder's legs must mean.

Whereupon he turned over on his other side and fell instantly asleep.

The next morning conviction was not quite so strong, but it remained conviction. As he shaved, Roger argued against his idea, battered it, pummelled it, and generally did his best to reduce it to pulp. Nothing of the sort happened. The idea continued to stand, upright and smiling, and quite refused even to be shaken.

Impressed, Roger went out after breakfast to test it.

There was only one test he could think of to apply, and that involved an interview with the constable whose arm Zelma Deeping had clutched in Gray's Inn Road. This constable, therefore, Roger sought out and finally ran down on his beat not a hundred yards from the same block of Mansions. He introduced himself, and the constable, who remembered seeing him in intimate conversation on the very scene of the crime with no less a person than Chief Inspector Moresby of the C.I.D., felt no compunction in giving such information as the gentleman seemed to require.

'Now tell me this very carefully,' Roger said in his most impressive manner. 'When you opened the door of the room, did it open quite easily or did it seem to be obstructed in any way?'

'Well, it opened easily enough, sir, but the chair was lying close up against it, and of course that had to be pushed back as the door opened.'

Roger nodded as if that information, at any rate, was no news to him. 'Do you remember if the chair was actually lying up against the door, or did the door strike on it when it was partly open?'

The constable ruminated. 'Well, sir, it's difficult to say now, but to the best of my recollection it was lying right up against the door. At least, I don't seem to remember it striking on it. I should have gone steady if I'd felt it do that.'

'Yes. And when you got inside, the chair was lying just as we saw it later? On its back, with the feet pointing at an angle away from the doorway?'

'That's right, sir. It wasn't touched any more till the Superintendent and Mr Moresby went.'

'And the wrapper was where I saw it, over the back of that green chair?'

'Yes, sir. Nothing was touched at all but the body, which I lifted down to make sure life was extinct.'

'That's right. Well, I want to have a look at the flat. Is there still a constable there?'

'No, sir. The place is locked up, but the porter's got a key. Nobody's allowed in but the police; but if I walk back with you and tell the porter, that'll be all right, sir.'

They paced majestically along the pavement. Even at so solemn a moment Roger could not help wondering whether any of the passers-by were under the impression that he was in custody and, if so, what particular crime they would favour him with.

On the constable's gruff injunctions Roger was shown into the flat and left there. He waited till the outer door was closed, then hurried into the sitting-room and examined the inner side of the door with minute attention. After a lengthy search he found exactly what he had hoped to find—two very slight dents in the surface, so shallow as to have hardly more than dinted the paint, about eighteen inches apart and a couple of feet from the bottom, on the side farther from the hinges; from each dent ran a faint scratch right to the bottom edge of the door. Roger measured their distance apart with a pocket tape-measure, scrutinised them through a strong magnifying-glass which he had brought for the purpose, and made one or two other measurements. Then he rose from his hands and knees, opened the door to its fullest extent and with the magnifying-glass began minutely to examine the paint-work on the inside of the frame, on the hinge side of the door.

'Ah!' he exclaimed happily, as a deeper dint, from which the paint had been chipped, caught his eye. He pounced down on his knees and began poking about with a finger in the dust at the angle where the lining met the floor. Fragments of a nutshell emerged into the light. He picked up the largest and looked at it.

'Walnut!' he muttered, with satisfaction. 'Yes, of course. That would be much better.'

Putting the pieces of shell back where he had found them, he rose and made his way out of the flat. Not for the first time in his life Roger was uncommonly pleased with Roger.

On the steps he ran straight into Anne Manners.

'Oh!' she exclaimed, and blushed rather nicely.

'Anne Manners,' said Roger sternly. 'Subordinate Anne Manners, or rather, insubordinate Anne Manners—what are you doing here?'

'Investigating,' said Anne Manners, with a certain defiance.

Roger grasped her elbow, turned her round and walked her down the street. 'This is the time for my elevenses,' he said, taking no notice of her vehement protests. 'A cup of malt extract and a rusk. You're coming too.'

'I'm not!' said Miss Manners, who never had liked malt extract and had always hated rusks.

'You are,' said Roger. 'I've got a few questions I want to ask you, Anne Manners.'

As Anne had no wish (*a*) to cause a crowd to collect by belabouring Roger with her umbrella; (*b*) to be picked up and carried in broad daylight down Gray's Inn Road and into Holborn, she went quietly.

Seated some minutes later in the best restaurant in Holborn, with a cup of coffee and cream by her side and a plate of opulent and delightfully indigestible cakes in front of her, Anne consented to thaw.

'Very well, very well,' she said, unable to help smiling at her companion's insistence. 'I'll tell you. I wanted to talk to the porter about beards.'

'Beards?' repeated Roger. 'Oh! I see. Anne Manners, this is very clever of you. Beards, I take it, in connection with elderly solicitors?'

Anne nodded. 'Exactly.'

Roger regarded his subordinate with admiration. 'Do you mean to say you'd hit on the solicitor too, Anne? Really and truly? Quite on your own?'

'Oh!' Anne exclaimed excitedly. 'Then you think so too? He's the man, Mr Sheringham. I'm sure he is. What made you think so?'

'Wait a minute,' said Roger. 'You realise that according to the porter's evidence he can't possibly be the man, don't you?'

'Evidence!' said Anne scornfully. 'I *know* he's the man.'

'Well, between ourselves, so do I. And I think I know how he comes to be the man, in spite of the porter. But what I don't know is who he can be. He's disguised, of course. The gold-rimmed spectacles and all that. Obviously a disguise. Why, a silk hat's almost a disguise in itself nowadays.'

'I know who he is,' said Anne, and looked extremely wise. 'At least, I think I do. I just wanted to ask the porter a few questions to see if I could make sure.'

'And he certainly wouldn't have answered them. So you know who he is, do you? I suppose this is what you were being so mysterious about at tea yesterday?'

'I believe I did refer to it,' said Anne with dignity, and took another cake.

'Would it be too much for your superior officer to ask you to tell him who it is?'

'Much,' said Anne, through cake. 'I said I'd tell you at tea today, and so I will. But not before. I think we shall have got a little more proof by then.'

'"We!"' Roger repeated. 'Are you working with Jerry on this?'

It is difficult to look dignified when struggling with an éclair, but Anne did her best. 'Certainly not. With Mr Pleydell. As a matter of fact,' Anne confided, 'I did ring you up, just after breakfast, but you were out; so I rang Mr Pleydell up instead.'

'What about?'

Anne looked dubious. 'I'm not sure that I ought to tell you.'

'Why ever not?'

'Well, we thought it would be rather fun to see if we could find out by ourselves, and not tell you till we were sure.'

'Pleydell's getting very playful, isn't he?' said Roger drily.

'It was my idea, I think. Anyhow, I'll tell you this much. Yesterday afternoon I thought how silly we'd been; we'd quite overlooked a most important line of inquiry. Don't you see what ought to be the man's weak spot in Lady Ursula's case?'

'The possibility of having been seen with her, do you mean?'

'*No!* That's just what it isn't. If he thought he'd been seen *with* her, he wouldn't have killed her. Obviously his weak spot is the possibility of having been seen without her—coming away from the studio!'

'Ah!' said Roger.

'Don't you see,' Anne went on excitedly, 'that if the police have been making inquiries about that at all, they'll only have been interested in a man answering to Gerald Newsome's description, won't they?'

'I rather doubt that,' said Roger. 'The police aren't fools, you know. However, go on.'

'Well, what we ought to do is to comb the neighbourhood

with inquiries about a man with a *beard* coming away at that time. Of course I couldn't do that myself, so I thought we ought to get a firm of private detectives on to it at once. I rang you up, but you were out, so I rang up Mr Pleydell, and he promised to have it done at once. He seemed to think it an awfully good idea,' Anne added, with pride. 'He said it might quite well put us on the right track at last.'

'But if the beard is a disguise,' said Roger stupidly, 'he may not have—'

'The beard isn't a disguise!' Anne interrupted impatiently. 'The other things may be, but not the beard. Come, Mr Sheringham, don't you see? Isn't there a beard in this case already? Oh, I suppose I may as well tell you now, though I didn't tell even Mr Pleydell this. Why, surely it's obvious. I mean—'

'Good God!'

'No,' said Anne. 'Arnold Beverley.'

CHAPTER XXII

THE LAST VICTIM

ROGER arrived in Sutherland Avenue that afternoon for his vigil in a somewhat mixed frame of mind. He was certain that, at last, he was on the right lines; he was certain that he could not possibly complete the vast amount of investigation necessary within a mere twenty-four hours; he was certain that the police would make a colossal mistake if they really did arrest Gerald Newsome; he was certain now that Anne was mistaken in her identification of the solicitor with Arnold Beverley; and he was certain that he himself had not got the faintest idea who the man really was. On the whole he was not sorry for the prospect of a couple of quiet hours in which to reflect on these difficult matters.

Throwing his hat on to the table which, with a comfortably solid armchair, constituted the sole furniture of the little room, he dropped into the latter with a sigh of relief. The strain of the case was beginning to tell on him, and he felt tired. When it was over (if it ever was) he would go away and take a holiday somewhere.

He had ascertained from Pleydell on the previous afternoon that the bell worked perfectly and the ten-minute signals came through without a hitch. Glancing at his watch as he settled himself in the chair, he saw that it was exactly half-past two. As if to confirm its accuracy a short, sharp tinkle sounded from the corner in which the bell had been installed. Roger laid the watch on his knee in order to check the intervals and tried to concentrate.

As regards Anne, he was not unduly perturbed, even after the candid remarks which Newsome had addressed to him.

The more one considered it, the more fantastic it seemed that, out of all possible victims, the murderer should hit on Anne. As to the attraction supposed to be exercised on a murderer by the scene of the crime, which might be believed to lure him back to Sutherland Avenue, Roger did not put any credence in it at all. But Anne had conceived the idea and she thought she was doing something towards avenging her sister by carrying it out, so by all means let the poor kid go on with it.

Thus Roger.

Slowly the hands of the watch crept on, to a quarter to three, three o'clock, half-past; and punctually at every ten minutes the bell in the corner uttered an abrupt little ring. But to Roger no illumination came. He concentrated and concentrated; he cried, presumptuously, in his spirit, 'Let there be light,' but no light appeared; he wandered dizzily through the endless mazes of the case, and every time found himself in a fresh blind alley. By four o'clock he had given it up in despair and was longing whole-heartedly for tea and companionship.

He looked at his watch. The time was three minutes past four. He started guiltily. Had the bell rung at four o'clock or hadn't it? He had been so immersed in his own woes that the rings of late had only been subconsciously noted. But now he was aware of a blank. No, he was sure there had been no ring at four o'clock.

He stood up. It was no good leaving a thing like this to chance, he must run across at once. After all, perhaps he had minimised the danger. What if the murderer had got hold of their plan and, fearing they might be on his trail, had determined to take this opportunity to rid himself of one of his pursuers? That was a possibility he had never considered. He looked at his watch again before putting it back in his pocket; it was practically five past four. He hurried towards the door. As his hand touched the knob the bell in the corner spoke at last; but this time its ring was loud, long and insistent—the signal of alarm.

Roger rushed down the stairs three at a time and into the next house.

The sitting-room door resisted his efforts to open it.

'Anne!' he called at the top of his voice, regardless of what the people in the flats below might think. *'Anne!'*

There was a bump and a thud in the passage beside him, and Newsome appeared, tumbled out of his cubby-hole. 'What's the matter?' he asked anxiously.

'Alarm signal,' panted Roger, pushing at the door with all his strength. 'Can't get an answer The man's inside, I think.'

Newsome joined him, adding a sturdy shoulder. Trying to find some other way of attacking it, Roger looked up; and what he saw made him feel for a moment quite sick. At the top of the door was a hook, screwed firmly into the wood, and from it, disappearing over the door, was a thin strip of some silky-looking material.

Roger shook Newsome's shoulder and pointed at it. 'Charge the thing together,' he grunted. 'Not a second to lose.'

They drew back, paused for an instant, and then flung them-selves forward, shoulders against the heavy cross-piece of the old-fashioned door. This time the obstruction, whatever it had been, gave way, and the door flew open.

'Guard the doorway!' Roger gasped, as they tumbled into the room. He utilised the force of his motion to fling himself round the edge of the door. Hanging on the back of it, her feet a good twelve inches above the floor, was Anne.

In the same movement Roger lifted her up and shouted to Newsome to unfasten the stocking from the hook on the farther side, loosening the portion round her throat at the same time. As Newsome freed the stocking from the hook, Roger carried Anne over to a couch and laid her gently along it.

'Get the fellow, Jerry,' he said, without looking round. 'I'll see to Anne.' He bent over her.

She was quite unconscious, and her face was horribly distorted, but to Roger's unspeakable relief she was still breathing. Without even a glance round the room he began to flex her limbs and apply the usual methods of relief to her strained lungs.

'I say,' said Newsome's voice behind him, 'this is ghastly. Is she—is she alive?'

'Yes, she'll be all right in a minute. Have you got him?'

'There wasn't anybody! The room was empty, except for—Anne.'

'Nonsense!' Roger retorted. 'He must be in here somewhere. Look round. And keep your eye on the door. He'll make a dash for it. I'll look after Anne. She's getting better already.'

Newsome made a circuit of the room, looking into every available hiding-place, without result. The fox had gone to ground.

'Then run out and telephone to Pleydell to come up here at once,' said Roger, still bending over the unconscious girl. 'Hurry!'

'Look here, hadn't I better get a doctor first?' suggested Newsome, gazing down at Anne, whose bloodless lips were only just beginning to lose something of their ghastly hue. 'She looks awful. We must—'

'Go and telephone Pleydell!' Roger cut in, speaking in an authoritative voice. 'I'm in charge here now, Jerry, officially; and I want Pleydell up here as soon as he can get. We've got to consult whether to inform the police about this or not, and it all depends on what Anne has to tell us. She's all right; she'll be round in a few minutes. And we don't want a doctor unless we can't avoid it; he'd ask too many awkward questions. Go and telephone, there's a good fellow; I don't know whether there's an instrument downstairs or not. You can find out.'

Newsome hesitated for a moment, then he went. Roger resumed his ministrations.

Before Newsome returned, five minutes later, Anne's eyelids were fluttering and her hands were making little movements by her sides.

'Thank God!' Newsome muttered, noting these signs of returning animation. 'Pleydell's got a directors' meeting on,' he said to Roger. 'He's not in his office. I left word that they were to get hold of him at once and send him up here, on a matter of life and death.'

Roger nodded, and the two stood watching Anne. The next moment her head began to turn slowly from side to side on the cushion which Roger had placed under it; one hand went jerkily up to it and clutched her forehead.

'My head!' she whispered, in a cracked little voice. 'Oh, my head.'

Roger started violently and bent over her again, touching the back of her head with infinitely gentle fingers. He frowned.

'Curious!' he muttered, and went on feeling.

Still almost completely dazed, Anne began to mutter. 'I'm— I'm going to be—to be—'

Roger wheeled round suddenly on Newsome. 'Jerry! Get out!'

'What?' asked that astonished gentleman.

'Get out!' Roger snapped. 'This is going to be no place for you. Hurry!' He herded the protesting Newsome forcibly from the room and locked the door on him.

Hurling some dried leaves out of a large flowervase he snatched it up and ran back to the couch. He was just in time.

'Wet nurse, dry nurse, three bags full,' Roger was murmuring distractedly three minutes later, administering frantic first-aid with a silk handkerchief in one hand and a cushion-cover in the other. 'There, Anne, dear, are you feeling comfier—not to say tidier?'

Anne smiled at him with watery eyes. 'Roger Sheringham,' she said, 'you're a *dear*. But I'll never be able to look you in the face again without blushing.'

Roger cast a harrassed eye unostentatiously under the couch to make sure that the evidence was out of sight. 'He hit you on the head, didn't he?'

'I should say he did,' Anne agreed, feeling the back of it with cautious fingers.

'I guessed as much,' Roger nodded, 'and just managed to get Jerry out of the room in time. Anne, did you see him?'

'Yes!' Anne was recovering quickly now. 'Roger, it was the solicitor!'

'It was, eh? Top-hat, beard, spectacles and all?'

'Yes; *and* gloves. I only caught one tiny glimpse of him, and he hit me before I could even open my mouth to scream. Or rather, I think I was so petrified with terror that I simply *couldn't* scream. I never heard a sound till he was right inside the room. I was reading and looked up, and there he was, with his right arm all ready lifted to hit me.' She shuddered violently. 'Roger, I was *terrified!* Oh, and I'd thought once I was so brave.' She began to laugh weakly, while her eyes filled with tears.

Roger tried to soothe her, but she continued to giggle fool-ishly. 'Anne, stop!' he said in desperation. 'Stop, or I'll kiss you.' And she did not stop, so he did kiss her—once, twice, three times, four, five, lots of times . . .

It took Anne quite half a minute to realise what Roger was doing, and then she did stop. She stopped Roger too.

'Roger!' said Anne, blushing fiercely.

'If you get hysterical again, I'll kiss you again,' Roger threat-ened, unabashed. Anything to take her mind off what she's gone through (he was thinking behind his smile), and this seems the very best way.

'If you do, I'll be sick again,' Anne retorted promptly.

Roger judged that the cure was complete.

'But oh,' Anne murmured, holding her forehead, 'my head does ache.'

'You poor child! Anne Manners, you're the pluckiest girl I've ever met. And you've solved our problem, remember.'

'But we still don't know who he is.'

'We're jolly soon going to,' replied Roger grimly. He dived under the couch and retrieved the evidence, wrapping it decently in the cushion-cover, and marched out to give it burial. 'I'll be back in a minute,' he said airily.

'Very well,' said Anne, looking at the ceiling and pretending hard not to know what he was doing.

Outside the door a wild-eyed Newsome confronted him. 'Is she all right?' he babbled. 'I heard her making the most awful—'

'She's all right,' Roger cut him short. 'Go in and see for yourself.' He stalked on to the cemetery.

Some twenty minutes later, when Pleydell arrived, Anne was sufficiently recovered to be lying back in a chair and submitting to having her forehead bathed in eau-de-Cologne by Newsome. Roger gave Pleydell a hasty account of what had happened, and the latter, evidently deeply shocked, congratulated Anne warmly on her pluck and her escape.

'Wedged the door with a chair underneath the handle, eh?' he said, looking at the splintered object that had held up their attempts to enter.

'Yes,' said Roger, 'it must have been very cunningly balanced.'

'But in spite of everything, you couldn't identify the man?' Pleydell asked Anne.

She shook her head. 'I'm afraid not. He hardly gave me time, either.'

Pleydell frowned. 'This is very serious. Sheringham, do you realise that Miss Manners is by no means out of danger yet? This was no chance attack, you may be sure. He had some object, and it isn't attained. When he learns that, I'm very much afraid that he may make a second attempt.'

'Yes, I'd thought of that,' Roger nodded. 'We must get them away from here, both of them. Miss Carruthers won't be safe here either.'

'I quite agree. I think they should go as soon as possible. It's out of the question for them to appear at the theatre tonight, even if Miss Manners were fit to, which she isn't.' He thought for a moment. 'I have a small cottage in Surrey, on the Banstead Downs. I can put that at their disposal.'

'That's very good of you, Mr Pleydell,' Anne said gratefully. 'Thank you so much.'

'Is that wise, though, do you think?' Roger demurred. 'I'm inclined to think they'd be safer in London, at one of the big hotels. Supposing they were traced down to Surrey, you see. Isolation in a cottage might be even more dangerous than here.'

'I see your point,' Pleydell said, and paused. There was a moment's silence. 'Oh, Newsome,' he went on, 'would you do something for me? I was called away from my meeting in a hurry, of course, and I find I've brought an important document with me. They'll be entirely hung up for it. Could you slip down to the city with it and hand it in at an address in Leadenhall Street for me?'

Newsome looked a little surprised at this rather cool request, and still more so when Roger proceeded strongly to back it. 'Yes, Jerry, there's nothing you can do here, and we mustn't forget in all this excitement that Pleydell's time is, quite truly, money. Cut along to Leadenhall Street, there's a good chap. And you can change and come back to my rooms afterwards. I'm dining with some people in Kensington, for my sins, and they asked me to bring an extra man. You're going to be the extra man.'

'But I say,' expostulated the recipient of these commands.

'Jerry,' said Roger, with mock severity, 'I'd have you remember that you're under orders. Now you've got 'em, so cut!' His voice was light, but there was an undertone of real command in it.

Newsome looked sulky, but prepared to obey. 'Oh, all right, I suppose, if you make such a point of it,' he said, with no very good grace.

Pleydell drew a long envelope out of his breast-pocket, scribbled an address on it, and handed it over. 'Thank you very much,' he said courteously. 'That will save a great deal of trouble.'

Newsome nodded and went out without a further word.

Pleydell turned to Anne as if no rather uncomfortable atmosphere had been generated. 'I think,' he said quietly, 'if you are feeling well enough, that you should pack at once, Miss Manners. It is no good losing time, and the sooner you are out of here, the better.'

'Oh, yes,' Anne said cheerfully. 'I can manage now, I think.' She rose and went out of the room.

Pleydell, who had opened the door for her, shut it carefully. He waited for a moment, then walked up to Roger. In that short instant his normally rather sallow face had become suffused with blood, and Roger could see that he was trembling all over. 'Now can you doubt, Sheringham?' he said, in a low voice that vibrated with passion. '*Now* can you doubt?'

With the utmost deliberation Roger drew out his pipe and began to fill it. 'Newsome, you mean?' he said matter-of-factly.

His pointed ordinariness had its intended effect. Pleydell pulled himself together, though it cost him a visible effort to do so. 'The only one on the premises, the only one with the opportunity, the only one who even *knew*,' he said, in tones which still shook a little in spite of his attempts to keep them even. 'God, I could hardly keep my hands off *his* throat.'

Roger nodded casually. 'I'm afraid there can't be any doubt of it now. I couldn't believe it at first, but—well, as you say, it's impossible to think anything else now. You understood that was why I helped you to get rid of him?'

'Yes. He mustn't learn where Miss Manners is going, at any cost. My God, Sheringham, if he tries it again I *will* take the law into my own hands, now I'm certain. Nobody has a better right than I to punish that man.'

Roger, praying hard that no further hysterics should be inflicted on him (he could hardly try the same cure with Pleydell), grew more and more normal as the other grew warmer. 'Oh, I shouldn't do that,' he said, as if he were talking about the next day's big race. 'You'll get your revenge all right when you see the judge calling for his black cap. This is a police-matter, you must remember, and after this last effort it passes into their hands. And I know for a fact,' he added confidentially, 'if it will make your mind any easier, that Newsome's arrest is only a matter of hours.'

Pleydell's eyes gleamed. 'Is that so? Then I think I may forgo my private vengeance. Yes, of course you're right, Sheringham. This is a police matter. But do you know how hard it is to realise that simple fact? All this time I've looked on it as *my* matter, *my* matter, and nobody else's. I tried to get the police to move (you were there yourself), and it seemed that they did nothing. I—'

'Oh, yes, they jolly well did,' Roger interrupted. 'They've put together a perfect case against Newsome; and this will clinch it. Don't you worry, Pleydell; the police have been busy all right.'

'I'm very glad to hear it. But I shan't rest till he's under lock and key. Think—any moment he may attack some other unfortunate girl.'

'That's all right,' Roger said soothingly. 'Didn't you hear me make sure of that? You can depend on it that I'm going to keep him under my eye for the short time he's still at liberty.'

'Thank you. I would have done so myself if you hadn't. Now about these two girls. I agree that Surrey might be unwise. Where do you suggest?'

'The Piccadilly Palace,' Roger replied at once. 'They'll be far safer in a big, noisy place like that than in a smaller one. I'll take them there myself.'

Pleydell nodded. 'Excellent. Ring me up about them this evening, will you? It's very good of you to undertake all these duties, Sheringham. I feel I'm shirking my share. But as it happens today is a very busy one with me, and though I'd gladly shelve everything if I can be of any real use, I will be extremely grateful if you can take on the smaller duties for me.'

'Of course,' Roger said heartily. 'That's quite all right. You push off at once, if you're busy. There's nothing at all for you to stay for. I'll see to everything.'

And that, I suppose, Roger reflected as Pleydell went, just

about sums up the Jewish outlook. They'd give up everything in the world to save the life of a dying friend, or even to ensure that he had a really luxurious funeral if he wanted one; but that doesn't prevent them from asking the undertaker for a cash discount. And why should it? We call it callous, but it's only practical. That's our trouble; we can't distinguish between real and false sentiment. And the Jews do.

But it had been a nervous ten minutes, for all its aftermath of peaceful moralising.

CHAPTER XXIII

THE TRAP IS SET

WHEN Gerald Newsome, obedient to discipline but not unresentful, arrived at the Albany that evening, he found a surprisingly cheerful trio awaiting him. Kensington, apparently, had vanished from the map. Certainly it seemed that neither Roger, Anne nor Miss Carruthers had the slightest intention of going to such a foolish place. In the Albany they were going to dine, and the Albany had been commanded to do its best for them.

'I must apologise for talking to you like a sergeant-major, Jerry,' Roger said to his bewildered guest, whom he took the opportunity of waylaying in the hall. 'But I could see that Pleydell was thirsting for your blood, and I had to get you out of the way before he began drawing it.'

'My blood? What on earth for?'

'Because he holds very strong opinions about you, my poor Jerry. He's quite convinced that you're the villain of this piece, and I knew it wasn't the least use trying to shake his convictions. I had to humour him by pretending to agree with him. At present we're both gloating over your impending arrest tomorrow.'

'Good Lord!'

'Well, really one can't blame him,' Roger pointed out. 'In addition to all the other evidence against you, we're now faced with the fact, to be explained away somehow, that you are really the only person who could have attacked Anne. He thinks you jumped out of your little cubby-hole, complete with whiskers and gold-rimmed spectacles, and simply fell on her.'

'Damn the fellow!' said the indignant suspect.

'No, as I said, one can't blame him. But you're safe from him here, I fancy; though he did mention that he was itching to get his fingers round your throat. Now that's enough shop till after dinner. Anne's got to recover completely during the evening, and I want to take her mind off this business completely. I've unhooked the telephone, and we're all under orders to talk of nothing but frivolities till further notice. Now come along and have some of your cocktails.'

'Anne? Is she here?'

'She is. And so is my excellent friend, Miss Carruthers.'

'Great Scott! Then—then we're not going to Kensington after all?'

'Where is Kensington?' queried Roger blandly.

And the result was a very cheerful little dinner-party and, so far as one could see, the complete recovery of Anne.

One thing Newsome was surprised to learn, and that was that both the girls were going to spend the night under their host's bachelor roof.

'I tried to get rooms at the Piccadilly Palace, you see,' Roger explained lightly, 'but the place was full up. And if it's safety that's wanted, what could be safer than the Albany? Why, the place is a veritable fortress at night.'

'Shop!' said Anne, and Roger bowed his head.

But when the two girls had gone into the sitting-room and Roger and Newsome were left alone, Roger dropped the bantering air he had worn all the evening and became very serious indeed.

'This is a perfectly damnable business, Jerry,' he said, 'and I simply don't know what to do about it. We've *got* to get that man under lock and key somehow, and pretty quickly too. Anne's life isn't worth a halfpenny if we don't, I'm convinced.'

'I say,' Newsome gasped. 'Is it really as bad as that?'

'Well, I may be exaggerating, of course, but I don't think so. And then there's your arrest tomorrow. That's bound to stop police activities for a time, till they do find out that you're the wrong man.'

'And you haven't any idea at all who this damned man is, who disguises himself as a solicitor?'

'Well, I don't mind admitting that I have got a theory now. But it's really only a theory. And I may be miles off the track. *I* don't know.'

'Can't you get hold of any evidence to support it?'

'None, that I can think of; at least, not without a search-warrant. And even then almost certainly none either. I *can't* prove it, though I feel in my bones I'm right.'

'Who do you think it is?'

Roger hesitated. 'Well, I don't think I'll say that yet, even to you. But I'll tell you that if I published my theory in *The Courier* there'd be such a shout of laughter throughout the entire country that my ear-drums would immediately burst. And you, Jerry, would probably be shouting as loud as any of them. I'm afraid that at first hearing my theory might sound, to put it mildly, a trifle fantastic.'

'But do you think you're on the right lines?'

Roger got up and began to pace restlessly up and down the room. 'I *think* so. In fact, I'm almost sure. When the idea first occurred to me, only a little time ago, I nearly laughed at myself. But I've applied every conceivable test since then, and it seems to stand up to them all right. It stretches the probabilities here and there, it's true, but not into impossibilities by a long chalk. Oh, damn it, I'm certain I'm right. But I *can't* prove it! And I've simply got to, if you're to marry Anne and bring up a family of small Jerries.'

'What!' exclaimed his astonished audience. 'I say, Roger, you don't think—I say, she wouldn't think of—Good Lord, do you really think she—'

'Stop blethering! We're up against the stiffest proposition either of us has ever encountered, not excluding the War, and you sit there and bleat like a sheep about would she, and do I think and does she think, and do I really think. Do I really think? My hat, I've got to really think tonight, I can tell you. And so have you, so begin at once.'

'Oh, hell!' muttered the discomfited swain, and lapsed into silence.

Roger continued to prowl.

'I remember saying once that Scotland Yard's methods would never solve this case,' he burst out after a minute or two, 'but that French ones might. I still think I'm right about the first part, but French methods haven't proved very successful yet, have they?'

'Was that a French method this afternoon?' asked Newsome, almost timidly.

'As French as a haricot bean,' said Roger shortly. 'And if only the brute hadn't been wearing his whiskers, we'd have got him by now.'

'I say, I've been wanting to ask you ever since: how on earth did he get away?'

'Thought he'd done the job, and was going down the stairs when he heard me bounding up like a bull elephant. If I'd been in carpet-slippers I'd have run straight into him. As it was, all he had to do was to step aside, into a bathroom or anywhere, wait for me to pass, and then walk calmly out.'

'And you knew something was up because the ten-minutes' bell didn't ring? By Jove, it was lucky that was arranged.'

'Partly. I was just going on that account, when suddenly the alarm signal went off. The fellow must actually have stepped on it himself, of all ironical things. Thank heaven for that, at any rate. Anne might have been dead now if he hadn't. The luckiest accident!'

'My hat!' Newsome breathed. 'But, I say, it's funny that, isn't it? I thought the idea was that he'd found out about the arrangements, and wanted to eliminate Anne in spite of them. He evidently hadn't found out that one.'

'So it would seem,' Roger said absently. 'Oh, Jerry, my excellent but thick-skulled Jerry, isn't there *anything* you can suggest? We've got about eighteen hours to get this creature, and it would take me about eighteen weeks to collect enough evidence to prove my case in the orthodox way, even assuming I could do so at all, which I very much doubt. Because we've got to remember that this fellow is just about as cunning a maniac as there's ever been.'

'Any other sort of French method?'

'A trap!' Roger mused. 'We ought to set a trap for him. If he can't be found out, he must be made to give himself away. *How?*'

They debated this matter in silence.

Suddenly Roger halted in his stride. 'Supposing,' he said slowly, 'supposing we staged a Could it be done? Good Lord, I do believe it could. It's a horrible risk, but really . . . Well, it all depends on Anne. I must . . . Oh, yes, I think that might work. It's our only possible chance, anyway.'

'What, Roger?' Newsome asked, bulging with curiosity.

'Another leaf from the French notebook. Look here, run along and ask Anne to come in here, Jerry, will you? And then stop in the other room and make charming conversation to Moira. Everything depends on what Anne's got to say.'

'But what *is* the idea, man?'

'I'll tell you when I've talked to Anne. Quick, Jerry, I'm simply bursting with excitement.'

'Roger, you are the most irritating devil,' grumbled Mr Newsome, but went.

In a moment Anne arrived. Roger, sitting on the edge of the table, contemplated her with professional rather than human interest. Yet the human interest she might have been expected to arouse was quite strong.

'You wanted me, Roger?' she said.

'Yes. How are you feeling now, Anne? Pretty well recovered?'

'Oh, yes, thank you. My head still aches a bit, and my throat is a little sore, but otherwise I'm quite recovered.'

'I wonder what you'll be feeling like tomorrow morning,' Roger said.

'Perfectly all right, I should imagine. Why?'

Roger got up and conducted her with ceremony to a chair. 'Sit down, Anne. We've got to hold very serious converse. I want you to realise this first of all; as long as this man is at liberty and unsuspected, your life, to put it frankly, isn't worth fourpence. In fact, I put it at a halfpenny to Jerry just now.'

'Oh!' said Anne, wide-eyed.

'Moreover, if he isn't laid by the heels actually by midday tomorrow, your Jerry will be arrested; and I can tell you that once a suspect is arrested it's no easy matter to get him released.'

Anne nodded. 'Yes?'

'Well, it seems to me that it's up to us to get him before it's too late. You and I, Anne. We're the only ones who can do it. And neither of us can do it without the other. Most of all, I can't do it without you. No,' Roger corrected himself, 'that's not true. I could with Moira, I suppose. But we'll talk about that later.'

'Oh! You've got a plan, Roger?'

'I have, my child. A perfect brute of a plan. I hate and loathe my plan, but I'm blessed if I can see another. And it ought, with any luck at all, to work. But before I tell it you, I want to make this clear. If this man remains at liberty, not only you, but dozens of other girls are in deadly danger. You realise that?'

'Yes.'

'Well, I want to ask you this question; in order to provide me with a chance (and it's only a chance, mind) of catching the beast, are you prepared to risk your life?'

'Yes, Roger.'

'I don't mean a slight risk. I mean a really dangerous risk, with the chances possibly balanced against you. I shall take every possible precaution, naturally, but there aren't many I can take. You must realise that first of all.'

'Roger,' Anne said earnestly, 'at present I've only got one aim before me. I've left home to achieve it; I've planted myself in a new world which I really don't like at all; I display myself every night in public in the minimum amount of clothing the censor will allow, which I simply detest—and all to gain my object, the discovery of my sister's murderer. Of course I'll take any risk you like.'

'Anne,' said Roger fervently, 'I am about to kiss you.' And he did so.

'So now,' said the blushing Anne, having been duly kissed, 'perhaps you'll tell me what this plan of yours is.'

Roger did so. But this time he was careful not to mention his supposed identification of the murderer. It was an important part of his plan that Anne should be in ignorance of who her attacker had been. If Roger shared his suspicions with her, she could hardly avoid the infinitesimal gesture or glance that would put him on his guard; and the whole point of Roger's plot was surprise.

Anne listened intently. 'Why,' she said, when he had finished, 'there's no danger in that.'

'You think so?' said Roger grimly. 'And supposing I didn't rescue you in time, or there was a struggle, or anything unforeseen happened?'

'I shall be quite content,' said Anne, 'to trust myself entirely to you, Roger.'

'You darling!' said Roger. 'But you realise that it's going to be quite damnably uncomfortable, to put it at the very least? I may have to leave you till you've actually lost consciousness, if the psychological moment doesn't arrive before, you know.'

'Oh, it'll be horrible, of course,' Anne said, with a prim little smile. 'I shall simply hate it at the time, and probably I shall be quite unnecessarily frightened as well. But none of that matters. If you think there's a good chance of catching him in this way, then you can do just what you like with me. Besides,' she added in a lower tone, 'just think of all the other lives I may be able to save through a few minutes' discomfort.'

They discussed the details for some time, and then Anne was ordered off to bed. Moira, who was far too excited by all these stirring events to remember her carefully acquired refinement and had been in consequence a much more amusing companion than ever before, was summoned from the sitting-room and given strict injunctions that Anne was to be got to sleep at once and caused to sleep all night long.

'Like hell she shall!' affirmed Sally Briggs (late Moira Carruthers). 'If I have to sit up all night singin' at her.'

As soon as the two men were left alone, Roger fulfilled his promise and told Newsome of his intentions. He had expected Jerry to be difficult, and Jerry was difficult. Very difficult indeed. He had many things to say, and he said them all.

Finally Roger took a peremptory line. 'Very well, Jerry,' he said. 'If that's your attitude, you can't be present. This thing's going through; Anne's said so, and it's her responsibility, not yours. I was going to ask you to take on the responsibility of rescuing her when I give the word; but if I can't trust you to sit still through it all, however horrible and dangerous it seems to you, until I *do* give the word—why, then I simply won't have you present at all. I'll stage it the day after tomorrow instead, when you're safe in jail.'

After which, of course, Mr Newsome could put up no further fight.

'And now,' said Roger, 'I've got just a little telephoning to do.'

CHAPTER XXIV

THE TRAP IS SPRUNG

THE party from Scotland Yard was the first to arrive the next morning, for Roger had asked them to come at half-past eleven, whereas the rest were not expected till twelve o'clock. It was with an air of disapproving amusement that Chief Inspector Moresby, Superintendent Green and the Assistant Commissioner himself greeted their host and consented to imbibe the glasses of old pale sherry which he had prepared to soothe their feelings.

'Now remember,' he said, having seen a portion of the sherry safely down on its soothing path, 'remember that you're here quite unofficially. It isn't because you're from Scotland Yard that I've asked you to come and watch my little cat-and-mouse act. Nothing of the kind. It's simply because Sir Paul Graham, Mr Green and Mr Moresby are friends of mine and I thought I'd like to have them to my party.'

'Humph!' said Superintendent Green, unsmiling.

'Ah!' said Chief Inspector Moresby, smiling.

'Sheringham, you're incorrigible,' said the Assistant Commissioner, also smiling. 'But I don't approve, you know.'

'And on the other hand,' Roger retorted, 'you don't disapprove, because you don't know what on earth I'm going to do.'

'Well, what *are* you going to do?' asked Sir Paul.

'That,' said Roger, 'is just what you don't know, isn't it? Have some more sherry.' He refilled the glasses, to a refrain of politely protesting murmurs which he disregarded; as, indeed, their makers fully intended him to do.

'Well, anyhow,' persisted the Assistant Commissioner, 'what do you want us to do?'

'Just sit still and look on at the little drama Miss Manners and I are going to perform. And above everything, not interfere by so much as a grunt till I show I'm ready for you. I warn you, you'll find it a ticklish business to sit still and say nothing, but I want your three promises to do so, even though you think I'm killing Miss Manners under your very eyes. Do you agree?'

'I don't like this,' said the Assistant Commissioner uneasily.

Roger became as persuasive as he could. This, he knew, was the moment upon which everything depended. If Scotland Yard refused its presence, the whole plan became useless. He pointed out with all the eloquence at his command that any methods were admissable in such a case, unorthodox as these might seem, and that Scotland Yard was not being invited actively to co-operate, but merely to sit aloof and step in only if they cared to do so; and he pleaded pathetically to be allowed just this one chance of saving Jerry Newsome from arrest and the police from the blunder of arresting him and of proving a fantastic theory of his own which they would simply laugh at if he were to voice it prematurely.

In the end Sir Paul consented. It was the argument concerning Newsome which probably brought him to agree to grace this unconventional scene with his own presence and that of two of his chief officers; for Sir Paul was by no means as convinced as were the two officers that Newsome was the man they wanted. Like Roger, he simply could not see him in the role; and the circumstantial evidence, after all, though nearly always infallible if strong enough is not invariably so.

Much relieved, Roger emptied the bottle among them and proceeded to give them their instructions. Moresby and Green were not to be in evidence at all; they were to lurk behind a screen which had been drawn across a corner of the room, and only come out when Roger called for them. The Assistant Commissioner was to be introduced, if any introduction was necessary, as Mr Blake and his connection with Scotland Yard not revealed; he would sit in a dark corner and make himself as unobtrusive as possible. Would he do that? He would.

'Well, Mr Sheringham,' said Chief Inspector Moresby jovially, 'we shall expect some startling results from you after all this.'

'I think you'll be startled all right, Moresby,' said Roger.

Superintendent Green continued to say nothing in a very masterly way. Even Roger's excellent sherry had not softened that dour man. Except while actually imbibing it, his face was eloquent of his opinion that of all the time-wasting, silly businesses, this was going to be the silliest and waste the most valuable time. Superintendent Green, it was clear, was not going to be an appreciative audience.

Having completed his arrangements, Roger called in Anne and introduced her.

'Now Anne,' he said in businesslike tones, 'I want you to tell these three doubting Thomases that you are doing this of your own free will, that you fully understand the risks you are going to run even to the extent of losing your life, and that you don't want them to interfere with what I am doing to you until I myself give the word.'

'That is so,' Anne agreed gravely. 'And I should like to add that even though I knew it meant certain death, I think I should still go through with it because I am sure that if necessary one life should be sacrificed to save the others that this man will certainly take if he's not caught, and also that if Mr Sheringham had refused to carry out his plan with me after consideration, because he thought it too risky, I should not have rested until I'd found somebody else who would.'

There was a short silence after Anne had spoken. Even Moresby looked more or less serious.

'It is a fact, then, that this scheme involves real danger to Miss Manners' life?' asked Sir Paul uncomfortably.

'The gravest,' Roger assured him.

'Then I suggest,' said Sir Paul, 'that for your sake, she put in writing what she has just told us.'

'That's a very good idea,' said Anne, with equanimity. 'I'll go and do it at once.'

The Assistant Commissioner, who had entertained vague hopes of frightening her out of this hare-brained business, looked nonplussed.

Anne went out of the room.

'You realise, Sheringham,' said Sir Paul, 'that what she said doesn't make the slightest difference legally? If you do cause the girl's death, you will be responsible in the usual way.'

Roger nodded. 'Oh, yes, I know that, of course. But I thought you'd like to hear her own opinion. By the way, I've been guilty of a gross dereliction of duty. It will interest you gentlemen to hear that, although I haven't yet reported it, Miss Manners was attacked yesterday by this brute and very nearly lost her life then.' He gave the details briefly and answered such questions as the three asked him.

'Newsome!' said Chief Inspector Moresby, without hesitation.

'Newsome, of course,' grunted Superintendent Green, in disgust.

'Really,' said Sir Paul, almost convinced in spite of his feelings, 'it does look as if Newsome is the man.'

'So Pleydell said,' agreed Roger equably. 'And yet he isn't, you know.'

'And you really think you know who it is?'

'I'm convinced of it. But this business will prove once and for all whether I'm right or not. And it's the only thing that will.' He handed to Sir Paul an ordinary envelope, sealed. 'By the way, here's the name of the man I suspect. Put it in your pocket and don't open it till the show's over. I should hate you to say afterwards that I'd been afraid to commit myself in advance.'

Sir Paul took it with a slight smile and stowed it away in his breast-pocket.

'And now,' said Roger, 'I think you'd better take up your positions. The others will be arriving at any minute.'

They had been so far in Roger's study. He now led them across the hall into the sitting-room. This was a room of tolerably large dimensions, long and not very narrow. There was a window in one end and two in one of the sides; the door opened in the middle of the end wall opposite the window. Across one corner at the window end the screen had been placed, and in the other corner was Sir Paul's chair. Roger saw them into their places, and then drew the curtains half-way over all the windows so that the two corners were thrown into shadow.

He had only just completed these arrangements when the front-door bell rang, and he excused himself.

George Dunning was the first arrival, puzzled but good-humoured as ever, and Roger took him at once into the study, where Newsome had now materialised, from his lurking-place in Roger's bedroom. In the spare bedroom Anne was completing her document, a little frightened now, but determined not to show it, and watched over anxiously by a far more frightened Moira, who was under orders to stand by to render such first-aid as might prove necessary, but otherwise to put in no public appearance.

In the study Roger, Newsome and George Dunning were exchanging stilted conversation, the last far too well-mannered to ask what on earth the strangely urgent invitation he had found waiting for him when he got home on the previous evening, might portend.

The next arrival, however, Sir James Bannister, was less diffident.

'Mr Sheringham?' he asked, as Roger opened the door to him (his man had been sent out for the morning).

'That's right,' Roger agreed cheerfully, allowing him to enter.

'I received a message from you asking me to call here this morning on a matter affecting not only my personal honour and reputation, but my actual physical safety, Mr Sheringham,' said Sir James weightily. 'These are serious matters, sir. May I ask you to explain yourself?'

'Certainly, Sir James. Take off your hat and coat and come inside. I shall explain things to you in a few minutes.'

Sir James raised his heavy black eyebrows, but consented to do as he was requested. Roger took him at once into the sitting-room and sat him down on one of a semicircular row of chairs which had been set out across the end of the room facing the door. Newsome, as had been previously arranged, brought Dunning in at the same time and the two of them took other chairs.

It was now a minute or two past twelve o'clock, and the rest of the audience arrived almost together, the first, a stranger to Roger, in a beautifully cut blue overcoat, the effect of which was marred only by a too-bright tie and a pair of patent-leather boots with cloth uppers, proving to be the great Billy Burton himself, most popular of whimsical stage humorists, whose yearly earnings amounted to just about five times as much as the Prime Minister of his country. Almost on his heels came Arnold Beverley, and with him Pleydell.

The last Roger detained for a moment in the hall. 'Haven't got time to go into it with you, Pleydell, but I want you to back me up. I couldn't get hold of you last night, but I think I'm on the verge of great things. All I want you to do is to sit tight (you'll see my idea in a minute) and remember that all the responsibility is mine. Come along, and I'll show you where to sit.'

Pleydell looked surprised, but there was no time to explain anything further, and Roger hurried him into the only vacant chair at the end of the arc, just in front of the corner where Sir Paul was sitting. 'Be ready to back me up if I want you,' he whispered, a little anxiously. Stepping past him, he dropped a note unostentatiously in Sir Paul's lap before making his way to the middle of the room.

Roger drew a quick little breath as he glanced at his audience. Among those seven men facing him was, he felt utterly convinced, the callous but unbalanced brain that was responsible for the deaths of at least four girls and was probably planning already the murder of others. And now the crucial moment had arrived, by which he was to stand or fall. Roger was not often nervous, but his heart beat a little irregularly as he thought of the tremendous responsibility which the next few minutes must bear.

'Gentlemen,' he said, in an ordinary, conversational voice, 'most of you know why I have called you together this morning so urgently. Let me explain. You may have seen in the newspapers recently the reports, from time to time, of a novel form of suicide in which the victim, always a girl, hangs herself with one of her own stockings. Quite unofficially I have been looking into these cases, in an amateurish way, and the conviction has been forced upon me that they are not cases of suicide at all, but of murder.

'If this is the case, gentlemen, a very serious state of affairs has arisen. In the middle of our community there is a man at liberty with a brain so unbalanced that his supreme joy in life is the killing of defenceless girls. He is worse than a homicidal maniac, for in all other respects he may be quite sane. I will not trouble you now with the way in which this conclusion has forced itself upon me, though I shall be ready to give anybody any information on this point later; but the important thing is that there is not a jot of evidence, in the legal sense, to support it. Not one jot! I am therefore, as you will see, in a very difficult position. I *know* that these deaths are not suicides, but murders; but if I went to Scotland Yard and told them so they would, on the only kind of evidence I could produce, simply laugh at me.

'It has therefore occurred to me to form a committee of respectable citizens drawn from representative lines of our national life, to relieve me of the responsibility of my knowledge and consult as to what should be done. You, gentlemen, are the committee I have, quite gratuitously, selected. It is up to anyone to refuse to have anything to do with it, as I need not say; but first, I ask you to hear me a little further.' Roger paused and moistened his lips. The audience were quite still, and their intense interest was evident.

'To discover the means by which these unfortunate girls met their deaths has necessitated a long and arduous inquiry,' he resumed, encouraged. 'The many details had to be worked out or deduced each by itself, much had to be imagined, much was only brought to light after weeks of work. To explain all these steps and enumerate the various points in detail would take far too long. I therefore propose to give you here and now a representation of how this man goes about his work.

'I warn you, the thing will not be easy to watch. It is my intention to bring home to you the gravity of the state of affairs by showing you exactly how these girls have died. There will be no faking or rigging. A lady has kindly placed herself at my disposal, and I am going to bring her within an inch of death before your very eyes; and I should tell you that, so strongly does she feel on the subject, that she has told me that if the experiment results in her actual death (as I am bound to confess that it may) she will consider the sacrifice worth while if only public opinion can be stirred up to hunt this brute down. That is all I have to say, except to ask you to sit absolutely still and silent while the representation is being performed, and to remember that any well-meant attempt at interference when matters have reached a critical stage will almost certainly have, the opposite effect and result in causing the lady's death. Please use every ounce of self-restraint you possess!'

As Roger had anticipated, murmurs of protest rose the moment he had finished speaking, but disregarding them he went to the door and threw it open. At once Anne walked in, pale but perfectly collected. Roger had coached her well in the time at his disposal, and she began to speak at once.

'I want to add to what Mr Sheringham has said,' she said, in her rather precise tones, 'that the responsibility for what is going to happen is entirely mine. I want nobody to interfere or do anything at all except sit quite still, even if I scream for help or seem to be quite at my last gasp. If you do, you will spoil everything. Thank you. I'm quite ready, Mr Sheringham.'

Roger turned to the audience. 'What you are now going to see,' he said, 'is an exact replica of what must have happened each time one of those girls died. You must imagine that you are in the room of a flat belonging to one of the girls.' He hurried out of the room.

Anne picked up a book and, seating herself in a chair, began to turn the pages. In a moment Roger entered the room again, and she jumped up.

'Why, hullo, Mr Sheringham!' she said, in a pleased voice. 'You're quite a stranger.' They shook hands.

'I was passing,' said Roger, 'and thought I'd like to look in and see you. Where's Phyllis?'

'She's gone out to do some shopping, and then she's going on to lunch with a friend.'

'I see. You're all alone, then?'

'Yes, quite.'

'Good. I was wondering if you'd come out and have some lunch with me, perhaps. You haven't any engagements, or anyone coming round to see you?'

'No, nobody. I'm quite free till the theatre this evening.'

'Excellent. Well, what about getting your hat on and coming out?'

'Yes, I'd love to. Will you wait here?' She turned towards the door, and Roger drew a black object from his pocket shaped not unlike a small pestle, and concealed it behind his back. 'I'll open the door for you,' he said, following Anne.

'Thank you.' She stood aside while he opened the door. 'I won't be a minute,' she said, and began to walk out. Immediately her back was turned, Roger made belief to strike her on the back of the head. Without a sound she sank back, and he caught her in his arms, lifted her off her feet, and laying her on a settee near by, tiptoed to the door.

A little gasp had sounded from the audience as Anne collapsed, but a tense silence now prevailed.

With infinite caution Roger stole just outside the room and stood for a moment listening. Then, drawing a small hook from his pocket, he screwed it quickly into the top of the further side of the door, opening the latter wide so that the audience could see exactly what he was doing. Closing it again, he walked over to the settee and, slipping off her shoes, began to unfasten one of her stockings, which were of pale-coloured silk. Stripping it from her leg, he proceeded to tie the two extreme ends tightly together, testing the strength of the knot with his knee. He placed the loop over her head so that it was lying loosely round her neck, and put the shoe back on her foot.

Somebody in the audience pushed a chair back sharply, but otherwise there was no sound.

Taking no notice of them, without even a glance in their direction, Roger picked up a chair and placed it squarely in front of the half-open door, its back towards the door, shifting its position as if at some pains to get it exactly right. Satisfied at last, he strolled back to the settee, his hands in his pockets, and again stood looking down at its occupant.

Anne began to show signs of returning consciousness. She moved her head more freely, and made little fluttering motions with her hands. Immediately Roger picked her up and carried her over to the door.

There, amid a tense silence, he propped her in such a position that she was half-sitting on the chair back, her feet on its seat, and holding her there he gave the loop round her neck three or four twists, passed it over the top of the door and slipped the other loop so formed over the hook. Then he lifted her up in both arms, pushed the door shut and, dragging the chair up to it with his feet, replaced her in the same position as before; but now that the door behind her was firm she could be so balanced as to remain there without being held. He stepped away from her.

Slowly Anne's eyes opened and she gazed round the room as if dazed, her hands gripped the chair-back under her, her lips fluttered, she seemed to be trying to speak.

Roger waited till it was clear that she had practically recovered all her faculties, then darted forward and, lifting her up, kicked away the chair. 'Darling Anne!' he whispered, his face as white as hers. 'Be brave, my dear!' And lowering her with slow deliberation, he stood back. Her head well above the top of the door, her feet at least eighteen inches above the floor, Anne hung by her neck. A little choking cry had broken from her as Roger lowered her, but now she was plainly incapable of uttering a sound.

There were stifled noises from the audience. Some were leaning forward in horror, others had half risen. A voice, low but authoritative, said: 'Keep still, everyone, please.' It was Newsome; who had risen from his chair at the other end of the arc from Pleydell and was standing with his back to the screen, his face deadly pale, but gallantly doing what he had been told.

All eyes were fixed upon Anne in horrified fascination. She had been hanging there only a few seconds, but already her face was crimson and contorted; the veins were swelling rapidly as if they were going to burst through the skin, her lips were drawn back in a hideous grin; her feet scrabbled on the door as if trying desperately to find some lodging-place, one hand was tearing at the stocking round her neck, the other clutching at the air in front of her.

It was a horrible spectacle, and normal flesh and blood could hardly bear it. Everywhere there was the sound of chairs falling as their occupiers pushed them back in rising. Cries of protest began to fill the room. Though he was trembling himself in every limb, Newsome had to restrain Sir James Bannister by sheer force from rushing forward.

Disregarding entirely the din, Roger strolled forward nonchalantly, his hands in his pockets, towards the corner occupied by Sir Paul. In front of the latter still sat Pleydell, the only one still remaining in his chair.

'That's how you do it, Pleydell, isn't it?' Roger asked easily.

Pleydell looked up at him with bright, mad eyes. 'No,' he said in a thick voice. 'I hold them up every now and then, to stop them—' He broke off abruptly.

'Hold him, Graham!' shouted Roger, and hurled himself towards Anne.

Just as he reached her, the convulsively struggling body went suddenly limp.

CHAPTER XXV

ROUND THE GOOD XXXX

ROGER leaned back in his chair and drew in two or three satisfying lungfuls of smoke. 'So the good old French method, of reconstructing the crime in the presence of the suspected person, can claim one more triumph,' he said. 'It's a pity Scotland Yard is so conservative, isn't it?'

'For all that, Mr Sheringham,' observed Superintendent Green, 'conservative methods pay all right, in most cases.'

'But they never would have in this,' Roger retorted, 'and so I've said from the very beginning. Haven't I, Moresby?'

'You have, Mr Sheringham,' Moresby agreed. He could not help himself; Roger certainly had said that. More than once.

It was three o'clock, rather more than two and a half hours after Pleydell had been removed, raving and struggling, from the Albany, and a quartette was sitting in Roger's study composed of the triumphant novelist himself, the Assistant Commissioner and the two officers in charge of the case. In the next room Anne was still lying down after her ordeal, with Moira holding one of her hands and Jerry Newsome the other, completely happy in the vindication of the desperate plan in which she had played so gallant a part. Her lapse into unconsciousness had been but momentary (although it seemed hours at the time, her period of suspension had actually been only forty seconds, according to Roger's wrist-watch) and her recovery considerably more rapid, and less unpleasant, than on the previous day, when she had had a severe blow on the head to contend with as well.

The terrible shock of realising himself unmasked before all those witnesses had toppled Pleydell's brain, merely balanced on the verge as it had been, finally over into the abyss of complete insanity. In his own financial line he had been a genius, and genius being already abnormal the curtain between it and the more ultimate abnormality of madness is always thin; in Pleydell's case it had always been not merely thin, but ragged; a severe shock at any time and of any sort, such as financial disaster, might have sufficed to tear it down altogether; and now that the shock had come, down it had gone. A general sigh of relief had gone up when the fact became realised. It was far the best thing that could have happened, for had Pleydell remained sane, repudiated his confession and pleaded not guilty, it was still a little doubtful whether he could have been convicted on such actual evidence as there was against him.

The Assistant Commissioner, in his relief generous without stint of praise and congratulations, had stayed to lunch in the Albany, and now the two officers, their prisoner safely disposed of and the formalities duly performed, had come back to listen to their amateur colleague's story. To them, no less than to the Assistant Commissioner himself, the identification of Pleydell with the maniac they had been hunting, had come as a complete and paralysing surprise.

'And we can't say that you were watching them all and hit on him as the most likely, Mr Sheringham,' Moresby admitted, 'because you'd written his name in that envelope you gave the Commissioner beforehand.'

'That's why I gave it him,' Roger grinned. 'I knew you'd say something like that if I didn't.'

'And Mr Sheringham dropped a note on my knee at the beginning, telling me to keep my eye on Pleydell, too,' Sir Paul added.

'I was afraid he might get violent,' Roger explained. 'That's why I put you in a place of vantage behind him.'

'When did you first begin to suspect him, Mr Sheringham?' asked Superintendent Green. The Superintendent had thawed considerably since twelve o'clock, but it was evident that he still considered an amateur had no right at all to succeed where the Yard had failed.

'Yesterday afternoon,' Roger replied. 'After the attack on Miss Manners, that's all. I won't say he hadn't crossed my mind before that, but never really seriously. And when I did come to consider him seriously, of course, I soon became positive. The more I thought about it, in fact, the more obvious it became. And I knew the real criminal, whoever he was, must have a key to Newsome's front door, a false beard and a pair of gold-rimmed spectacles, to say nothing of that pestle-shaped weapon of hard rubber; so that's how I was able to include the list of those things as waiting for you in Pleydell's rooms, in the envelope I gave Sir Paul beforehand.'

'Yes, and there we found them right enough,' admitted Moresby readily, 'though, as you said, they weren't much in the way of real proof. But how did you get over his alibis, Mr Sheringham? I don't understand that even now. How did he kill that girl in Pelham Mansions at the same time as he was eating lunch with you at your club?'

Roger took a pull at the tankard by his side. Out in the world a grandmotherly government was forbidding its citizens to quench their noble thirsts with good XXXX; in the Albany, with the help of a nice, round-bellied cask, such feeble puerilities could be disregarded.

'Fill up, you two,' said Roger. 'There's a gallon or two left, and I hate stale beer. I'm going to begin at the beginning, so fortify yourselves.'

With happy grins the two representatives of the same grandmotherly government took the necessary steps towards fortifying themselves.

'Monte Carlo is the beginning,' said Roger, 'so I'll begin there. Well, the truth is that there never was a murder at Monte Carlo at all. The French police were right; that was a perfectly genuine suicide. So there goes alibi No. 1. But that was what gave Pleydell his idea. He arrived just afterwards, you remember, and must have heard plenty of talk about it. The thing tickled his imagination. He may have been overworking or his health may have been bad; anyhow, he had probably got into a queer state. You can picture him brooding over that girl hanging on the door by one of her own stockings. He loved it. Nothing would satisfy him but that he must see such a thing happen. So the first thing he does when he gets back to England is to do it.

'You must remember that Pleydell suffered badly from mega-lomania. I'd noticed that on several occasions. "If I say a thing is, then it is; if I say the impossible shall be done, then it shall." But he was so quiet about it, while the usual megalomaniac is so bombastic, that one simply didn't recognise it for what it was. Anyhow, that gave him the idea that all was possible to him; that if it amused him to see girls die in this way then it was only right that girls should die for his pleasure; and that of course *he* could never be even suspected, much less found out.

'I was with him once in the street when we met Miss Carruthers and was rather surprised to find that he knew her. It turned out, however, that he was financially behind the show she's in. It never occurred to me at the time, but of course there was his connection with Unity Ransome. Perhaps he didn't even go to Sutherland Avenue with the idea of killing her. He may have seen his opportunity and just taken it. Probably that is what happened.

'As for the note left in that case, and the next, I can't tell you exactly how he induced the girls to write them; but you can picture well enough the sort of thing that must have happened. Perhaps he offered them a new fountain-pen and wanted to see how it suited their writing; perhaps he was pretending to tell their characters from their handwriting, anything like that. All we can say definitely is that he dictated and induced them, somehow or other, to take down his words verbatim. But it evidently wasn't easy, because in the last case, where he had no time to waste, he contented himself with cutting out a verse from a handy volume of poetry.

'Well, the death of Janet Manners whetted his appetite. He stood off for six weeks, then he went for that poor little prostitute, Elsie Benham. That, of course, was his safest line. There's no connection to be traced in those cases at all. But I don't expect he was worrying about being traced. He would be immune from that sort of thing. And so next we have him actually killing his own fiancée.'

'Now that I do *not* see how anyone could be expected to tumble to, Mr Sheringham,' said Moresby, without much grammar, but with considerable feeling.

'Why not?' Roger retorted. 'Neither of us did, as it happens, but that was because we both fell into the same error. We assumed that the engagement was a happy one. As a matter of fact it wasn't anything of the kind. That never came out at the inquest, of course, but it was common gossip among their own small circle of intimates. That complete idiot Newsome only thought to mention it to me at one o'clock this morning, after I'd been questioning him about the two of them for a couple of hours on end. But you made a worse mistake than I did, because when you heard that Newsome and Lady Ursula had been very thick at one time, you thought that her subsequent engagement to Pleydell gave Newsome a motive for killing her. Knowing Newsome, I never thought that. What it actually did was to give Pleydell the motive.'

The Assistant Commissioner, who had heard all this before, nodded sagely.

'From what I can gather,' Roger went on, 'Lady Ursula was always in love with Newsome, and engaged herself to Pleydell in sheer desperation when she became convinced that Newsome wasn't in love with her. He had no idea of this, of course, and hasn't now; but it's quite plain to me. Well, that didn't make for a happy engagement, did it? As I see it, they were continually quarrelling, and Lady Ursula was always on the verge of breaking it off, till they fell in with each other that night (Pleydell never had a real alibi for that night, you remember) and had one final grand bust-up when Lady Ursula, very nervy and suffering from a bad headache, finally gave him his congé. Probably they went into that studio to have their quarrel in private, and Pleydell, his megalomania utterly outraged, simply took what he considered the proper steps to restore it to self-respect. There was a struggle in that case, because he hadn't got his weapon with him, and he had to tie her wrists and ankles, and no doubt he gagged her in the way I first suggested, Moresby, when we reconstructed the case, if you remember.'

Moresby nodded. 'Yes, I remember. With a scarf or something like that, you said. But what about the note, Mr Sheringham?'

'Ah, yes, that note,' Roger smiled. 'I felt in my bones all the time that the note was taking you on the wrong track, Moresby, but you wouldn't listen. You see, one thing struck me forcibly about that note, but I didn't mention it to you because I knew you wouldn't pay any attention. It was the way it was folded. You pointed out that the main fold didn't come in the middle, and so something must have been cut off the top; but you quite missed the point later on that, if it was the man for whom it had been left who made use of it afterwards, the fold *would* have been in the centre, because he would have cut the top off *before* he folded it, not after. That told me (as soon as I heard from the valet that the note had not been left in an envelope) that it was not the man for whom it had been left who used it, but someone else who had got possession of it, folded it and carried it off before cutting it. You see?'

'Oh, Mr Sheringham, come!' expostulated Moresby. 'That's too subtle altogether.'

'That's exactly what I knew you'd say,' Roger replied equably. 'So I didn't say it. But I deduced from that subtle bit of reasoning that somebody might be in illegal possession of one of Newsome's keys; and lo! when I questioned his valet, I found that one of his keys actually was missing. Newsome had had his pocket picked some weeks ago, and his keys and wallet stolen. It was Pleydell, of course, looking for letters from Lady Ursula; and no doubt he thought the keys would come in uncommonly handy too.

'The truth is patent enough, if one reads between the lines. Pleydell knew all about Newsome and Lady Ursula, and he was mad-jealous of Newsome. He was always trying to get some evidence that the two were on more intimate terms than those of happy-go-lucky friendship; hence the pocket-picking. I've no doubt he was in the habit of shadowing Lady Ursula; at any rate he must have seen her go into Newsome's flat the day before the murder. That may have clinched his suspicions; we can't tell. Anyhow, as soon as the valet was out of the way, he went in too, with that handy key, and found the note. He took it, seeing at once the use to which he could put it if occasion arose. Oh, Moresby, why didn't you take a hint from me and try what would happen if one assumed that Newsome was speaking the truth and it was the facts, not he, that were at fault?

'Well, I don't know whether Pleydell realised at the time, though he certainly did later, that he had, wittingly or unwittingly, built up a very pretty case against Newsome. The next thing to do was to develop it. And so we come to the last murder.

'So far we've had murders with two different motives. Out of the series of four only the first two were pure lust-murders. Lady Ursula's was a vengeance-murder, or a megalomania-murder if you like. The last was a murder committed with the sole motive of increasing the strength of the case against the man he loathed. By being preferred to himself in Lady Ursula's affections, you see, Newsome had committed the unforgivable sin. He must be eliminated at all costs, and very cunningly the trap was laid.' Here Roger paused to prevent a little more beer from going stale.

'Pleydell *was* a cunning man, you see. Oh, very cunning. Do you know what brought him to Scotland Yard, Moresby? Not any vague suspicions, as we thought at the time, but that paragraph in *The Evening Clarion* which you showed me, saying that the police were taking an interest in Lady Ursula's death and hinting at exciting developments. Pleydell knew well enough that the police don't take an interest in death unless something like murder is suspected. He did a bit of hard thinking, put himself in our minds, and proceeded to act precisely as we should expect him to; and very well he played his part too. But he wanted more than that. He wanted to keep abreast of our investigations and know every minute just what we thought, were doing, and were going to do. And there I admit frankly that I was the mug. I offered him what he wanted with both hands.

'Well, Pleydell didn't mind the police investigations. Not he. He welcomed it. And it amused him terribly. There was no question that he himself could ever be suspected, you see, and now he could go right ahead with his case against Newsome. And he went. Having worked out his plot, he proceeded to put it into operation. He went in disguise to a girl in one of his shows (did you know he was behind *Her Husband's Wife* too? I found that out from Miss Deeping on the telephone last night), so that he wouldn't be recognised if seen outside, rang her bell, whipped off the disguise and went in. No doubt he'd telephoned to her in advance or knew in some other way that the coast was perfectly clear till well after lunch. Well, he'd worked out a very clever alibi, and had no time to waste. The first thing he does is to tell the girl that a friend of his called Gerald Newsome is extremely interested in her (all this is only guesswork, of course, but it must be near enough to the facts) and has consulted him about putting up the money for a show in which she would be the star. (Of course he'd have chosen a girl who did know Jerry.) Newsome has said something about taking her out to lunch that day to discuss the proposition; has she heard from him?

"'No,' says the girl, thoroughly excited, she hasn't. "Then if I were you I should ring him up at once and clinch it," says Pleydell; "and tell him one o'clock, not earlier, because I want to talk it over with you myself till then." And naturally the girl promptly does it. So there is Newsome's presence guaranteed for one o'clock, with the certainty that the porter will see him enter. I was assuming, by the way, that Pleydell knew enough about Pelham Mansions to have heard about that porter; that also was confirmed last night, as I'll explain later.

'Now, this next bit of deduction, I must tell you, is one that I really am proud of. It's all based on those dints in the girl's legs. I'd already made up my mind, you see, that the solicitor-looking man was the murderer, and his trimmings were a disguise, though I hadn't the least idea then who he was; but I was sure that his object was to establish an alibi. And I had become convinced, independently, that the girl was alive inside when Newsome rang the bell, but under forcible restraint. I shouldn't say "deductions", by the way; this was pure induction. I took these various assumptions and deliberately built up my case to prove them. Very naughty, wasn't it, Moresby?

'Putting myself in his place, then, I asked myself how I could cause that girl to die exactly three-quarters of an hour after I was safely out of the way. That puzzled me for some time, till I began to wonder—wasn't there some method by which, having made her unconscious, I could place her in such a physical position that the very act of regaining consciousness would make her bring about her own death? To have thought of that question was the great step; the answer soon came. Yes, by stunning her with some yielding instrument on the principle of the sandbag by means of a blow hard enough to keep her unconscious for an hour or so without cracking her skull. That would leave no bruise, you see, and would be quite undiscoverable at a post-mortem unless the actual brain were examined, which would be highly unlikely. I needn't explain to you experts, of course, that a blow with an instrument of that nature stuns by bruising the brain which, being a little loose inside the skull, is thrown violently against the bone on the farther side. I didn't actually hit on the idea of hard rubber as the material then, but of course when Miss Manners explained to me later the short glimpse she had caught of the weapon which stunned her, I realised what it must be.

'Well, having stunned her in that way, with a blow sufficiently forcible to keep her unconscious for about an hour, the next thing he could do, I imagined, would be to prop her on the back of a chair, leaning back and balanced against an open door, with the stocking already in position round her neck and fastened to the hook, and the chair tilted in such a way that the slightest movement would destroy the balance of the whole erection. The door would then swing to, you see, the chair on whose back she was half-sitting, half-lying, would follow it, sinking gradually to the floor as the door closed, and the girl would be left hanging. And the particular beauty of the plan is that the first movement made by a person who has been knocked out is a rolling of the head, which would effect nothing, but the second is a sort of stretching movement of the legs and the body. I've been knocked out myself more than once, and I know. The latter movement, of course, would cause her feet to press on the seat of the chair, which would at once push herself, and the door, away from it. The next impulse, by the way, is to be sick, but the immediate strangulation would prevent that.'

'And you worked all that out just from those dints in her legs, Mr Sheringham?' asked Superintendent Green, with real respect at last.

'More or less,' said Roger proudly. 'Together with the particular chair he used, with a very high back, and the fact that she was not wearing her wrapper; if he had gone to the trouble of removing that from her it must have been with some particular reason, and the only reason I could see was that it was getting in the way of whatever he wanted to do with her. And what is more, Superintendent and Chief Inspector both, having worked it out I went round to the flat to examine the door for the two tiny dints which the knobs on either side of the chair-back should have made in the paint-work, and the infinitesimal scratches they ought to have left as they slithered down to the floor. And there I found them.'

'Well,' said the Superintendent, nobly burning all his boats, 'that's as clever a piece of reasoning as ever I heard.'

'Thank you,' said Roger. 'And all by the inductive method, which you people don't use. By the way, one other thing had occurred to me. A limp body is a difficult thing to balance like that, and I thought he would anticipate some difficulty in preventing the door from shutting prematurely. What, in that case, would be better than a nut, wedged in between the frame and the door? It would hold the balance, you see, and yet crack when the extra pressure was applied. And there, in the dust at the bottom, I found the fragments of a walnut-shell.'

'Well, I'll be blowed!' quoth Chief Inspector Moresby.

Expanding like a flower before the warmth of these official compliments, Roger continued. 'And it was the wrapper, I should add, which told me that Pleydell's first action on getting inside the flat was to tell her the exciting news connected with Newsome, and that he struck her down as soon as she'd hung up the telephone receiver. That was a simple deduction from what Miss Deeping had to say about the habits of her friend concerning visitors and wrappers.

'Well, that was that. All the murderer had to do then was to put on his disguise again and walk out, and his alibi was established by the porter. At first, when I began to realise that the solicitor was our man, I had thought that, knowing the habits of the porter, he had sneaked back as soon as the latter had gone to lunch, but I was right in thinking I had made a mistake there and the man wanted not only the porter's negative evidence, but somebody else's positive testimony as well. I provided the latter for him, by paying for his lunch. And when Newsome rang the bell later, according to plan, the girl was still alive inside. Could anything have been neater? And the case against Newsome after that was nothing less than glaring, as Pleydell knew it would be.

'And that brings us to the attack on Miss Manners yesterday. Pleydell would have been better advised to forgo that; it gave him away at last. And the curious thing is that, lost to everything else as the girl lay helplessly at his mercy, he not only forgot to give the ten-minute signal himself, as of course he intended, but actually stepped on his own alarmbell! Could anything be more ironical. What a perfect mixture of superhuman cunning and complete idiocy. Yes, that last attempt was a real madman's effort. He realised, of course, as soon as he'd done it, and darted out to hide on the lower landing till I had fled past; but by that time he'd spoilt his own game.

'At first I was hopelessly at sea. I'd never expected for a moment to get any results with such a poor little trap for such a very clever spider. I began by thinking that it must be one of our five suspects, and wondered if it really could be Beverley, as Miss Manners had told me the same morning.

'This attack cleared up certain points on which I had been still doubtful, and confirmed others. It definitely settled the question of the weapon, and explained the absence of any struggle, except in Lady Ursula's case; it also showed that I had been wrong in my first reconstruction, regarding the scarf, but that did not help much. Then it occurred to me that there might be a double object in this case, not only to eliminate Miss Manners, but also to throw still further suspicion on Newsome; for I was convinced by this time that somebody was deliberately trying to do just that thing, and with a malicious vindictiveness that argued a substantial motive. Did that give me a pointer? Who had anything against Newsome? So far as I could see, only Pleydell; and as I told you, I laughed at myself.

'Then I thought: *why* should anyone want to eliminate Miss Manners? Even if the existence of our trio of inquiry were known, she was the least important member of it. Why not eliminate Pleydell or myself? Could there possibly be any reason for her elimination beyond her membership of our trio? Because it was clear that this was not a haphazard attack (or so I thought); there was some hidden reason for it. And at once I remembered a conversation she had had with me that same morning.

'Briefly, she had suggested then a new line of inquiry: to put out feelers as to whether a man, not answering to Newsome's description but wearing a beard and gold-rimmed glasses, had been seen in the neighbourhood of Miss Macklane's studio *after* the crime. That was significant, you see; and she had already arrived at the independent conclusion that the bearded man at Pelham Mansions was the real murderer, though she thought he was Arnold Beverley and I had an open mind. But what now occurred to me as in the highest degree interesting was that she had mentioned this to Pleydell earlier in the morning and he had as good as asked her not to say anything about it to me, and had got her to agree that it would be fun to follow it up behind my back. You see? There was evidently something in it, and he didn't want it investigated. Moreover, he had heard her say the day before that she had a new idea and that we had been blind, and she had promised to tell me after tea the next day. If Pleydell were the murderer, I thought, that would give him a real motive for getting rid of her before she had told me anything.

'Well, that put me on to the idea of Pleydell in real earnest. And immediately things began to fall into their places. Pleydell was not in his office in the city when we rang him up immediately after the attack. Why not? Because he was in Maida Vale. He arrived in Sutherland Avenue much quicker than he could have done from his board-meeting. Why? Because he was so anxious to see if he were suspected after the incident of the alarm bell. His first action on being alone with me was vehemently to accuse Newsome afresh. Why? To put me off himself. And one of the first things he said was that it must be Newsome, because he was "the only one who knew". Why did he say that? Newsome wasn't. Pleydell really had passed the word to the other suspects, about the sittings. But what was significant was that Pleydell was "the only one who knew" that Newsome was on the premises.

'And there were hundreds of other little things of the same kind, not only in that case, but in all the others. In fact, once I had begun to see seriously whether Pleydell wouldn't fit, he fitted everywhere. I spent an interesting ten minutes soothing him by pretending to agree about Newsome and doing my utmost to get the girls out of his clutches. I told him I was going to take them to the Piccadilly Palace (where doubtless he would have followed and attacked Miss Manners again in the middle of the night), but when we got there I told the others to wait in the taxi while I booked their rooms; then I ran inside, waited a minute, and ran out to tell them that the place was full. I didn't want them to suspect Pleydell, you see, because I wasn't sure; but I did want to get those two safe inside the Albany for the night.

'Well, if I wasn't sure before dinner, I was after. Apart from the few but very significant things I found out from Newsome and on the telephone, I got a report I'd asked for about the other inhabitants of Pelham Mansions. One of the girls there was reputed to be kept by Pleydell. That, to my mind, clinched it.

'Then I was up against the problem of proving it. And there was no real proof. At least, none that could not quite easily be explained away. I was morally convinced, but what, as Moresby says, is the good of that? And as for attempting to assemble any convincing proofs within eighteen hours, to prevent you people from arresting Newsome—well, I ask you! So I thought of the usual French method of re-constructing the crime and testing the suspect's reactions, and wondered whether anything could be done in that line. And the more I thought of it the more I was sure not only that it was the only possible way, but that some sort of reaction might be confidently expected—*if* we made the scene convincing and horrible enough.

'So I hit on that quite impossible plan, enlisted plucky little Miss Manners (to whom, and that undeserving Jerry Newsome who's going to get her, I drain this tankard), cajoled Scotland Yard into sitting through the performance, forced myself through quite the most unpleasant ten minutes of my life—and there we are. Oh, and of course I couldn't warn Pleydell, even by innuendo, what the real object of the mummery was, and so I had to spin that yarn about a representative gathering of citizens, and all that nonsense. That's all.

'But I do wish Pleydell hadn't gone quite mad at the end. I should like to have had a chance to probe into his mind a little further first. His psychology, of course, is absorbing. I don't suppose for a moment that he considered himself a murderer, you know. He killed, but he didn't murder; his mind, when the action was applied to himself, is sure to have conceived some subtle differentiation. And he really had rather a nice sense of humour, you know, with it all. He must have been hugging himself all this time, not only looking on at the futile hunt for himself; but even assisting in it. How his tongue must have been in his cheek, when I think of some of the things he's said to me. Well, well, it's a pity that quite the most interesting brain that any of us is likely to meet has turned out to be a mad one; but I suppose one can't have everything. And that really does appear to be all.' The remaining contents of the tankard descended the way of all good beer. '*Facilis descensus taverni*,' said Roger, smacking his lips.

He looked round at the three thoughtful faces and grinned widely. He was feeling rather more pleased with Roger Sheringham than ever before, and he wanted a victim. Moresby was the selection. Roger felt he owed Moresby just what that Chief Inspector was going to get.

He rose and clapped him happily on the shoulder. 'Do you know what's the matter with you real detectives at Scotland Yard, Moresby?' he asked kindly. 'You don't read enough of those detective stories.'

THE END

THE DETECTIVE STORY CLUB

FOR DETECTIVE CONNOISSEURS

recommends

"The Man with the Gun."

Philip MacDonald

Author of Rynox, etc.

MURDER GONE MAD

MR. MacDonald, who has shown himself in *The Noose* and *The Rasp* to be a master of the crime novel of pure detection, has here told a story of a motiveless crime, or at least a crime prompted only by blood lust. The sure, clear thinking of the individual detective is useless and only wide, cleverly organised investigation can hope to succeed.

A long knife with a brilliant but perverted brain directing it is terrorising Holmdale; innocent people are being done to death under the very eyes of the law. Inspector Pyke of Scotland Yard, whom MacDonald readers will remember in previous cases, is put on the track of the butcher. He has nothing to go on but the evidence of the bodies themselves and the butcher's own bravado. After every murder a businesslike letter arrives announcing that another "removal has been carried out." But Pyke "gets there" with a certainty the very slowness of which will give the reader many breathless moments. In the novelty of its treatment, the humour of its dialogue, and the truth of its characterisation, *Murder Gone Mad* is equal to the best Mr. MacDonald has written.

LOOK FOR THE MAN WITH THE GUN